BACKLASH

OTHER BOOKS AND AUDIO BOOKS
BY TRACI HUNTER ABRAMSON:

Undercurrents

Ripple Effect

The Deep End

Freefall

Lockdown

Crossfire

Royal Target

BACKLASH

A NOVEL BY

TRACI HUNTER ABRAMSON

Covenant Communications, Inc.

Cover images: *Steel Sheet Used for Target Practice Bullet Holes* © Catscandotcom, *Broken Shop Window* © Assalve, *People Silhouette* © Maikid, *Terrify* © boryak. Images courtesy istockphoto.com.

Cover design © 2010 by Covenant Communications, Inc.

Published by Covenant Communications, Inc.
American Fork, Utah

Printed in USA
First Printing: September 2010

16 15 14 13 12 11 10 10 9 8 7 6 5 4 3 2 1

ISBN-13 978-1-59811-987-9

For everyone who has discovered that marriage is worth the journey.

ACKNOWLEDGMENTS

My continued appreciation goes out to all of the usual suspects, especially Rebecca Cummings, who helped me prepare this novel for submission in record time. Who needs sleep, right?

Thanks to my family for their continued willingness to let me spend time in my fictional world and for reminding me to eat while I'm there.

Thank you to my friends and extended family for believing in me even when I forget to.

Finally, thank you to the wonderful people at Covenant for all of your support in every aspect of bringing this book to light. My special gratitude goes to Kathryn Jenkins for your continued encouragement and to Samantha Van Walraven for all of your insight throughout the editing process.

PROLOGUE

Commander Kelan Bennett moved silently through the dense foliage of the jungle, his weapon already drawn. Three of the men under his command moved in tandem with him, each of them dressed completely in black. Tristan Crowther was on point, checking the underbrush for booby traps or anything else that might threaten their mission. Quinn Lambert, the other enlisted man on his squad, had their back. Moving parallel with Kel was Brent Miller, his second in command.

Tension vibrated off each of them, a necessary adrenaline that heightened their senses and kept them poised for any obstacle. As US Navy SEALS, they were trained for this. The night was their ally, the water their friend.

The submarine that had slipped them into Nicaragua's territorial waters undetected now waited for them out in the dark ocean a short distance away, but they couldn't leave until they completed their mission. They wouldn't leave until they had their missing man.

Seth Johnson was somewhere inside the fortress, the home and headquarters of arms dealer Akil Ramir. An impromptu undercover mission had given Seth the opportunity to unearth some much needed intelligence, but now it was time to bring him home. The coded message Seth had sent to them two days before included only brief information—a place, a date, and a time. And that time was less than two minutes away.

In front of him, Tristan stopped and held up a hand to signal everyone else to do the same. In the shadows, Kel could see him pull a knife from his belt and then lean down, presumably to diffuse some kind of trip wire.

The silence of the night was interrupted by a burst of gunfire. Tristan quickly finished his task and gave the sign to go ahead. They were nearly into position at the edge of the jungle where the lights of the fortress were visible. Ten more seconds and—gunfire sounded again, this time two quick bursts followed by shouts and the sound of a helicopter taking off.

"Cover him," Kel ordered, hoping and praying that Seth was heading their way. He shifted his weapon, his eyes sweeping the grassy area surrounding the fortress. Then he saw them. Vanessa Lauton, the CIA spy who had infiltrated Ramir's organization, was running straight for the beach, and Seth was right behind her, turning his weapon back toward the dozen guards who had just rounded the corner of the building in pursuit. Suddenly, Vanessa was down.

Kel fired in tandem with his men, successfully slowing down the guards. "We've got snipers on the roof. Give us some cover fire," Kel told Quinn and Tristan. He motioned to Brent, who followed him out into the night, both of them firing their weapons as they sprinted to the beach where Vanessa had fallen.

When they reached Seth, Kel took a quick look, relieved to see that Vanessa wasn't injured. He squeezed off another burst from his HK-47 and told Seth, "We've got a zodiac behind those trees. Get her out of here. We'll cover you."

"Got it." Seth kept his hand on Vanessa's arm and pulled her down the beach.

Kel and Brent faced the oncoming threat, retreating toward the jungle as they continued to fire. Then he heard the real danger: the Z-10 attack helicopter angling toward them. He and Brent both raced for the water to use the waves for cover as the Z-10's guns started firing. A spray of saltwater washed up over his boots, and then Kel saw it—a steady stream of bullets marking the beach coming directly for him. He dove for the water right as metal struck flesh and a searing pain exploded in his leg.

1

Marilyn Bennett opened the mailbox outside her house, pulling the contents free. She flipped through the envelopes twice, not surprised to find that she hadn't received what she really wanted.

Carrying the mail and two bags of groceries, she walked into the house and hit the button on the answering machine to listen to her messages. As the first message played, a reminder about a staff meeting the next day, she dropped her bags onto the kitchen counter and started putting away her groceries.

Impatiently, she listened to three more messages: one from Heather Addison, her longtime visiting teacher; and two from other officers' wives reminding her about a fundraiser they wanted her to help with. When the last message played, she let out a sigh. No word from her husband. Again.

She wasn't even sure how long he had been gone this time. She glanced into the living room where her wedding photo hung on the wall. Her husband had looked incredible that day in his dress whites, just as he had at the church dance where she had met him. Her constant worry eased for a moment as she remembered that night.

Kelan Bennett had seemed larger than life when he had walked into the cultural hall of the church in Baltimore. She had stared at him. Everyone had. The white uniform stood out against everyone wearing the normal church attire, but it was his presence that captured her attention. He looked like he could take on the world in battle and come out on top without much effort.

He wasn't terribly tall, only about five feet ten inches, his light brown eyes direct. Though his brown hair was cut short, it didn't look like the typical military-style haircut. In fact, had he not been wearing a uniform, she doubted she would have pegged him for the military type at all.

She remembered the blush that had crept into her cheeks when his eyes had landed on her and he'd given her that little smile of his. Then a petite blond had approached him. He had danced with the blond and two other girls while Marilyn had watched them wistfully. Then with a confidence that she admired, he had crossed the twenty feet between them. She had felt awkward and plain that night before he had asked her to dance, but he made her feel beautiful. He had complimented her eyes, even though she knew that the pale blue color was ordinary. A shiver had run through her when he had toyed with the tight spiral curls she was forever fighting into submission. Somehow overlooking the mousy color, he said it reminded him of the desert at sunset.

Perhaps what she remembered the most was the way they had talked. She had always known she was a good listener. Kel had seemed to appreciate that about her, but he had also been interested in hearing what she had to say.

The romance that had begun that night had been a whirlwind of excitement and adventure unlike anything she had ever experienced. They went out every night those first two weeks before he had to return to his base in Virginia Beach. Confidences had been shared surprisingly early, creating a foundation to build on. Then he'd had to return to work.

The loneliness had barely started to set in when he had convinced her to come spend a few weeks at the beach. He had a friend who was out of town who'd offered to let her stay in his condo. Then Kel had convinced her to meet him in odd places as he traveled to various assignments. He likened her to an anchor, his anchor. The image shouldn't have been romantic, but Marilyn thought it was.

When he called and told her he was in Italy and wanted her to come spend a week with him, she had thrown caution to the wind, ignored her mother's warnings about dating a man in the military, and jumped on an airplane. For the first time in her life, she had been daring and unafraid. He had taken leave to spend time with her, showing her the Italian countryside. At the end of the week he had knocked on her hotel room door with a dozen roses in his hand, and she knew. She knew he was going to propose that night, and she knew she was going to say yes.

A few short weeks later, they were married, and she thought she had found her happily ever after. Then reality set in. She had married a Navy SEAL. She had married a man who spent most of his time away from home, leaving whenever the phone rang and not returning until his job was done—a job he couldn't tell her about.

Her inherent shyness and her insecurities had started coming back then. She could feel herself pulling back into her shell, that safe place where no one could hurt her, the place where no one could really know her. More than once she thought that she should walk away from this mistake she had made. Surely Kel deserved someone who was more confident and independent.

Maybe someone else would be able to give him the children he so desperately wanted. She still wasn't sure why she hadn't been able to get pregnant, even though she and Kel had hoped to start a family more than two years before. The doctor attributed the problem to Kel's career and their lack of time together. But Marilyn was afraid it was something more.

So often she had hoped for a child, someone who would be there to love even when Kel wasn't home. Then she would remember her own childhood. What if she had a child only to have to raise it on her own? The doubts were always right there at the edge of her thoughts, but then Kel would come back from an assignment. He would do something sweet like bring her flowers or pick her up in the middle of the day to take her to lunch. As much as she hated this life, she kept stumbling over the same problem. She still loved her husband.

Her phone rang, and she abandoned the groceries to pick it up, only to find her mother on the other end. "Hi, Mom."

"Hi, honey. How are you doing today?"

"Fine," Marilyn said vaguely. "Just a little frustrated that I haven't heard from Kel for a while."

"I don't know how you do it, living like this," Barbara said to her daughter, a combination of sympathy and disdain in her voice.

"One day at a time," Marilyn muttered. Not emotionally equipped at the moment to deal with her mother and one of her hour-long lectures on why she shouldn't have married a military man, Marilyn glanced over at her kitchen counter. "Hey, Mom, I just walked in the door, and I have groceries I need to put away. Can I call you back later?"

"Of course," Barbara agreed easily enough before saying good-bye.

Marilyn replaced the phone in the charger and then began unloading her groceries once more. She had just finished putting the last TV dinner into the freezer when she glanced out the window and saw them pull up, saw the two men get out of the government car. She stood anchored to the spot where she stood, hoping, praying that the two men weren't coming to knock on her door. Everything seemed to move in slow motion as one man held up a paper, presumably to check the address. He then looked at her mailbox and nodded to the other man.

No! The voice screamed inside her head, but still she didn't move. For five years now, she had been dreading this possibility. Every time her husband shipped out, her heart ached until he returned home. She couldn't count the number of times she had begged him to leave the SEAL teams or how many arguments had ensued when he refused to give up the life he felt he was destined for.

The men headed up her short sidewalk and rang the doorbell. As though she were moving on automatic pilot, she somehow found herself standing in the entryway, her hand on the doorknob. She didn't want to pull the door open. She didn't want to face the news these men had come to bring her, but she couldn't stop herself from answering the door.

"Mrs. Bennett?" one man said. She must have nodded because he continued, "I need you to come with me, ma'am. Your husband has been injured."

She stared at him, blinking twice as she replayed his words. *Injured.* She was sure he had said *injured*, not *killed*. Kel was still alive. She couldn't ask how badly he was hurt. She couldn't get past the incredible relief that flooded through her at the news that her husband was still living and breathing. Instead, she simply stared as tears of relief flooded her eyes.

The men at the door misinterpreted her tears. They began to explain the situation, the fact that her husband was being transported to the naval hospital in Bethesda, Maryland. They were going to take her there to see him, to see for herself that he was still alive.

One of the men reminded her to get her purse and then walked her out to the car. His words blurred together as he helped her buckle into the backseat. *Gunshot wound . . . medevac . . . surgery.* Then they were on their way, Marilyn praying that her worst nightmare wasn't about to come true.

* * *

Kel struggled to open his eyes from the drug-induced sleep. His mind was still foggy, as if he were underwater and couldn't quite break through the surface. Then the memories came rushing back with sudden clarity. He remembered the searing pain when his leg was hit. He remembered Brent and Seth helping him into the zodiac boat after they completed their mission. And he remembered that they had successfully recovered the two people who had the intelligence they needed, the information that could help stop an impending terrorist threat.

His arms were heavy, and he struggled to lift them, but he reached down to where the bullet had imbedded in his leg only inches above his knee.

"Take it easy." The words were meant to soothe him, but he could hear the underlying concern.

Kel shifted his eyes toward the sound of his wife's voice. "Hey," he managed as her face came into focus.

"Hey, yourself." She managed a timid smile as she pushed herself out of the chair beside his bed and reached for his hand. "I was starting to wonder if you were ever going to wake up."

"How long?"

"A couple of hours." She rubbed her thumb back and forth across the back of his hand. "The doctor said the surgery went well. If everything goes okay, you can come home in a week or two."

His brain began to clear, and the ramifications of his injury hit him full force. Unwilling to consider that the injury might be career-ending, Kel asked, "Did he say how long until I can go back to active duty?"

Marilyn's hand tensed in his, and she shook her head.

Kel saw it then. The fleeting hope in his wife's eyes that he wouldn't be able to go back, that his career as a Navy SEAL would be over. "You don't want me to go back."

"We don't need to talk about this now." Marilyn looked toward the door, and she pulled her hand free. "I'll go tell the doctor that you're awake."

Kel opened his mouth to stop her from leaving, to try once again to explain to her how vital his job was, not only to him but to the security of their country. She reached for the door handle, and his lips drew into a firm line instead. Silence filled the room as she looked back at him for a long moment before pushing the door open and disappearing into the hallway.

* * *

Marilyn listened to the doctor repeat what she had heard several hours ago after Kel had come out of surgery. Her first response was an incredible wave of relief. Kel was alive, and he would be able to walk again. Then he explained his concerns. The gunshot wound had caused some nerve damage, but they wouldn't know for several weeks if it was permanent. The doctor was also concerned with the swelling of Kel's knee, a problem that didn't appear to be related to the gunshot wound.

Kel sat propped up in his hospital bed taking in all of the information. He seemed so calm, as though this crisis was just a minor setback on the way to his next mission. He asked questions, using medical terms Marilyn had never heard of, as though he too were a doctor instead of a patient. Rehab and physical therapy were discussed at length while Marilyn sat quietly absorbing their words.

The doctor was quite insistent that even though Kel would be well enough within a week to return home, he wanted to keep him longer to allow him to undergo rehab in Bethesda where the navy was better equipped to speed his recovery.

Marilyn tried to digest this latest information and the ramifications it would have on her life as well as Kel's. If the doctor had his way, they would be in Maryland for at least six weeks, maybe more.

When she thought they were finally done, Kel asked one more question. "Is there any chance you can get me access to a secure line? I need a status report."

"Not likely." The doctor shook his head. Then he glanced down at Kel's chart and appeared to read a few lines. His eyes whipped up to look at Kel, and the two men appeared to communicate without saying a word. Finally, the doctor said, "I'll see what I can do."

"Thanks, Doctor."

Marilyn stood and moved closer to the bed. "What was that all about?"

"Nothing."

"You mean nothing you'll talk to me about."

"Marilyn, please don't do this." Kel's eyes were pleading. "You know I can't talk to anyone about my job, not even you."

"Maybe I should leave you to get some rest." She looked away, even though she knew he had already seen the hurt in her eyes. "I need to figure out where I'm staying tonight."

"Excuse me for interrupting," a young nurse spoke hesitantly from the doorway. "Senator Whitmore is here to see you."

"You can send him in," Kel told her.

Marilyn turned back to face Kel, her mind reeling. Why would a senator be visiting her husband?

The tall man stepped through the doorway. His hair was more silver than gold, his blue eyes direct as he nodded to her. "You must be Marilyn. I'm Jim Whitmore."

"Nice to meet you," Marilyn managed. A senator was visiting her husband and knew her name? Stunned, she moved aside so the senator could come farther into the room.

"How's our patient?"

"I'll live," Kel said simply. He hesitantly glanced at Marilyn and then asked, "Do you have any news for me?"

"Nothing yet," Jim told him. "I should know more tomorrow."

Kel nodded, seeming to accept that he would have to wait for whatever information he thought the senator could give him.

"Tell me what the doctors have told you," the senator insisted. Then he listened as Kel gave him the highlights—a week or two in the hospital and another month in rehab followed by intensive physical therapy. Finally, Jim turned to Marilyn. "Did I hear you say you needed a place to stay?"

"One of the men who brought me up here said they could probably get me a hotel nearby for at least a couple of days."

"You're welcome to stay with me and my wife. Our house is over the border in Virginia, but it's only about a twenty-minute drive."

Marilyn immediately shook her head. "I couldn't impose like that."

"It wouldn't be an imposition," Jim insisted. "I assume you will want to stay in the area while your husband is recovering. Or do you have a job you have to get back to?"

"She works from home," Kel told the senator. His eyes met Marilyn's, and she could see the need there. "I'm sure if she could get her computer from the house, she could work up here—that is, if she even wants to keep working."

Kel had mentioned this before, the fact that she didn't *need* to work. Marilyn had never told him that she had already cut back from four days a week to two. While she was tempted to free herself of that burden once and for all, she wasn't sure she was willing to give up the extra income or the excuse her work gave her to be on her computer. "I don't know . . ."

"Either way, we can have someone go by your house and pick up your computer and some clothes for you," Jim suggested.

Someone else go through her things? Without her there? She shook her head. "That's okay. I would need to pick up my car anyway."

"Honey, I know you have to be exhausted," Kel said softly. "Why don't you go home with the senator and spend the night. Then tomorrow we'll have someone take you down to Virginia Beach, and you can pack up whatever you need."

She found herself nodding, too overwhelmed to do anything else. "I guess that would work."

"Good." The senator reached over and shook Kel's hand before turning to Marilyn. "I'll give you a few minutes alone. I'll be waiting in the hall when you're ready to leave."

"Thank you," Marilyn said, pleased to see that he had closed the door behind him. Then she turned to Kel. "Why did you do that?"

"Do what?" Kel asked.

"I can't possibly stay with someone I don't know for six weeks, maybe more."

"Come here." Kel reached for her and took her hand as soon as it was in reach. "I don't know if I can get through this without you, and I don't want you to have to stay in some dinky hotel room for weeks on end."

"But . . ."

"The senator's house is huge. You won't bother them, and I'm sure they won't bother you." Kel's voice became persuasive. "Please, Marilyn. I really want you here."

She stared down at him, surprised to see the sincerity there. Feeling truly needed for the first time in her marriage, she nodded. "All right. I'll give it a try."

2

Kel's comment repeated itself over and over in her mind as Marilyn sat beside the senator in his car. *The senator's house is huge.* How did Kel know what the senator's house looked like? *You won't bother them, and I'm sure they won't bother you.* The way he had spoken suggested that Kel knew the man sitting beside her well, and she had no idea why. And even more, why had he visited the senator regularly, and why had he never invited her to come?

"It must be hard seeing your husband lying in that hospital bed," Jim Whitmore said after driving for several minutes in silence.

Marilyn nodded, remembering too vividly the rush of emotions she'd experienced when she'd seen the two men approaching her front door. "I'm so glad it wasn't any worse."

"Me, too," Jim nodded. "From what I understand, my son-in-law was standing next to Kel when he was shot."

"Your son-in-law?"

"Brent Miller." Jim glanced over at her quizzically. "I assume you know my daughter, Amy."

Marilyn nodded slowly. She knew Amy Miller, the Saint Squad's intelligence officer. But how was it that no one had ever mentioned that Amy was Senator Whitmore's daughter? Especially since they lived in Virginia, the senator's home state. Granted, she didn't spend a lot of time with the other members of Kel's unit. Being around them always made her uncomfortable and even a little jealous. No matter how much time Kel spent with her when he was home, she always felt like his squad was more important to Kel than she was.

She tried to push those thoughts aside. "I didn't think to ask before. How is your wife going to feel about you showing up with a houseguest?"

"Grateful."

"Huh?"

Jim smiled at her. "Life gets pretty crazy from now until Congress breaks in August. I called to let her know I was bringing you home. She said that she's looking forward to having someone around the house for a change." He slowed the car as he approached a stoplight. "Amy is supposed to be arriving sometime tonight or tomorrow, but I don't expect to see her much while she's in town."

"Amy's coming?" Marilyn asked, a new crest of unease rising up inside her. She liked Amy well enough, but she found it difficult to really connect with a woman who spent more hours with her husband every day than she did, a woman who understood what her husband did when he was away from home, an understanding that she couldn't claim for herself.

"Last I heard. Of course, with her profession, we never really believe she's coming until she's standing in front of us," Jim said lightheartedly. "You know what that's like."

Marilyn simply nodded. She couldn't count the number of times Kel had shipped out at a moment's notice, always a different variation of the same story. Their conversations on each of those occasions could have been recorded and simply replayed.

Can you tell me where you're going or how long you'll be gone? she would always ask. His response was always the same. *I'm sorry, hon. You know I can't tell you, even when I do know.* Then he would hug her and kiss her good-bye, promising to call or e-mail as soon as he could. "As soon as he could" was sometimes an hour later. Other times weeks went by before she heard from him. A few times it was even longer.

Marilyn's thoughts were interrupted when the senator slowed and pulled between two of the oak trees that lined an oversized, grassy lawn. The driveway curved around in front of the enormous house, but the senator pressed the garage door opener and continued straight into the three-car garage. A sporty little coupe was parked on one side of them, and an older SUV was parked in the spot nearest the door that appeared to lead into the house.

"Come on inside," Jim said as he climbed out of the car and headed for the door.

Marilyn followed, her hand tightly gripping the strap of her purse. Not for the first time, she wished she had taken the time to change out of her baggy khakis and simple T-shirt before going to the hospital. She stepped onto the tile floor of the enormous kitchen. Standing in front of the stove was a striking woman, her dark hair swept back from her face with a barrette that gathered it at the base of her neck.

"You're home." Her smile was genuine and welcoming as she leaned forward to kiss her husband. She then turned to look at Marilyn, who awkwardly closed the door behind her. "And you brought me company."

"Katherine, meet our new houseguest," Jim told his wife. "This is Kel's wife, Marilyn."

"Welcome. I am so glad to hear Kel is okay." Katherine turned the stove down and then crossed to where Marilyn stood just inside the door. "You must be exhausted. Let me show you your room and give you the lay of the land before dinner."

"I feel so bad to be imposing like this," Marilyn managed, as Katherine swept her out of the kitchen and started through a living room that was the size of a small apartment.

"Don't be silly." Katherine waved away her concerns as effortlessly as her husband had done at the hospital. "We have plenty of room, especially now that the kids are all out of the house. Besides, I love to cook, and I hate to eat alone. Hopefully your schedule will work out that you'll be home for dinner every once in a while."

Marilyn followed Katherine into the front entryway where a large picture of the Washington D.C. Temple hung on the wall facing the front door. They moved past the stairs and what appeared to be Jim's study as they entered a long hallway. Finally, Katherine opened a door at the end of the hall.

"If this room doesn't suit you, you can take one of the upstairs bedrooms, but I thought you would like your privacy," Katherine told her. "It's always a bit awkward at first staying with someone when you're used to living on your own."

Marilyn felt a little wave of relief and nodded. She stepped inside the room, barely managing to keep her jaw from dropping open. An antique four-poster bed filled the center of the room. A loveseat was angled in the corner near the window, a small desk occupying the space opposite of it. "It's perfect, thank you."

"The bathroom is through there." Katherine waved to the door on the right and then nodded at the slim laptop on the desk. "You're welcome to use the laptop there. It has Internet access and the basics. Our son Charlie left it here when he got a new one last year. If you have your own, we can move it out of your way."

"No, this is perfect," Marilyn said, offering Katherine a small smile. "Really."

"Well, I'll let you get settled in while I go finish fixing dinner," Katherine told her. "And like I said, please make yourself at home."

* * *

Kel stared at the television screen, waiting for the next segment of the news to come on. He hated not knowing what was happening. He hated knowing that if he did get any information off of the news about the impending terrorist attack, it would mean his squad had failed.

Shifting in his hospital bed, Kel absorbed the pain that shot through his leg and took a deep breath to steady himself. He still couldn't believe that he was here, wounded. He had gone over the mission in his mind so many times, trying to figure out what he had done wrong and what he could have done to avoid the bullet that had put him here.

The mission into Nicaragua had been risky, but this wasn't the first time he had been on a mission that was a little dubious in nature. Everything had gone perfectly until the gunfire had started, until Seth and Vanessa had been unable to slip out of the fortress undetected. Still, his squad had reacted quickly, and they had succeeded in accomplishing their mission. But now his squad was out there fighting to protect their country without him.

He closed his eyes, panic enveloping him as he considered what it would be like to have to stay out of the action for long, to not know what was happening or what threat was taking place that he might have been able to stop. *Please don't let this end my career,* he prayed silently.

Unwilling to let the doubts take over, he pushed that thought aside and watched the news headlines come on. It only took a few minutes for Kel to realize that the terrorist attack he was worried about wasn't yet public knowledge. If everything went the way he hoped, the public would never know about the threat in Arizona or the possibility of the nuclear power plant located there turning into a nuclear weapon.

He trusted his men implicitly, and he prayed that they would be able to do their job well enough to avoid disaster.

The elite five-man unit from SEAL Team Eight, known as the Saint Squad, had been under his command for the past five years. Their nickname had come from the fact that all of the members of his squad belonged to The Church of Jesus Christ of Latter-day Saints. They were an oddity in the teams, both in how they lived and in how they fought. Yet, everyone knew that their unit was special in ways no one could quite define.

Kel could rattle off the Saint Squad's impressive success rate, but the numbers wouldn't matter if they failed when it counted most. A successful attack on the nuclear power plant outside Phoenix would likely affect the entire western United States. He prayed that his men would be inspired and somehow manage to put a stop to Akil Ramir's plans.

He was pretty sure that if Marilyn hadn't been present when the senator arrived, he could have gotten an update. As it turned out, he had been unwilling to risk upsetting his wife to get the information he so desperately wanted.

Kel rubbed a hand over his face, wishing he understood his wife. He thought of the first time he'd met her, the way he had asked her to dance on a whim. She had seemed a bit out of place, like she wasn't quite sure what to do around so many people. Perhaps he had been drawn to her because he knew what it was like to feel vulnerable.

He hadn't expected to dance with her for the rest of the night, but once they had started talking, he hadn't wanted to stop. Marilyn understood him in a way no one had before, at least not since he had lost his family. She was sensitive, humble, and unassuming. He appreciated her natural beauty and the fact that she wasn't constantly worrying about fixing her makeup or messing with her hair.

While they were dating, he felt a void being filled, a void he hadn't fully recognized before. The only difficulty he had encountered during their courtship was when he had met Marilyn's mother, Barbara. He could still remember that first meeting.

"So you're in the navy?" she had asked in a voice that was sugar coated and shallow.

"That's right, ma'am. I'm a Navy SEAL."

She had looked over at her daughter, bitterness tainting her words. "Well, I suppose someone has to do those jobs."

Marilyn had been embarrassed by her mother's comment and the subtle and not-so-subtle insults that had followed. Clearly still hurting from losing her husband many years before, Barbara made sure Marilyn knew she didn't approve of her dating anyone who chose to face danger as a regular part of their job. So accustomed to her daughter following her advice, Barbara had seemed genuinely surprised when Marilyn had defied her and decided to marry Kel anyway.

Despite Barbara's obvious disapproval, everything had been great between Kel and Marilyn while they were dating and after they were first married. He had taken her to the temple, and they were active in church, but somehow the perfect life they dreamed of always seemed to be just out of reach. The children he had expected to bless their lives had never come, and their hope for a family of their own continued to dim as time passed.

Although the constant separations had been difficult on both of them, especially on Marilyn, Kel could appreciate that they were both willing to fight through the challenges to preserve their marriage. Marilyn had trained as a legal transcriptionist so that she could work at home. Her job gave her the flexibility to take her work with her when she was able to accompany him on temporary assignments. Those assignments didn't happen often, but when they did, Kel often felt like he was able to see glimpses of the woman he'd married, the woman willing to go out with him and look for adventure.

A knock came at the door a second before it opened. Kel glanced toward the door, expecting to see an orderly with his dinner. Instead, it was the doctor who walked into his room. "I just got off of the phone with a young woman asking about you." The doctor looked at him quizzically. "Amy Miller?"

"And?"

"She said to tell you that she's coming home and that your boys are going fishing," Dr. Pollard told him. "Do you know why she insisted I tell you this right away?"

Kel nodded. He understood perfectly. Amy coming home meant that she was coming to work at CIA headquarters, which was practically down the street from her parents' house in Virginia. His boys "going fishing" translated to the rest of his squad going to Arizona in search of the mole who was feeding information to the terrorists they were currently trying to stop. Keeping his face solemn, he told the doctor, "Thanks for the message. I really appreciate it."

"Get some rest," Dr. Pollard said now. "Tomorrow we'll see if we can get you up and moving."

"I'll try," Kel agreed, though he didn't know how he was supposed to sleep when he should be working beside the rest of his team.

3

Marilyn sat down at the round table in the kitchen, grateful that Katherine Whitmore had chosen to eat here rather than in the massive dining room around the corner. Jim had been on a business call in the study when she had emerged from her room and made her way back to the kitchen, but right after she came in, Jim followed.

She wasn't sure exactly what she expected, but when she saw the simple meal Katherine had prepared—meatloaf and mashed potatoes—she was pleasantly surprised. She thought that a senator would expect fancier fare than this. Then again, she supposed she would have expected the Whitmores to keep a household staff rather than to see Katherine fixing her own meals.

They all sat down to eat, Jim blessed the food, and immediately Marilyn felt the awkwardness surfacing. She hated it, this difficulty she had always struggled with to make conversation with people. Taking a little breath, she forced herself to ask one of the many questions that had been building up inside of her. "I never thought to ask how you met my husband."

"Let's see." Jim grinned across the table. "I believe the first time I met Kel was when he was politely trying to tell me I didn't have the proper security clearances to be in his office."

"What?" Marilyn forgot about her awkwardness, now fascinated.

"I always thought it took a lot of guts for someone to tell a senator to get lost, especially when that senator has a personal stake in what you're doing," Jim told her.

"A personal stake?" Marilyn repeated.

"I don't know if you remember when Amy was taken hostage in Abolstan."

"How could I not remember? It was all over the news." Marilyn nodded. "That must have been incredibly difficult for your family."

"It was an awful time, but so much good came from it," Katherine told her. When she noticed the confused look on Marilyn's face, she added, "If the Saint Squad hadn't gone in to rescue the hostages, Amy never would have met Brent."

"I never thought of it that way." Marilyn spoke softly, her heart aching now. She looked at these two relative strangers, these kind people who had taken her into their home, and wondered if they knew that they had just told her more about her husband's past assignments in one conversation than he had in five years of marriage. Never once had Kel mentioned going to Abolstan or that he had led the efforts to rescue the hostages. Although the food in front of her had lost its appeal, she forced herself to take another bite.

"Of course, Jim wasn't terribly fond of Brent in the beginning," Katherine said with humor in her voice.

"Really?" Marilyn asked.

"You can't blame me," Jim said, feigning insult. "This boy shows up and basically wages war on me to steal my little girl away."

"Right, honey." Katherine grinned. "In other words, he wasn't ready to let his little girl go."

"Especially to someone like Brent."

"You mean someone who was a SEAL?"

"You're married to one." Jim nodded. "You can understand the reservations I had."

Marilyn nodded. She did know. She just didn't know until after she had Kel's ring on her finger. "What changed your mind?"

"When I saw how happy they were together, it was hard to object," Jim told her. "Still, when I first met the Saint Squad, I was treated like I was an intruder. Especially by your husband."

"Kel definitely takes the 'need to know' factor seriously."

Jim nodded. "In his line of work, he has to."

Katherine gave a casual shrug as she changed the subject to more practical matters. "I forgot to tell you earlier that I put a few things in the guest bathroom when Jim said he was bringing you home with him. Nothing fancy, just a nightshirt, a toothbrush, that sort of thing."

"Thank you."

"I know you probably want to go visit Kel at the hospital in the morning, but I thought afterward I could drive you to your house and help you pack anything else you need."

"You don't have to do that." Marilyn looked up at her, stunned. "That's a three-hour drive each way."

"I don't mind," Katherine insisted. "It will give me something to do tomorrow. Besides, I wanted to go visit Kel in the hospital anyway."

Marilyn shook her head in amazement. "Are you both always like this?"

Now Jim looked at her, confused. "Like what?"

"This," Marilyn motioned to the food in front of her with one hand and waved the other in the direction of the guest room. "Taking people in that you don't even know, helping them when they don't even know what help they need yet."

Katherine and Jim looked at each other for a moment. Then both of them grinned and nodded. Katherine let out a little laugh. "I guess you could say this isn't the first time we've been fortunate enough to help someone out."

"It's all her doing." Jim laughed. "To hear my brothers talk, I was a big bully growing up."

"He's still a bully," Katherine said, lowering her voice as though sharing a government secret. "But I've trained him to use that particular skill for good now instead of evil."

"I like to call it 'positive persuasion.'"

Marilyn couldn't help but laugh. "Whatever you call it, thank you for letting me stay here."

"We really are happy to have you," Katherine insisted. She turned toward the living room when they all heard the front door open and then close with a thud. Footsteps followed, and a moment later Amy stepped into the kitchen.

"Did you save me some?" Amy asked, her bright blue eyes sparkling with mischief.

"You're really home!" Katherine jumped up out of her seat and hugged her daughter, her daughter who, at six feet tall, was a good four inches taller than her mother.

Amy was passed from her mother to her father, and Marilyn enviously watched the warmth of the embrace between Amy and Jim. When Jim released her, Amy turned and looked at her. "Hi, Marilyn. I didn't know you were here."

"Your parents offered to let me stay here while Kel's at Bethesda. I hope you don't mind."

"Why would I mind?" Amy brushed her comment aside as she turned and opened a kitchen cabinet to retrieve a plate. "It's great to have you here. Maybe you can keep my mother occupied while I'm working this week."

"Actually, she just offered to drive me down to Virginia Beach tomorrow to pick up a few things."

"That's great." Amy nodded her approval. "Hey, if you're going down there anyway, any chance you can pick up some clothes from my place, too? I didn't exactly pack the right wardrobe for CIA headquarters."

"Sure, honey," Katherine agreed. "Just give me a list of what you want, or you'll have to deal with what I pick out."

"I'll give you a list," Amy insisted a little too quickly. She sat next to Marilyn and leaned closer. "She still thinks that brown is my best color."

"Oh, stop that. I just like that one suit you bought last fall."

"I'm just teasing, Mom." Amy reached for the bowl of mashed potatoes and scooped some onto her plate. She then turned to Marilyn once more. "How is Kel holding up?"

One shoulder lifted as Marilyn answered the best she could. "Okay, I guess."

"I know it's got to be killing him being tied to a hospital bed, especially knowing that the rest of the squad is still out in the field."

"I'm sure it is," Marilyn managed. She took a quick sip of water and then looked over at Katherine. "I'm a bit tired. I think I'm going to turn in if that's okay with you."

"Of course." Katherine's voice was kind and sympathetic. "Please make yourself at home, and let us know if you need anything."

"Thanks." Marilyn nodded. "I'll see you in the morning."

* * *

Marilyn sat down at the desk and turned on the laptop. Even though her body was exhausted, her mind was on overdrive. She knew she should probably check her e-mail or at the very least call her mom with the latest news about Kel, but instead she found the word-processing program and opened it up.

And she started to write.

She could feel the tension draining as she poured her emotions into the characters she knew so well. She wrote of a woman who was confident and self-assured, a woman who knew what she wanted and wasn't afraid to fight to make her dreams come true. She wrote of the man she loved so much, a man who always seemed to be putting everything else in his life before her.

Tonight Marilyn didn't have the luxury of looking back on the hundreds of pages she had written before, but that gave her a different kind of comfort. Perhaps her characters could have a new beginning, a new chance to find the path to happiness.

4

Kel was dreaming. He knew he was dreaming, but he couldn't wake up. His father and stepmother were standing in front of him, each of them holding hands with the little girl with bouncing curls and serious brown eyes.

"It was good to have you home, son," his father was saying.

His stepmother smiled in agreement. She had come into their lives seven years before, almost a decade after his mother had died from cancer, and Kel loved her with all his heart. Her voice was a little teary when she spoke. "Don't stay away so long this time. Before you know it, college will be over, and you'll be away at sea for who knows how long."

Even though he knew it wasn't real, Kel could hear himself responding as he crouched in front of the little girl. "I'm going to have to come back more often if Maggie doesn't stop growing so fast. I hardly recognized her when I got here."

"You did, too." Maggie smiled at him with her four-year-old innocence and dimples in her cheeks. She let go of her parents' hands and wrapped her arms around her big brother. Kel could smell the baby shampoo in her hair from her bath that morning, and he could feel the incredible softness of her skin. Mostly, he could feel that unconditional love Maggie gave him, even though he had been away at college for half of her life.

"Don't grow up too fast," Kel told her just as he had the last time he had seen her. Then he was boarding the train, even though his mind was screaming for him to stop, to go back and give them all one last hug, to at least take one last look.

Then the train jerked forward, and Kel turned to look back, only now they weren't there. All he could see was the rubble. He knew what the

Alfred P. Murrah Federal Building had looked like before April 19, 1995, before the day of the Oklahoma City bombing. He also knew what was beneath the rubble after the blast went off. Or rather, he knew *who* had been buried beneath the rubble.

He couldn't look anymore. He tried to turn his head, tried to turn off the images that had been haunting him for the past fifteen years. A hand grabbed his arm, and he knew it was the police officer coming to tell him the news. Then suddenly he heard a woman's voice, and the trance was broken.

"Commander?" the nurse repeated. "Are you okay?"

Kel's eyes opened, and he squinted under the bright hospital lights. Slowly, he nodded and let his eyes close for a moment longer. He took in a breath and then a second one before nodding once more. "Yeah, I'm fine."

"The doctor wanted me to tell you that he's scheduled some tests for this morning."

Still somewhat dazed, Kel nodded and managed to say, "I'll be here."

* * *

Marilyn turned the corner to the kitchen and stopped suddenly. In front of her was Katherine Whitmore standing at the kitchen counter, a fresh batch of blueberry muffins on a cooling tray in front of her and her husband's arms wrapped around her waist. Marilyn simply stared, not wanting to intrude.

At only seven in the morning, she hadn't expected to find anyone up yet, but from the looks of the kitchen, Katherine had been up for some time.

She listened to the humor in Katherine's voice as she spoke to her husband. "If you think you're taking this whole batch to your office, you have another thing coming."

Jim kissed his wife's neck. "But my staff loves me when I bring something from home. You can make another batch."

"And I can make something for your staff tomorrow if you really want me to, but you aren't taking these muffins," Katherine insisted, turning in his arms to reach up and kiss him.

Marilyn started at the sound of Amy's voice behind her. "They always make me a bit jealous when I'm here."

"What?"

"You know, being able to get up each morning and spend a few minutes together." Amy shrugged a shoulder. "I always thought I would have that when I grew up, but I never dreamed I'd end up married to a SEAL."

Marilyn nodded in agreement, some of the nerves in her stomach loosening. "I know what you mean."

"I guess it just proves you can't choose who you fall in love with." Amy gave Marilyn's arm a squeeze before moving past her and raising her voice. "Good morning."

Jim and Katherine turned to face Amy and Marilyn, both of them looking completely at ease, even though they still had their arms wrapped around one another. "Good morning," they replied in unison. Jim gave Katherine another quick kiss before releasing her and reaching for a muffin.

Katherine grinned over at him before shifting her attention back to Amy and Marilyn. "You should probably grab one while you can. He's determined to sneak these out of the house for his staff."

"I don't sneak," Jim countered. "I just wait until you aren't looking."

Katherine's laughter rang out. "Yes, I see how that sounds so much better."

"They smell great, Mom." Amy reached for one of the plates that was sitting on the counter, handed it to Marilyn, and then grabbed a paper towel for herself.

"Thanks," Marilyn said, waiting for Amy to serve herself before setting a muffin on her plate.

Katherine grabbed one, too, and looked over at Marilyn. "What time did you want to head over to the hospital?"

"Whenever you're ready," Marilyn told her. She had considered insisting on letting the navy get her back to Virginia Beach, but the more she thought about it this morning, the more she realized how tortuous that would be. Even though she didn't know Katherine very well, surely driving with her for three hours would be better than being escorted by a couple of men she had never met.

"We can leave right after breakfast if you want."

Amy put some butter on her muffin and then spoke to her mom. "I put the list of things I need and my house key in your purse, Mom."

"You're leaving already?" Katherine looked at her daughter suspiciously.

"I have a lot of work to do today," Amy said simply. "Don't hold dinner for me tonight. I'm not sure how late I'll be."

Jim looked over at her and said, "Subway?"

"Yeah." Amy nodded and quickly left the room.

Marilyn looked at Jim quizzically, but he turned his attention back to his breakfast. A minute later he stood up. "I'd better get going." He leaned down and kissed Katherine good-bye. "Give me a call when you get down to Virginia Beach."

"You mean, leave you a message when I get there."

Jim grinned. "Same thing."

Katherine nodded. "Have a good day."

Marilyn finished her own breakfast, still a little confused by the Whitmore's family dynamics. She couldn't say she had a lot to compare it to since her own father, a policeman, had died in the line of duty when she was only five years old. As long as she could remember, it had been just her and her mom. At least it had been that way until she had finished her associate's degree at the community college and finally dared to move into her own apartment in Baltimore.

She sometimes wondered if the reason she and Kel had clicked when they first met was the understanding of what it was like to lose someone close to them. Even though she had only been a child when her father was killed, Marilyn could still remember the smell of his shaving cream when he would let her sit in the bathroom and watch him get ready for work. He had been her hero, looking so invincible in his uniform.

Although Kel didn't speak of his family often, she knew that he still struggled with the incredible loss the day of the Oklahoma City bombing. He had told her once how relieved he had been when he'd heard the initial reports that day that the children in the day care facility were all okay. That tidbit of information had given him hope, hope that at least one member of his family had survived. But as the day went on, the truth had come out. The children in the day care weren't okay after all.

The horror of innocent children dying in such a horrendous way put an ache in her heart even now, and Kel still struggled to talk about his little sister's death. His parents' deaths were equally difficult, but she found that he could sometimes tell her about what they were like when they were still alive. Little Maggie he couldn't talk about at all.

When Katherine pushed back from the table, Marilyn brought herself back to the present. She picked up her plate and asked, "Can I help you clean up before we go?"

"That would be great." Katherine smiled. "Thank you."

With a little nod, Marilyn pulled open the dishwasher and wondered if maybe her fictional characters might want to live in a house like this one.

5

"What kind of books does Kel like to read?" Heather Addison asked as she approached the bookshelf.

Marilyn looked at her longtime friend and tried to push aside a wave of embarrassment. "I'm not sure."

Heather's eyebrows lifted over expressive brown eyes. "You aren't sure?"

Marilyn shook her head and began loading a canvas bag with books. She hoped Kel would like something out of the eclectic collection she was bringing him. "You know what it's been like. I hardly ever see my husband, and when I do, we don't exactly talk about books."

"I guess that's true." Heather nodded sympathetically. "It's pretty sad that it takes Kel getting shot for you to have time to spend together."

"I know." Marilyn thought of her visit that morning, fully aware that Kel was already getting bored with hospital life. "The worst part is that I keep hoping that he won't be able to go back to the teams. Then I feel guilty for thinking that way."

Heather turned toward her, sympathy showing on her face. "I'm sure he knows that you only want to spend more time with him."

"Maybe." Marilyn shrugged. She considered what life would be like if Kel didn't fully recover and couldn't imagine it. Kel's interests were varied, but most included actively doing something—running, swimming, hiking, camping. Doing anything outside made him happy. Inside activities that appealed to him were extremely limited.

Heather reached out and gave Marilyn's arm a friendly squeeze. "Trust me. Everything will work out."

"I hope so," Marilyn said, doubt lingering in her voice.

Heather's eyes narrowed, and she cocked her head to one side as she studied Marilyn more closely. "Have you talked to your mother today?"

"No." Marilyn shook her head. "I haven't talked to her since I called to let her know how Kel's surgery went. Why?"

"Because you always start second-guessing everything when you talk to your mom," Heather told her.

"She's just worried about me."

"She's also paranoid," Heather pointed out. "Not that I don't love your mom, but she has a tendency to look on the not-so-bright side of things. With the way she disapproves of Kel's career, I'm surprised he doesn't try to block her calls."

"She's the only family either of us has left. Besides, she's a lot better now than when I first got married."

"I guess that's true," Heather agreed. "But don't let her get you down. Trust that everything will work out, and it probably will."

"I'll try," Marilyn managed. "But I still don't know what I'm going to do after you move."

"You'll talk to me all the time on the phone," Heather said without missing a beat. "I still can't believe we've both lasted this long. Two navy wives living in the same place for five years." Heather's eyebrows lifted. "Pretty amazing."

Marilyn nodded, fighting a sudden sense of loss. "I'm sorry I won't be here to help you pack up."

"That's what the movers are for. Besides, you'll probably get back before I leave." Heather's cell phone chimed, and she reached into her pocket to silence it. "I hate to pack and run, but I've got to go meet with the Realtor."

Marilyn reached out to embrace her friend. "Keep in touch."

"You know I will." Heather hugged her and then moved toward the door. "And call me if you need to talk."

Marilyn simply nodded and watched Heather disappear outside. She let out a sigh, staring at the door for a moment as she sniffled back the tears that threatened. Heather was her only real friend, and now she was moving across the country. Marilyn couldn't begin to imagine what life would be like if Kel made it back to the teams now that she wouldn't have anyone else here to rely on.

She let out a sigh and tried to shake off her negative thoughts. Realizing that Katherine would be back from Amy's house any minute, she moved down the hall and entered the bedroom she and Kel used as an office. She crossed to the closet and pulled out a deck of cards and a couple of other games that were small enough to transport easily.

She then turned and stared at the bulky desktop computer, considering whether to pack it up or not. Even though Kel insisted that he had some money stashed away for a rainy day, Marilyn had saved nearly every penny of her transcription money over the past few years. Her money wasn't so much for that rainy day, but rather to prepare for if and when Kel ever left the military.

After writing on the Whitmore's laptop the night before, she wondered if perhaps it was time to break open her savings account and buy one of her own.

With a sigh, she turned on the computer and logged on to check her e-mail.

She then indulged herself and opened the file that contained the latest version of her novel. She scrolled down to the end, reading the last few paragraphs she had written.

Isabella glanced at her watch again, even though she knew what time it was. He was late. Again.

She thought of the evening she had planned. The special birthday dinner, the elegant place settings in the dining room, complete with candlelight.

Her teeth clenched together as she thought of the hours she had spent in the kitchen making his favorite homemade rolls. I should have known, *she thought to herself. She should have known he would stand her up again.*

With a shake of her head, she walked into the dining room. One by one, she blew out the candles.

Marilyn itched to fiddle with the scene, to explore more possibilities, but instead she downloaded the file onto her flash drive and then turned off the computer. When a knock came at the door, Marilyn stepped out of the office into the hall. Then the door opened before she moved to answer it.

"Hello?" Katherine called out as she stepped inside.

"Come on in." Marilyn waved her inside. "Did you get everything Amy wanted?"

"More or less." Katherine smiled innocently.

"Does that mean you added the brown suit Amy was talking about?"

"Well, it was right between two of the outfits she wanted. She can't blame me that it jumped into her suitcase with the others." Katherine gave a shrug. "What about you? Are you all packed?"

"Just about." Marilyn waved in the direction of the office. "I'm trying to decide if it's worth it to pack up my computer and bring it with me or if I should break down and buy a laptop of my own."

"You're welcome to borrow the one at our house as long as you like. You can even take it with you to the hospital if you want."

"Are you sure?" Marilyn asked hesitantly. After growing up on a shoestring budget, she was still hesitant to spend the money on such a luxury.

"Absolutely," Katherine insisted. "You'll need something to do when you're at the hospital, especially once your husband starts rehab."

"That would be great. I hate to the spend the money on one before I know if I'll really use it," Marilyn admitted.

"What can I help you with?"

"I think I'm all set except for these." Marilyn slipped the strap of the canvas bag over her shoulder and picked up the stack of games.

"Did you already pack some clothes for Kel?"

Marilyn smiled. "Oh, yeah. That was the only thing he asked me to bring him."

"Yeah, he doesn't look like the hospital-gown type to me."

Marilyn laughed. "You're right about that." She took one last look around the little house and then followed Katherine outside to where their cars were parked. "I'm going straight to the hospital, so I guess I'll see you at your house later tonight."

"We'll leave the door unlocked for you."

"Thanks again for everything."

"That's what friends are for."

* * *

Kel hated this. He could take the constant poking and prodding, but lying in bed all day and doing nothing was likely going to drive him crazy.

An orderly knocked on the door and carried in a tray. "I have your dinner, sir."

"Thanks." Kel shifted in his bed as the tray was set in front of him. He looked down at the food, wishing he had some interest in the chicken broth and Jell-O in front of him. Reluctantly, he picked up his spoon and forced himself to eat the broth, all the while wishing it were a steak, medium rare.

The door opened once more, but this time he smiled.

Marilyn shifted an overnight bag as she moved into the room and then dropped a canvas bag onto a chair. She took one look at the food in front of him and shook her head sympathetically. "Let me know when you can have some real food, and I'll smuggle in some lo mein."

"Deal." Kel smiled up at her as she leaned down to kiss him. "Did you bring me my clothes?"

She nodded. "I brought some books and games, too. I thought they might help you pass the time."

Kel looked up at her, a sudden sense of anxiety settling in his stomach. He watched her set the overnight bag down on the chair, unzip it, and pull out a change of clothes. With a glance down at his leg, reality struck him with new force. He needed help. He couldn't even perform the simple task of getting dressed by himself.

Marilyn looked up at him, concern crossing her face. "Are you okay?"

"I don't know if I can do this," Kel admitted. "How am I going to survive this place for six weeks?"

"One day at a time." Marilyn put her hand on his and squeezed, her eyes compassionate. "Don't think about tomorrow until you have to." She nodded down at the food in front of him. "Why don't you finish eating, and then I'll help you get dressed. You'll feel more like yourself when you have your own clothes on."

He kept his eyes on her for a long minute, realizing how relieved he was that she hadn't made him ask for help. Slowly, he nodded, but all the while he hoped he wouldn't need her help for long.

* * *

Something was very wrong. Marilyn didn't know what it was, but she could feel the tension in the air, not from the people in the house but rather from those absent. As far as she could tell, Amy never came home last night, and the senator had been oddly preoccupied when he arrived long after the sun went down. She had just been waking up that morning when she heard the senator's car pull out of the garage. The clock at her bedside had read 5:04.

Unsettled by the change in atmosphere, Marilyn turned to the one thing that always seemed to calm her down: writing. She had moved to the desk and fired up the laptop in the early morning light. She had planned to work from the file she had started several months ago, but instead she found herself continuing with the story she had started two days before.

Even though the characters had the same names as they did in her numerous other stories, for the first time she found them taking on their own personalities, making choices she hadn't already mapped out for them. The anxiety she felt infused itself into the situations she wrote for them as her fingers flew over the keyboard.

He hadn't called. He'd said he was going to call. He had promised.

She knew she shouldn't worry. It wasn't like this hadn't happened before, but still the nerves in her stomach churned. Maybe something was wrong. Or maybe he was still upset about their fight the night before. But he had said he would call. He said he knew he had to decide.

Maybe it was better that he hadn't called after all. She wasn't sure she was ready to know what his choice was. What would she do if he chose his career over her? More importantly, would she see him again?

Marilyn let the possibilities run through her head, and the words continued to appear on the computer screen. When the demands of her stomach finally slowed her creative momentum, she was surprised to look out the window to see the sun shining brightly. She glanced at the clock, stunned to see that it was after nine o'clock. Embarrassed that she had yet to surface from her room, she quickly showered and changed before heading for the kitchen.

She found Katherine in the living room curled up on the couch, a glass of juice in one hand and a book in the other. "Good morning," she greeted her with a warm smile.

"Good morning," Marilyn managed.

Before she could voice whatever apology she felt she should offer, Katherine motioned to the kitchen. "I'm afraid I'm being lazy today, so I didn't make any breakfast, but there are some Danishes on the counter, or, if you would rather, there is cereal in the pantry. Help yourself to whatever you can find."

"Thank you," Marilyn said, but instead of continuing to the kitchen she surprised herself by asking, "What are you reading?"

Katherine lifted the book so that she could see the cover of a recently released mystery novel. "Do you like to read?"

"Yeah, I do," Marilyn admitted. "It's one of my favorite things."

"Me, too. It never ceases to amaze me how a writer can string words together and come up with a book I can't put down." Katherine shook her head. "I started reading this last night before I went to bed and stayed up later than I should have. This morning I decided to indulge myself so I can find out what happens."

"Well, I'll let you get back to it." Marilyn smiled at her, wondering if she would ever be able to succeed in writing something people would want to read. "I'm going to head over to the hospital and see how Kel is doing."

"There are paper towels on the counter if you want to take a Danish with you," Katherine told her. "Also, the case for the laptop is in the top of the closet in your room if you want to take it to the hospital."

Marilyn smiled. Maybe the words that had come so easily this morning would continue if she found some time to write at the hospital. "I think I will. Thanks."

"Give me a call if you need anything," Katherine told her.

Marilyn nodded as she headed back to her room to retrieve the laptop. She was still a little awed by the fact that she had Senator and Katherine Whitmore's home and cell phone numbers programmed into her cell phone. The senator had even given her the number to his private line on Capitol Hill.

She moved back down the hall and called good-bye to Katherine as she left through the front door. As she climbed into her car and settled the laptop case safely in the front seat, she decided it was time her husband told her more about how he had come to know the Whitmores.

6

Kel stood by his bed, his hand gripping the edge of it as he struggled to put some weight on his injured leg. He had opted against taking the heavy painkillers the doctor prescribed. He was determined to get back in touch with his body and what it was trying to tell him. If he couldn't feel the pain, he wouldn't know how far he could push himself.

After Marilyn had left the night before, one of the nurses had helped him walk to the bathroom. If that hadn't been humiliating enough to need help to go the six steps across the room, he'd had the added embarrassment of not making it even two steps before he stumbled.

Today he was determined to win back some of his dignity. And his privacy.

Grabbing hold of the walker the doctor had insisted he use for the next few days, he shifted his weight onto his good leg and straightened his body. Gritting his teeth together, he moved his injured leg forward. He could feel the pull of the stitches, the ache from deep in his leg combined with an odd numbing sensation, and a sharp pain radiating from his knee. He quickly stepped forward with his good leg so he could take his weight off the bad one.

Taking a deep breath, Kel repeated the process. One step, then another, and another. By the time he reached the bathroom, he could feel beads of sweat on his forehead, and all of his muscles felt weak. Kel tried to focus on the victory of making it on his own, not wanting to admit that he had been reduced to someone who couldn't yet walk without assistance.

He was halfway back to his bed, leaning heavily on the walker, when the door opened wide and Marilyn walked in.

"What are you doing out of bed?" She rushed to his side, gripping his arm to help him back to the bed.

Out of breath, Kel let her help him. He sat on the edge of the bed and tried to catch his breath while Marilyn stood beside him and held him steady. Bracing against the pain that was sure to come, he shifted himself farther onto the bed and used his hands to lift his injured leg so he could reposition himself to where he could lie back down.

"Are you okay?" Marilyn asked now, reaching down to pull the covers over him.

Kel blew out a breath and nodded. He let himself catch his breath before he attempted to speak. "I just got a little winded when I went to the bathroom."

"Why didn't you call a nurse to help you?"

He looked at her then, wondering if she really understood him. "I needed to do it for myself."

Marilyn straightened a little, as though surprised by his intensity. "Okay." She set down a bag she had been carrying. "Does the doctor have any more tests scheduled for you today, or do you finally just get to rest?"

"I have an ultrasound scheduled for this afternoon, but as far as I know, there isn't anything until then."

"In that case," Marilyn pulled open the bag and looked up at him, "do you want to play gin rummy or Boggle?"

"You always win at gin rummy."

"Yeah, I know." Then she leaned down and kissed him. "Because it requires very little skill and a lot of luck."

"Let's try Boggle." Kel pushed aside the water jug on his tray to make room. "It's about time I beat you at something."

Marilyn pulled her chair closer and grinned. "You can try."

* * *

Admiral Carlos Mantiquez stood outside Kel Bennett's hospital room door. He had considered making this visit two days ago when the commander had been admitted, but he knew from experience that wounded sailors needed a little time to adjust mentally before they faced the practicality of their situations.

He shifted the stack of personnel files in his hands when he noticed Senator Whitmore heading his way.

"Admiral, I haven't seen you for a while. How are you doing?"

"Doing fine, Senator. How about you?"

"Better now that today is over."

Carlos nodded in understanding. The terrorist threat in Arizona had been averted, and the Saint Squad, including the senator's son-in-law, was heading home to Virginia.

Senator Whitmore motioned to Kel Bennett's room. "Have you told him yet?"

"Told him what?"

"That you want him to select his replacement." He gave him a knowing look. "You're standing outside of the commander's door knowing full well he is going to be out of the action. And you have a stack of personnel files in your hand."

"I was just about to discuss the options with him." Carlos shook his head. "I'm not sure how he's going to take this, though. As much as I would love to have the other squads in SEAL Team Eight pick up the slack, if we have a major event, I'm going to need the whole team ready to move. That includes the Saint Squad."

"Kel understands what's at stake. He has to know that his squad can't stand down until he recovers," Jim assured him. "Besides, he'll understand that he's only selecting a temporary replacement."

"I hope it's only temporary," Carlos said skeptically. "Do you think he understands that he might not make it back?"

"Mentally, yes. Emotionally, no." The senator shifted closer to the wall to let a nurse walk by. "I don't think he's willing to consider that possibility, and it's probably better for him at this point if he doesn't."

"You're probably right," Carlos agreed. "Having the right attitude is half the battle for these men when they're going through rehab."

"I assume you want to talk to the commander privately."

Carlos nodded. "I think his wife is in there with him now."

"I'll see if I can convince her to go for a walk with me so you can have a few minutes alone with the commander."

"I'd appreciate it." Carlos reached for the door and hoped the commander was ready for what he needed him to do.

* * *

Kel's first instinct when he saw Admiral Mantiquez walk into the room was to throw the covers off, push himself out of bed, and snap to attention. Realizing that his normal reaction would be out of place while lying wounded in a hospital, he instead sat up straighter and wondered what warranted a visit from an admiral and a senator.

His stomach clenched at the thought that his squad had been unsuccessful in Arizona, that somehow the terrorist attack had happened on US soil. Sensing his apprehension, the senator spoke first.

"I thought you'd like to know that your boys will be heading home tomorrow," Jim told him.

"Everything's okay?"

"Everything's fine." Jim nodded. He then motioned to Marilyn. "Admiral Mantiquez, this is the commander's wife, Marilyn Bennett."

"It's a pleasure to meet you." The admiral offered his hand as Marilyn stood up.

"You, too," Marilyn said softly, looking from the admiral to her husband.

"Marilyn, why don't we give these men a few minutes alone?" Jim motioned to the door.

"Okay," Marilyn said hesitantly, again looking back at Kel.

"It's okay, honey," Kel assured her. "Why don't you go down to the cafeteria and get some lunch."

Marilyn nodded and moved through the door the senator now held open for her.

Kel spotted the personnel files and reached out a hand. "I assume those are the top candidates for my replacement."

"They are." Admiral Mantiquez nodded. "I've thought about it a lot, and I feel it would be best to let Lieutenant Miller take over the Saint Squad while you're laid up."

"I agree." Kel nodded his approval, relieved that the man who would be taking over his command was someone he trusted implicitly. "Brent goes up before the promotion board in a couple of months. This will definitely help his chances, and I know he'll do a great job."

"I'm glad to hear that you have so much confidence in him." He offered a stack of five files to Kel. "These are some of our better prospects to fill the empty spot in your squad for the time being. I'd like you to look over them and give me your recommendation."

Kel looked down at the files, flipping the first one open. His eyes narrowed, and he opened the second one. Quickly glancing at the front page of all five files, he looked up at the admiral. "All of these are straight out of BUD/S training."

"That's right." Admiral Mantiquez nodded. "They graduate the day after tomorrow."

"Do you really think this is wise? Putting an unseasoned SEAL in with your best squad?"

"These candidates have a lot to offer, and your boys have a lot they can teach them." Mantiquez nodded. He motioned to the files. "Since those are confidential, I'll make sure the nurse provides you with a lock box. I want your recommendation by tomorrow."

Kel simply nodded as the admiral turned and left the room.

7

"You said no one would be able to stop us." Akil Ramir's voice vibrated with fury as he stared out the penthouse window of the hotel-style building he had turned into his safe haven, his fortress. Slowly, the longtime arms dealer and self-proclaimed terrorist turned to face his second in command, Halim Karel. "What happened?"

"I don't know yet," Halim spoke tentatively. "I'm still trying to get in touch with my sources."

Venom spewed from Akil as he hissed, "Find out."

Halim gave a nod and a slight bow, backing up until the elevator doors were behind him. Without another word, the man disappeared from the room, and Akil continued to seethe with hatred and anger.

* * *

The five men might as well have been interchangeable. Kel studied the files, studied each man's specialties. Two officers, three enlisted, all as green as they came. Not one of these men had any combat experience. Not one of them understood what real missions were like. Sure they had gone through BUD/S training, the basic underwater demolition course for SEALs. They could all swim five miles without much effort, they knew how to jump out of helicopters, and they could hotwire cars. They could fly airplanes or pilot boats. But could they be trusted?

Trust was essential. Without it, the SEALs would fail. How many times, he wondered, had he moved through a dark jungle and known where every one of his men was, even though he couldn't see them? How many mornings had he prayed with them that the Lord would guide them through whatever obstacles they might face?

Kel thought of those morning prayers, a ritual they had started shortly after the Saint Squad was created. Now he looked through the files again with a renewed interest. Which of these men would acclimate to that aspect of his squad? None of them was LDS. He was sure he would have noticed that before, but what kind of men were they?

He thought back to when he first started out in the teams. He could remember all too clearly what it had been like being the only man in his unit who didn't drink. He had always felt a bit like he was on the outside looking in, especially when the other men he worked with talked about their adventures together when they were on leave.

When Brent Miller had been assigned to Kel's unit, things began to change. Finally, he had someone else who shared the same values. Now, for the past five years, he had become spoiled working within a squad that was so solid in their values and in their faith. The men he served with had become more than just co-workers or teammates. They were his brothers, his family. Whoever he recommended to fill the open spot was going to feel like a stepchild, and it was up to him to find the man who had the best chance of conforming to their squad's high standards.

He noticed that one of the young officers was married and considered whether that might make the transition a bit easier, especially since Tristan was newly married. Kel read through the file once more, but when he read through the man's specialties, he realized the fit wasn't quite right. Communications was this man's strong point, but Seth Johnson already filled that need within the Saint Squad.

The door opened, and he looked up to see his wife come into his room.

"Did Senator Whitmore leave?"

Marilyn nodded. "Yeah. He said he had to get back for a meeting, but I'm supposed to tell you that he'll give you a call later." She hesitated, stepping closer when Kel closed the file he held and set it on his lap with the others. She was quiet for a moment, as though working up her nerve to say something. "How long have you known the Whitmores?"

"I don't know. About three years, I guess."

"You never mentioned it before," Marilyn said, a touch of sadness in her voice. "I never knew that Amy was Senator Whitmore's daughter."

"Really?" Kel looked at her, surprised. "I'm sorry, honey. I just assumed you knew."

Marilyn's voice turned defensive. "How would I know?"

"You were around when Amy first started working with us, before she was married to Brent."

"Kel, you always referred to her as 'Amy' or your 'civilian.' You never said, 'Amy Whitmore is working for me, and by the way, her dad's a senator.'"

"Marilyn, I wasn't trying to keep this from you. If you hadn't been in Florida visiting your mom, you would have met the Whitmores at Brent and Amy's wedding." Kel reached for her, somewhat relieved when she let him take her hand. "Amy's background has always been one of those common-knowledge things. It never occurred to me that you didn't realize who she was."

She let out a sigh but seemed to accept his answer. "What did the admiral want to see you about? Or can you tell me?"

Kel checked his normal response of refusing to talk about work, instead motioning to the files. "He wants me to select the man who will fill in for me with the Saint Squad."

"You have to choose your own replacement?"

"He won't really be my replacement," Kel explained. "Brent Miller will take over command, but he'll need someone to fill in for him until I come back."

"I see." Marilyn sat down and leaned back in her chair. "Have you decided who it should be?"

He shook his head. "No. I've eliminated one as a possibility, but the other four are pretty equal on paper. I think I'll have to pray on it before I decide."

"Really?" Marilyn looked at him with surprise and wonder in her eyes. "You would pray about something work related?"

Kel laughed now. "Marilyn, in my line of work, I pray about everything work related."

"I never realized that."

"Believe it or not, inspiration is one of the tools we rely on a lot."

Marilyn nodded, considering. "That's good to know."

* * *

Petty Officer Alex Meyers walked down the hall, wondering how his new charge would respond to taking orders from an enlisted man. In his twelve years working in rehab and physical therapy, he found that the higher the rank, the more difficult the patient. When he entered the commander's room at 0600, he decided this time might be different.

Instead of lying in bed as Alex had expected, the commander was standing by the window across the room from the bed. Even more impressive than the man being vertical was the fact that the walker was beside him. If this man was willing to rely on the tools at his disposal instead of refusing them for pride's sake, he imagined they would get along just fine.

Commander Bennett turned to look at him. "If you're going to tell me I should be in bed, you'll be wasting your breath."

"I gather you've had a few run-ins with the nurses." Alex nodded in understanding.

"Oh, yeah."

"Well, I'm actually here to get you out of bed," Alex told him. "I'm Alex Meyers. It's my job to get you up and moving again."

"Good." Commander Bennett nodded. "It's about time I had someone on my side."

"Just remember you said that when I'm telling you to try something you don't think you can do."

"Deal."

"Are you ready to get started, Commander?"

"I'm ready." He gripped his walker and nodded his head. "And call me Kel."

8

"Are you having any luck?" Marilyn asked, motioning to the files Kel was looking through when she walked in.

Kel shook his head. "It's going to be hard finding someone to fit the dynamics of our squad without getting a chance to meet them."

"What do you mean, 'the dynamics'?"

"It's hard to explain." Kel looked at her as though searching for the right words. "When you rely so heavily on teamwork, it's crucial that everyone can trust each other. My squad has been together so long that we know what everyone else is doing whether we can see them or not. How do I find someone who can step into that environment and be sure that they won't let everyone down?"

"Is there any way you would be able to meet these men?" Marilyn asked. "Or maybe Brent would be able to."

"I get the feeling that the admiral doesn't want to wait long enough to give us that luxury," Kel told her. "They are all new graduates of BUD/S, so he wants to have a name before their orders are cut."

Marilyn sat down in the chair by the bed and nodded. "Tell me about them. I mean, tell me what you're allowed to tell me about them."

"Like what?"

"Can you tell me where they're from? How old they are? That kind of thing?"

"Let's see. This one is from Michigan." Kel laid the open file on his lap and opened the next one. "Then we have Chicago, Miami, and San Diego."

"Do they get to say where they would prefer to be stationed?"

"In the teams, everyone knows you don't have much of a choice," Kel started, but he still took the time to flip through the files. "Two don't show any preference. The one from San Diego asked for a West Coast station, and the one from Michigan wants OUTCONUS."

"Huh?"

"Outside of the continental US"

Marilyn nodded with new understanding. "If the guy from San Diego wants to stay close to home, he might not be the best fit since he'd be disappointed to get this assignment." Marilyn tilted her head to one side and continued hesitantly, "I don't know much about what you do, but you've always seemed really proud of how well your team works together. If this guy won't appreciate the opportunity, I wouldn't think you would want him."

"You're probably right." Kel pulled one file from his lap, closed it, and set it aside. Then he looked over at Marilyn with an odd expression.

"What?"

"I'm impressed." Kel gave her a nod of approval. "I've been staring at these files for hours and haven't gotten anywhere. Now I feel like I'm making progress."

"Maybe you've been staring at them too long," Marilyn suggested.

"Or you might be the inspiration I was waiting for," Kel told her.

Marilyn smiled at that. "What about their basic skills?"

"They're all pretty much the same. The one who wants to be stationed overseas is stronger in foreign languages, but the other two are better in most of the other skill areas."

"Which is more important to you?" Marilyn asked.

"Probably the basic skill areas," Kel admitted. "My foreign language skills are probably the weakest on my squad, so it isn't going to hinder them to have someone equal to me instead of better than me in that area."

"Plus, if he's that good with languages, he would probably be more useful in an overseas assignment where he wants to be in the first place."

"Okay. That brings us down to these two." Kel shifted the two files so that he could look at the information on both at the same time. "There is really no significant difference between them." He shook his head and leaned back against his pillow. "I keep thinking that the biggest obstacle for the new guy is going to be the religious issues."

"What do you mean?"

"If I get someone who wants to spend all of his free time hanging out at bars and chasing women, he's going to have a hard time connecting with the other guys in the squad."

"Yeah, but just because someone isn't Mormon doesn't mean they drink and smoke all the time or that they don't have standards."

"I know, but how can I tell from a stack of papers?"

"I have no idea."

"Me either." Kel shifted and started to set the files aside. Then he saw it. The clue he had been looking for. "Do you think a competitive swimmer would smoke or drink?"

"I doubt it." Marilyn shook her head. "And if he did, I doubt it would be much."

"I think we just found my replacement."

"Really?"

Kel nodded and smiled. "Our boy from Miami was the star of the Naval Academy's swim team. He swam all four years and was captain his senior year."

"It sounds like you should give him a try."

"That's what I'm thinking," Kel agreed. "Any chance you can hand me that phone there? I need to give the admiral a call."

Marilyn picked up the phone and handed it to him. "Do you want me to wait outside?"

Kel shook his head as he dialed the number. When the admiral came on the phone, Kel sounded confident when he said, "I've got that name for you. Jay Wellman."

* * *

Someone was after her, her breath ragged as she ran toward her car. She could hear the footsteps getting closer, her fingers numb as she fumbled with her keys. The car was just ahead, her ride to safety. She managed to press the unlock button, grasping the door handle and jumping inside. Somehow the key slid into the ignition even though her hands were shaking, and the car roared to life.

The car squealed into motion as she looked into the back window and saw the dark figure raise a gun, one she recognized as a . . .

Marilyn stopped typing, her train of thought interrupted as she hit a minor roadblock. What kind of gun would her bad guy carry? She considered a couple of options, not quite sure what the differences were, even though she was familiar with the names. She let out a little sigh, for a moment wishing that she could ask Kel his opinion. Of course, she couldn't. She could already imagine how embarrassed she would be if he knew this was how she spent her free time.

Usually, when he wasn't on an assignment, they spent most of their time together. Their shared interests weren't very complicated. They played games, watched movies, or went out to dinner or a movie. Since her hours were flexible with transcribing, she always worked when he worked so they would have more time together.

She knew he thought that all of her time at the computer was spent transcribing legal documents. Sometimes she felt a little guilty for deceiving him, but it wasn't like she had ever really lied to him. She'd just let him assume he knew why she was typing.

With Kel injured, she wouldn't have that excuse for long. She had called her boss and tried to quit her job the day she went down to Virginia Beach to get her things. Her boss had been very understanding, but he had been unwilling to take her resignation under the circumstances. Instead, he had insisted that she take a three-month leave of absence to be sure that quitting was really what she wanted. Marilyn already knew that when the three months were up she wouldn't want to go back.

Over the past several days, she had fallen into a comfortable routine. She got up early each morning and spent two hours writing before spending a few minutes with Katherine over breakfast. She then went to the hospital with the laptop in tow. Most of her time at the hospital was spent with Kel, but now that he had started rehab, she usually had at least an hour or two to write. At night she typically returned to the Whitmores' house where she ate dinner, made an occasional phone call to update her mom and Heather, and then spent another hour or two writing.

Her manuscript was growing longer by the day and was regularly taking turns that she hadn't planned. For once, she found an odd comfort in letting her characters take on lives of their own, not forcing herself to plan everything out with outlines and character sketches.

Still staring at the computer screen, she gave a little shake of her head. She hit the delete key a few times, changing the last part of the sentence so she wouldn't have to describe the gun.

With a sigh of satisfaction, she read through the last few paragraphs and got back to work.

9

Kel sat in one of the two chairs in his room, his elbow on the little table beside him. After more than a week in the hospital, he was no longer willing to be in bed unless it was time to sleep in it. His dinner tray was still on the table where he had eaten, and he held a book in his hands.

Alex wouldn't let him do much physically yet, but he could at least keep his language skills sharp. In the stack of books Marilyn had brought him were a couple of novels written in French, so he decided to pass the time with those.

When his door opened, he assumed it was someone coming to collect his dinner tray. Then he heard Seth's Southern drawl. "Hey, boss."

Kel looked up and grinned at the huge black man filling his doorway. Then his eyes settled on the woman beside him, the same woman he had been shot trying to protect. "Good to see that you made it back safely."

"How are you doing?" Seth asked, his voice serious. "Anything new from the doctors?"

"Don't worry about me. I'll make it back," Kel told him.

"Any idea of when you're getting out of this place?"

"They want to keep me for a few more weeks so I can do my rehab up here," Kel told him. "I'm not sure if that's such a good idea with my replacement showing up in a couple of days."

"Tell you what," Seth began. "Why don't you let us handle breaking in the new guy, and you concentrate on getting back to a hundred percent."

Before Kel could respond, Vanessa interrupted, "Do you think you can be up and around by July 2?"

"Yeah." Kel nodded. His tentative release date was the first of June. "Why?"

"We wanted to be sure you can make it to our wedding."

"You're getting married?" Kel saw it now, the diamond sparkling on Vanessa's left hand. "Congratulations."

"Thanks," Seth answered, but his face was still serious. "I also wanted to say I'm sorry about what happened. I shouldn't have had you come in after us."

"Don't go there, Seth." Kel shook his head. He had already spent far too many hours second-guessing his decision to go ahead with the mission, analyzing what he could have done differently that night. "We both made the best decisions we could with the information we had to work with, and we all made it out alive. We can't ask for a whole lot more than that."

Seth gave a curt nod. Then he nudged Vanessa farther into the room and closed the door behind him. "What do you know about the new kid?"

Kel glanced over at Vanessa, reminding himself that she was CIA and had top-secret clearance. "Have you met him yet?"

"He reports tomorrow."

"Name's Jay Wellman. I don't know anything about him except what's in his file," Kel began. "He's an Academy graduate, speaks Spanish and French, and his scores were strong on the shooting range."

"Brent said you were the one who chose him from the short list," Seth said. When Kel nodded, he asked, "What made him stand out?"

Kel shifted in his seat and thought back to how he had struggled to choose. "It started out with eliminating some of the other candidates for different reasons. Then when it came down to the last couple, I noticed that he was a competitive swimmer. Marilyn and I thought that being an athlete, he might have the kind of standards we live by."

"Marilyn?" Seth's eyebrows lifted.

"Yeah." Kel shook his head, still a bit awed by the help his wife was to him in the selection process. "It was the strangest thing. I kept reading through those files and praying about who I should pick. Then Marilyn comes in and after talking to her for five minutes, completely in generalities, the choice was made."

"Well, we'll try to go easy on him the first day or two," Seth said. "We'd better get going, but you take care of yourself."

"I will," Kel told him. "Thanks for stopping by."

Seth opened the door and then looked back at Kel. "You said this kid is a swimmer. Exactly how fast is he?"

"Fast." Kel laughed. "If you want to make him feel good, let Tristan challenge him to a race. That ought to give him some confidence."

Seth smiled now. "Seems to me I still owe Tristan for that little surprise he left me last time we were in Brazil."

"You did start that war when you left the tarantula in his room," Kel reminded him, remembering all too well the baby snake Seth had discovered curled up in his boot.

"Yeah, but this time he won't know I set him up." Seth gave him a knowing look. "I'll let you know how it turns out."

"Oh, I'm sure I'll hear about it." Kel laughed as Seth escorted Vanessa out the door.

* * *

Halim Karel crossed the plush carpet in the oversized dining room with purpose. As always, he was impeccably dressed in a tailored Italian suit, his handsome features belying his ruthlessness. He stopped opposite the seat Akil Ramir currently occupied. "I have something you should see."

Akil set down his fork and looked up. "What is it?"

Halim held up a printout of a newspaper article from the United States. "I had a couple of our men searching the Internet for recent articles on anyone injured by a gunshot wound."

"You're trying to find the man who was shot when Lina was taken?" Akil's eyes narrowed.

"I thought it might help us narrow down where she is being held." Halim handed him the printout and tapped a finger on the headline that read, "Local hero wounded." "I didn't really expect to find anything. Especially not this."

Akil scanned the article about the sailor who was injured in a training accident a few days before the paper had been printed. He looked up at Halim and shook his head. "What exactly am I looking at?"

"Look at the picture."

Akil shifted his eyes to the photo. Rather than the standard military photo that normally accompanied such articles, this one appeared to be a snapshot of the commander. It had been cropped so that he was the only one visible. But he wasn't the only one visible. Towering over him in the space behind him was the man they knew as Seth Billaud, the man who was supposed to be engaged to Akil's niece, Lina.

Now Akil looked up at Halim and stared. "How is this possible?"

"Perhaps your niece wasn't kidnapped by your business partner like we thought," Halim suggested. "Perhaps she was taken by Seth and his military friends."

"You think he infiltrated my brother's organization?"

"He must have." Halim nodded. "He knew this place, and we know he visited your brother in jail."

"Find him," Akil ordered.

"We've already tried, but no one even knows his real name," Halim told him. Before Akil could start a tirade, Halim continued, "But I do have another idea."

"What do you suggest?"

"Look at the date of the article," Halim suggested. He had already surmised that the wounded officer hadn't sustained his injuries in a training accident but rather in a firefight right outside where he now stood. "I don't think our sailor was hurt in a play fight."

"Says here he's being treated in Bethesda."

"I noticed that, too," Halim said calmly. "I think one of us needs to take a trip to the United States."

Akil stroked his mustache and considered. Then he nodded slowly.

* * *

Marilyn opened the door to her husband's hospital room, surprised to find that he wasn't there. She was pretty sure he didn't have any tests scheduled, and his rehab sessions were normally in the early morning and late afternoon.

His rehab seemed to be going well, and he had even graduated from using a walker to using a cane. His limp was pronounced, but Kel seemed confident that in time he would recover completely. Marilyn wondered how much time.

She wanted her husband to heal, but she was so enjoying the novelty of knowing where he was going to be each day. No one was going to call in the middle of the night and tell him he had to report for duty. He didn't have to leave on training missions that lasted weeks at a time.

She knew he was getting restless with his current situation, especially being confined to the hospital for so long. She had arrived the day before to find him arguing with the doctor, asserting that he should be allowed to do outpatient for his rehab. The doctor had shut him down, explaining that their policies wouldn't allow him to have the intensive help he needed if he wasn't still admitted to the hospital. Basically, everyone agreed that he was well enough to go home, or at least to stay at the Whitmores' house, but no one seemed to know how to cut through the red tape to make it possible.

Despite Kel's eagerness to leave the confines of the hospital, Marilyn couldn't help enjoying the time his stay had given them together. She felt like her marriage was becoming what it once was, what she still wanted it to be.

After waiting for a couple of minutes, Marilyn walked down the hall to the nurses' station. "My husband isn't in his room. Do you know where he is?"

The young nurse opened up a chart and pointed down the hall. "If you take your first left, it's the third door on the right."

"Thanks." Marilyn moved down the hall, wondering if she would be better off going back to Kel's room and spending some time writing. She didn't want to get too involved with her story, though, if he was going to be back soon. Resolved to find out what he was doing, she turned the corner and found the correct door.

She walked inside and looked around. Various exercise equipment was scattered around the room, although only a couple of exercise bikes were currently being used. Then she saw him.

Kel was on a stair-climber, his face contorted with pain. His green T-shirt was soaked with sweat, and he was struggling to catch his breath. Marilyn started forward, but a hand reached out and stopped her.

"He can do it," the man assured her. "Let him try."

"It's only been a few weeks."

"Let him try," he repeated.

Kel fought to keep up with the machine even though it was set to an incredibly slow pace. Then, with a shake of his head, he hit the off button and swiped at the sweat on his face. "I can't do it."

"You can do it," the therapist insisted. "You've worked through pain before. You can do it now."

The man who had stopped Marilyn interrupted. "I think the commander has had enough for now," he said, as he approached Kel. "I'm sure he'll be ready for this challenge tomorrow after he's had some rest."

Kel's gaze landed on Marilyn for a moment. Then he looked at the man standing beside her and nodded in agreement.

"Mrs. Bennett, why don't you wait for your husband in his room? He'll need a few minutes to shower and change before he heads back."

Slowly, Marilyn nodded. "Okay." With a last glance at Kel, she turned and left the room.

* * *

"What do you think?" Alex asked his supervisor, Commander Ruben.

"I think I don't like to hear a Navy SEAL say he can't do something."

"This is the third time this week he's been unable to do the stair climber," Alex told him. "Am I pushing him too fast?"

"No, he's ready." Commander Ruben considered for a minute. "His wife isn't going to push him through this, but I think I know what will."

"What?"

"The one thing that SEALs can never resist is a challenge." He picked up Kel's chart and reached for the phone. "And I think I know just the person to issue it."

10

Marilyn studied the letters as Kel placed them on the Scrabble board. He wasn't surprised when she looked up at him and shook her head.

"That is not a word," Marilyn insisted.

"It is too a word." Kel grinned at her, grateful that she had not insisted on talking about his earlier failure in rehab. "It means 'generous' in French."

"Nice try," Marilyn said, shaking her head. "But you know the rules. No foreign words. Even if it really is a word, it's not in the English dictionary."

Kel leaned forward and gave her a playful kiss. "Prove it."

"That's it," Marilyn told him. "I'm going out tonight to buy a dictionary."

After nearly a month in the hospital, they had both tired of the games Marilyn had brought from home, and this week they had graduated to Scrabble. Kel found that his wife was even more formidable in this game than she had been in the various games of chance they normally played together.

"You don't want to spend your hard-earned money on a dictionary," Kel told her. "Besides, if you do that I won't have a chance at beating you."

"Very funny." Marilyn leaned back in her chair. "Do you want to give up now, or should we play this game through?"

The door behind her opened.

"Knock, knock." Brent Miller's voice called into the room.

"Come on in," Kel begged him. "You can save me from my wife's endless torture."

"In that case—" Brent stepped inside, followed by his wife, Amy, along with Tristan and Riley Crowther, and another man he'd never met.

"What are you all doing here?" Kel asked, shifting to look at them. "I thought you were heading out for a training exercise tomorrow."

"It was postponed for a couple of days," Brent told him. "Besides, we had another mission that was more important."

"What mission is that?"

"The Nats game. Tonight." Brent motioned to Tristan, who closed the door to ensure some privacy. "Grab your shoes. We're breaking you out of here."

"That's funny." Kel shook his head. "I already tried to get them to let me do outpatient, but these doctors are determined to strangle me with red tape."

"Commander," Tristan drawled, amusement in his voice, "you aren't backing down from a little challenge, are you?" He stepped farther into the room and motioned to a dark-haired young man who looked to be about twenty-two. "Meet Roger. He'll be standing in for you tonight."

"Are you suggesting he *sneak* out?" Marilyn looked at Tristan like he was crazy. "You'll never get him past the nurses' station, not to mention the guards at the front entrance."

Every man in the room looked at her, eyebrows raised, disbelief in their eyes.

"Marilyn, maybe you and I should go get the car," Riley suggested and then turned to Tristan. "We'll meet you outside."

Marilyn let Riley lead her out of the room before she looked at her and asked, "Are they all nuts?"

"They're Navy SEALs. Of course they're all nuts," Riley said with a laugh. She put a hand on Marilyn's arm and ushered her down the hallway. "Come on. We don't want to talk about this here."

With a shake of her head, Marilyn walked down the hall, past the nurses' station, the doctors' lounge, a security desk, and then past the guards at the main entrance. Surely, her concerns about Kel leaving the safety of the hospital were unfounded. There was no way he was making it out of there.

* * *

"I assume you have a plan," Kel said as he slipped his shoes on.

"We thought about having you climb out the window, but we figured we'd give you another week to recover before we throw that one at you."

Brent motioned to Roger, who was dressed casually in a T-shirt and cargo shorts, very similar to what Kel was now wearing. "Roger will stay here while we're gone so that it looks like you're sleeping. We're going to take the back way out and go to the game."

"I guess I'm following your lead." Kel nodded to Brent. He stood up, only struggling a little to put weight on his injured leg.

Brent glanced down at his watch, and Kel could tell he was counting down. Then he pointed at Amy, who opened the door, held up one finger, and closed the door behind her.

A minute later Tristan opened the door and peeked out before motioning for Brent and Kel to follow. Roger climbed up into the bed and rolled onto his side so that his face couldn't be seen by anyone passing by. Then Kel was walking as casually as he could down the hall, shielded by the two taller men as they passed by Amy, who was currently talking to the nurses.

Instead of heading for the main entrance, they moved to the stairwell. Kel didn't want to think about his earlier struggles with the stair-climber in rehab. With a new determination, he moved with his men and put his hand on the rail. Pain shot through his knee when he took the first step, and Kel leaned on the rail to compensate for his leg's weakness, quickly taking another step so his weight was on his good leg once more.

"We've got four minutes to clear the stairs, and two minutes to make the back door."

"The alarms?" Kel managed to ask, as he continued his struggle down the stairs.

"We've got it covered."

Kel didn't ask how they were going to take care of overriding the alarms. He was still thinking about the four minutes his team had given him to make it down three flights of stairs. Normally, that much time would sound like an eternity. Now it sounded nearly impossible. He took another step, shifting his weight once more to the good leg. He could almost hear Alex's words echoing through his ears.

Stop favoring that bad leg or you're going to strain the good one. Trust that you can do it, and you can.

Kel blew out a little breath and took another step with his bad leg, this time letting his weight stay on it a bit longer. Slowly, he found a rhythm, one foot then the other. His hand still gripped the rail, steadying him as he reached the first landing.

"Keep going, Commander," Tristan encouraged him from behind. "We're right on schedule."

Three and a half minutes later, they emerged through the door onto the main floor and made their way to a back door. Brent checked his watch, holding up one hand as he signaled for everyone to wait. Then his hand dropped, and Tristan opened the door.

Kel stepped out into the night and smelled the sweet scent of freedom.

* * *

"I still can't believe you broke out of the hospital." Marilyn shook her head, bewildered. She had followed Riley outside to where Katherine Whitmore's SUV had been parked. A few minutes later, Amy arrived outside and told everyone to get in. She then drove over to a back entrance moments before their three husbands emerged without a sound. Then everyone was in the SUV, and they were headed for the stadium.

"I can't tell you how good it feels to be out of that place," Kel told her. He then shifted his attention to the front seat where Brent was in the passenger seat beside Amy. "Do I even want to know what you bribed Roger with to get him to double for me tonight?"

"I believe there was some mention of a weekend liberty."

Kel shook his head and chuckled. "So who are the Nationals playing tonight anyway?"

"The Devil Rays."

Marilyn straightened a little in her seat as she recalled the Whitmores talking that morning about going to watch their oldest son play tonight. "Amy, isn't that the team your brother plays for?"

"Yeah." Amy nodded. "That's why we picked tonight to go. When Matt's playing, I have a few more strings I can pull."

"You know, I've never been to a live game before," Marilyn said conversationally, surprised that she could say something like that in front of so many people.

"Really?" Brent shifted to look at her. "Then I'm glad you're able to come along. Tonight's going to be a lot of fun."

Amy passed the parking lot for general parking and continued to the lot right next to the stadium. She pulled in to where a guard was posted, the sign behind him clearly stating that permits were required. Amy showed the guard some kind of pass and was immediately waved through.

The parking lot was already crowded, but Amy passed the few open spots on the far side of the lot and continued toward the stadium. Then she slowed down and pulled into a spot right by the entrance. A sign at the front of the spot read simply, "Reserved: Whitmore."

"You have a reserved parking space inside the reserved lot?" Marilyn asked in awe.

"Not usually, but my brother pulled a few strings for me. Or maybe it was my dad." Amy shrugged a shoulder and grinned back at Marilyn. "I can't ever figure out who has what connections, so I normally thank both of them so that I'm covered."

"Let's go." Brent pushed the door open, and everyone climbed out. A few minutes later, they were in their seats and the first pitch was thrown.

"This is amazing," Marilyn said as she leaned closer to Kel. "This place is huge, but it feels like everyone is just hanging out at a big party or something."

Kel nodded in understanding. "I'm glad you're here."

"Me, too."

11

Halim stood in the shadows of Bethesda Naval Hospital, watching, waiting. He had spent three days staking out the hospital parking lot, hoping to catch a glimpse of Seth going to visit the man presumed to be his commanding officer. Other men and women arrived, steadily passing through the security at the front entrance and leaving the same way.

A delivery truck pulled past him and headed for the back doors. Halim had tried slipping in through that back entrance the day before until he had seen that there were guards stationed there every time a delivery arrived. For now he wasn't willing to resort to force.

The news that Lina Ramir was once again living in a federal prison had enraged Akil and those close to him. While Halim's first instinct had been to strike, to somehow break Lina out of prison, Akil had insisted they be a little more practical. Akil understood the Americans well and planned to wage a different kind of war when the time came. Once the softhearted American liberals learned on some news program that the military had abducted Lina, had taken her by force from her home in a foreign land, he was sure the public outcry would free her. Or, failing that, a slick, pricy lawyer.

Before they could deal with freeing Lina, Halim had to take care of one other obstacle first: finding the man who claimed to be her fiancé and making sure he was out of her life for good.

The doors of the front entrance opened once more. When a nurse pushing a patient in a wheelchair emerged from the building, a new idea began to form. Perhaps the answer wasn't how to get into the hospital, but rather when to be ready when the commander got out.

* * *

The tingling was still there, along with a pulling sensation, as Kel stepped with his injured leg. The bandages were off and the stitches were out, but he could still feel the slight limp he couldn't seem to overcome. Since the night he had sneaked out of the hospital with Brent and Tristan, Kel could feel himself making progress. But he knew that he wasn't anywhere near where he needed to be to get back to work.

Walking was still difficult, and the doctor insisted he use a cane for several more weeks until he could adjust to the numbness in his leg. He wasn't sure which was worse, the nerve damage that caused part of his leg to feel dead to him or the knee that seemed to swell up every time he thought about doing something new.

A torn or strained ligament was the diagnosis for his knee, but he knew the doctor couldn't do anything more than make an educated guess. Apparently, the possible presence of gun fragments in his wound prevented him from being able to have an MRI, which would have helped confirm the diagnosis. So for now, he would continue with rehab and hope that he would continue to improve.

"You're looking better," Alex said when Kel finished his allotted time on the stair-climber. "How's the swelling?"

"It still flares up after the stairs, but it's getting better when I only use the treadmill."

"That's not uncommon with a ligament injury," Alex told him. "If it doesn't get better after another month, you'll need to check back with the doctor to see if the ligament needs to be surgically repaired."

"Let's hope it doesn't come to that."

Alex shrugged. "I know it isn't easy, but six more months of rehab is a piece of cake compared to losing your active-duty status."

"I know," Kel agreed, but he prayed that his recovery wouldn't take nearly that long. The thought of spending another two to three months in rehab was daunting. He couldn't imagine adding another six months to that before he could go back to work.

Across the room another therapist wheeled a young lieutenant into the room. The man's left ankle was wrapped in an orthopedic brace, and he winced in pain as he gingerly put some weight on it.

"I haven't seen him here before. What happened to him?"

"Lieutenant Branders." Alex's tone echoed with disapproval. "He took a bad fall on a run near the Pentagon a couple of weeks ago, but he hasn't been very cooperative in helping us get him back into shape."

"Pencil pusher?"

Alex nodded.

Kel glanced back over when Lieutenant Branders grasped the parallel bars that were in place to help support his weight as he learned how to walk again. The man only took one step before he grabbed the bars and leaned heavily on them.

"It still hurts," the lieutenant complained. "I'm not ready yet."

"Sir, you are ready," the therapist insisted. "If you don't start walking on that ankle, the muscles are going to atrophy, and your injury could become permanent."

"I'm telling you, I can't do it," the lieutenant insisted. "Help me into the wheelchair."

"No," the therapist refused. "You need to try. All I'm asking you to do is try." He moved to the other end of the parallel bars and motioned to the lieutenant. "Walk over here to me, and then I'll take you back to your room."

"I can't do it!" the lieutenant shouted at the man, his face now red with anger. "Get me that wheelchair. That's an order."

Again, the therapist refused.

The lieutenant's rage exploded. Demands and insults spewed from his mouth, followed by threats. When the lieutenant began to pull rank, Kel felt his own anger bubble up.

"Lieutenant!" Kel's voice carried authoritatively with the single, hard-spoken word. The man looked up at Kel, fury still in his face. Kel limped closer before speaking again. "If you want to be treated with the respect your rank deserves, I suggest you start acting like a naval officer."

The muscle in the lieutenant's jaw clenched, but he didn't respond.

"These men are trying to help us however they can. I don't care if he's a seaman or an admiral. He deserves your respect, and you're going to give it to him. Do I make myself clear?"

Standing up a little straighter, he nodded. "Yes, sir."

"Good." Kel turned back to Alex and proved his point with his own actions. "Now, Petty Officer, what would you like me to do next?"

"Let me get you some ice for that knee, Commander. Then we'll let you take another run on the treadmill."

Kel nodded in agreement. "Whatever you say."

* * *

"Bethesda Naval Hospital, may I help you?" the cheerful voice came over the line.

"I hope so. My son is a patient there, and I was hoping to come into town to surprise him when he gets released, but he didn't seem to know when that would be. Is there any way I can find out without letting him know that I'm coming?"

"What is the patient's name, sir?"

"Commander Kelan Bennett," Halim read from the newspaper clipping in front of him.

"I can transfer you to the nurses' station on his floor. They should be able to help you."

"Thank you," Halim said, waiting as he was transferred. When a man's voice came on the line, he worried that he might have been transferred directly to the commander's room. Instead of repeating his fictional story, he said, "I understand Commander Bennett is a patient on your floor."

"Yes, sir," the young man said. "Would you like me to connect you to his room?"

"No, thank you. Actually, I'm looking for some information," Halim said in his best American accent. He repeated his claim that he was the commander's father and wanted to surprise him when he was released.

"Can you verify the commander's date of birth?" the young man asked now.

"Of course." Halim smiled, grateful he had taken the time to ferret that information out of Virginia's Department of Motor Vehicles office. He read off the birth date and was then asked for the commander's address as an additional security check. A few minutes later he jotted down the date that he would begin taking revenge on the men who had taken Lina from him.

12

She was stumped. Marilyn stared at the cursor blinking on the computer screen. For the first time, she didn't know what happened next. Her hero had altered from what she had intended into a man who was constantly struggling to balance his personal life with his work while somehow still managing to appear invincible. It was like he could do anything, except for be there when the heroine needed him. Her heroine had developed many of her own traits, her own doubts. Even Marilyn's fears of being alone had woven their way into the fabric of this woman who now lived and breathed within the pages of her novel.

Marilyn pushed out of her chair and wandered over to the window in the room she now considered her own. The bed behind her was neatly made, the bathroom scrubbed down, and her things all packed. When she walked away today, she would leave behind the little laptop that had become her constant companion.

She had so wanted to bring this story to a close, especially since Kel was getting released from the hospital in a matter of hours. With him around the house, she wouldn't be able to justify being at the computer for hours on end.

With a shake of her head, she decided it was okay to let her characters have a little time to figure out what came next. It was time for her to figure out what came next.

Kel's progress was coming along, the bullet wound now completely healed except for some residual nerve damage. No one was sure yet if that would impact his return to active duty. Marilyn only knew that Kel refused to consider any possibilities besides returning to the teams full time.

Marilyn didn't want to think about that yet. For now, she wanted to enjoy being back in her own home with her husband by her side. She wanted to see if this new bond between them would last once she no longer had his undivided attention.

She saved the file to her flash drive and turned off the laptop. Gathering her things together, she moved out of the guest room to find Katherine coming down the hall.

"I was just going to see if you needed any help." Katherine reached for the smaller of Marilyn's two suitcases. "Here, let me take that."

"Thanks." Marilyn followed her down the hall and out the front door. "I really can't thank you enough for letting me stay here with you."

"We've enjoyed having you." Katherine smiled warmly as she set the suitcase down beside the car. "You and Kel are welcome to stay with us anytime you're in the area."

"Thank you." Marilyn loaded her bags into the trunk and then turned to face Katherine. "Please tell Senator Whitmore thank you for me."

"I will." Katherine reached for Marilyn and gave her a hug. "You have a safe trip."

Marilyn nodded and climbed behind the wheel. As she pulled away, she felt a little pang of envy spreading through her. She loved the easygoing way the Whitmores had with each other, and she couldn't help but wonder if she and Kel would ever be able to find that for themselves.

* * *

"Are you ready?"

Kel looked up at his wife and grinned. "Get me out of here quick before they change their minds."

"Don't worry." Marilyn smiled back at him. "If they try to keep you, I'll call Brent and tell him to arrange another jailbreak."

Alex followed Marilyn into the room, humor in his voice. "I don't think that will be necessary."

Kel looked up at Alex and caught that knowing look in his eyes. "You knew about that?"

"You could say that."

Kel's eyes narrowed, and he shook his head as understanding dawned. "You set me up." With another shake of his head, he let out a short laugh. "You got my guys to break me out of here so I would tackle those stairs."

"You planned that?" Marilyn asked now, stunned.

"Your husband had hit a roadblock, and he needed to get past it," Alex said. "I needed him to get past it."

"I can't believe you would resort to such extreme measures."

He shrugged. "It worked."

"Yeah, it worked." Kel offered his hand in the way of a thank you. "Thanks to you, I'm getting out of here three days ahead of schedule."

"Glad to help." He turned to Marilyn. "Mrs. Bennett, if you want to go pull your car around, we'll meet you at the front entrance."

"Okay," Marilyn agreed. She picked up the stack of games that were still in Kel's room, along with his overnight bag. "I'll meet you downstairs."

Alex motioned to a wheelchair parked right outside Kel's door. "Now, am I going to have to wrestle you into this wheelchair, or are you going to come willingly?"

Kel looked him in the eye for a moment, considering. "I gather you have a lot of people try to refuse the wheelchair."

"Yes, sir." He nodded. "And as I always have to explain, it's policy that you be in the wheelchair when you leave the facility."

"So my fastest course out of here is to let you take me for a ride."

"That's right."

"Then let's go." Kel moved out into the hall with Alex and obediently sat down in the wheelchair.

Alex pushed him to the elevator and hit the down button. "By the way, I wanted to apologize to you. Your dad had planned to be here when you got released, but we didn't have his number to call to let him know that you were getting out earlier than expected."

Kel pushed out of the wheelchair and turned to look at Alex. "What did you say?"

Confused by the sudden tension in Kel, he explained, "Your dad called a couple of weeks ago and said he wanted to come into town to be here when you were released. We gave him the date you were scheduled for, but the nurse who took the call didn't write down his contact information." Alex paused. "Is something wrong?"

"Yeah." Kel nodded. "My father is dead."

"I don't understand." He shook his head. "By policy, we always check some personal data before we give out any information."

"What kind of personal data?"

"Standard stuff like the patient's birth date and address," he told Kel.

Kel's jaw tightened, his mouth pressing into a hard line. "Then this guy, whoever he is, knows where I live."

"Do you have any idea who it might be?"

"No, but I'm not taking my wife home until I'm sure it's safe," Kel told him. "I don't want her to worry, but if I don't get downstairs pretty soon, she's going to be suspicious. Can I get you to make a couple of phone calls for me?"

"Sure." Alex nodded quickly in agreement. "Just let me know what you want me to do."

13

Marilyn followed the directions Kel gave her, turning into the little inn overlooking the James River. They were still nearly two hours from home, but Kel had insisted he needed to make a stop along the way.

"Why did you want to stop here?"

"I have a surprise for you."

"What kind of surprise?"

"Come on." Kel climbed out of the car, carrying his cane, even though it rarely touched the ground. Taking her hand, he led her toward the entrance. He took the stairs slowly, and Marilyn matched his pace.

As they entered the lobby, she thought perhaps he wanted to stop and eat a nice dinner, but he didn't turn toward the quaint little restaurant with its wall of windows overlooking the river. Instead he headed for the reception desk.

"I have a reservation," Kel told the clerk. "The name is Bennett."

"Of course." The middle-aged woman smiled up at them. She set a form on the counter along with a set of keys. "Sign right here."

Kel scrawled his signature across the line she indicated and scooped the keys off the counter.

"You're room is up the stairs, last door on the left."

"Thank you." Kel reached for Marilyn's hand and gave her a little smile.

Still not understanding why they had stopped, Marilyn asked, "We're staying here?"

"I want to spend some time alone with my wife before I go back to the real world." Kel slipped his arm around her waist and steered her toward the sweeping staircase across the lobby. "Do you mind?"

She smiled now. "No, I don't mind." Then she shook her head, clearing away some of the confusion. "I just thought you would be anxious to get home."

"There isn't anything at home that can't wait for a few days," Kel assured her.

"I should go get our bags out of the car." Marilyn started to move away from him, but he held her firmly against him.

"Uh-uh." Kel shook his head. "We'll get them later."

She looked up at him and felt her heart beat a little faster. Not wanting to spoil her husband's romantic gesture, she let him lead her up the stairs, matching her steps to his. When they reached their room, Kel unlocked the door and then turned back to face her. Before she realized what he was doing, he scooped her up into his arms.

"What are you doing?" Marilyn gaped at him. "You'll hurt yourself."

Kel shook his head, his eyes locked on hers. "I love you, Marilyn."

"I love you, too," she managed, surprised by his intensity.

He leaned down and touched his lips to hers as she slipped her arms around his neck. She didn't think of anything but him as he moved into the room and closed the door.

* * *

Brent stepped beside Quinn in the shadows of Kel's house and turned to Seth. "What have you got?"

"Nothing," Seth said with a shake of his head. "We swept the house for transmitting devices and explosives. We even checked out Kel's car that's parked on base, but it's clean, too."

"We still have another day before Kel was supposed to get released from the hospital," Brent commented. "We'll stake out the house tonight. Have Tristan and the new kid take the first shift."

"Will do." Seth pulled out his cell phone and started relaying orders.

* * *

The lights were low in the hotel's restaurant, flames flickering from the candles on each of the occupied tables. Kel and Marilyn had requested a table by the window where they could look out at the lights reflecting off the water of the James River. Darkness had already fallen, and the peaceful sound of rushing water echoed from below them.

Kel reached across the table and covered Marilyn's hand with his. "You know, I never really thanked you for everything you did for me while I was in the hospital."

"Oh, I think you have." Marilyn smiled, her eyes bright. "Look at this place."

"I'm glad you like it here." Kel returned her smile. "Does this mean you won't mind staying for a few days?"

"Really?" Marilyn looked both surprised and a little wary. "I thought you would have to get back to work or something now that you were out of the hospital."

"I'm sure the admiral will find some paperwork for me to do until I'm back to a hundred percent, but he didn't seem to mind me taking a week off first."

"You took a *week* off?" Her jaw dropped open. "To spend with me?"

"Why do you look so surprised?" Kel's eyebrows furrowed at her reaction. "I always spend time with you when I'm not on assignment."

"Yeah, but not like this." Marilyn waved her hand in the air, a gesture that encompassed the inn. "We've never done anything like this. At least not since we've been married."

"I know life has been pretty crazy, but we have time together now." Kel shifted in his chair, and then his eyes narrowed. "You know, I never even thought to ask if you have to work this week."

Marilyn shook her head. "I haven't told my boss when I'm coming back yet. I thought you would probably need me around at least until you can drive again."

"I think regaining my ability to drive is going to be high on my priority list over the next week or two," Kel told her. "You're going to get sick of chauffeuring me around."

"I don't mind." Marilyn picked up her glass and took a sip of water. "Besides, I really like the way you say thank you."

Kel grinned. "Glad to hear it."

* * *

"You know what doesn't make sense?" Seth asked, continuing on with the real question. "Why someone would be targeting Kel."

"I've been wondering the same thing." Brent shook his head. "I can't think of anyone he's had a run-in with, at least not lately."

"There was the one lieutenant on the *Truman,*" Seth suggested. "What was his name? Lieutenant Kiefer?"

"You mean the guy you punched in the communications room?" Quinn asked, amusement in his voice.

"Yeah, that's the one." The corner of Seth's mouth lifted in a half smile. "Because of us, he got a bad rating and ended up reassigned."

"Where is he stationed now?"

"I don't know."

"Find out."

"Do you think someone is trying to retaliate against Kel because of one of our missions?"

"I don't know." Brent shook his head. "We don't usually leave loose ends, and it's not like our enemies to know our names."

Quinn tapped his fingers on his desk impatiently. "This doesn't make any sense."

"I know," Brent agreed. He looked up to see Tristan walk in with their new team member, Jay Wellman. His eyes narrowed when he noticed the bandage on Jay's hand. "What happened to you?"

"He sliced it when he was picking Kel's lock." Tristan gave an innocent little shrug.

Brent shook his head and tried to smother a grin. He looked up at Jay and said, "Next time one of these guys tells you to pick a lock, make sure they don't have the key first."

Jay's dark eyes widened as he turned to look at Tristan. "You had the key?"

"Never assume," Tristan said simply and then plopped down at his computer.

"How bad is it?" Brent asked, pointing at Jay's hand. "Do you need to go to the infirmary?"

Jay stood a little straighter and looked Brent in the eye. "I'll be fine."

Brent nodded and then turned to Quinn. "Check online and do a search for Kel's name." Turning to look at Seth, he continued, "And I want you to do a new background check on Marilyn."

"You think his wife could have something to do with this?"

"I doubt it, but we have to at least consider that this might have something to do with her."

"I don't like this." Quinn shook his head, a sour look on his face. "I don't like looking into the commander's personal life."

"I don't either, but like it or not, this may be the only way to figure out who was posing as his father," Brent told them. "And we need to know why someone wanted to know when he would be coming home."

14

Today was the day. Halim pulled into the driveway of the drab little house, a house that looked just like all the others on the street. He retrieved the black case from the seat beside him. From a distance he knew his bag looked like a briefcase. It was doubtful that anyone would suspect he was carrying a sniper's rifle.

A neighbor across the street was outside mowing his lawn and lifted a hand in greeting. Halim waved back, forced a smile, and then turned to walk up the two steps to the front door. He slid the key in the lock and stepped into the darkness.

The house was without furniture except for a camp chair he had picked up at the local Walmart. He crossed through the excuse of a living room and into the kitchen where he looked out the back window. The house behind him was still as quiet now as it had been the day he had rented this place nearly four weeks before.

The timing had worked out beautifully. Seven houses had been listed for sale or rent in this tiny neighborhood, including the one down the street from the commander's home and this one that backed up to it.

He still couldn't believe how trusting the people in this neighborhood were. His story that he had moved from California had been accepted by the numerous neighbors who had stopped by to welcome him into their midst. The kitchen counter was lined with their offerings of pastries, cookies, and fruit.

Reaching under some plastic wrap to retrieve a piece of banana bread, he wondered if perhaps his boss's method of striking at the United States from a distance was something he should reconsider. If all Americans were this trusting, perhaps his goals could be better achieved by living among them first—not that he wanted to be the man to do it, but it was something to consider.

Halim continued to watch the commander's house, knowing that the light burning in the kitchen had been on since before his arrival. According to his calculations, the commander should arrive within another hour or two. If luck was with him, Seth would be the man to bring him there.

* * *

"Aren't you about ready to get back home?" Marilyn asked as she walked out onto the balcony of their room. Rain was drizzling outside, sheeting off of the balcony on the floor above them. They had been at the inn for four days, and the novelty was beginning to wear off, especially since it had been raining for the past two days straight.

After being gone for so long, Marilyn was ready to get back to their little house. And she was ready to get back to work.

Ideas for her novel had been flooding her mind over the past few days, and her fingers itched to get them down on paper. She had finally snagged a notebook from the desk in their room and started jotting down notes when Kel wasn't looking. It hadn't been difficult to hide the little notebook in the side pocket of her purse, but she was quickly running out of pages as well as patience.

"Why don't we stay one more night?" Kel suggested. "Then we can head home and get back to real life."

Marilyn nodded in agreement, wondering if the weather might clear enough that they could take another walk down to the river's edge. Her eyes narrowed when she looked down at a truck pulling into the parking lot.

"What's he doing here?" she asked when she saw Tristan climb out of the cab.

Kel stiffened for a moment. Then he grabbed his cane and headed for the door. "I'll be right back." A moment later Marilyn saw Tristan walking toward the entrance, stopping when he noticed Kel hobbling toward him.

Neither of the men seemed concerned about the rain coming down on them, both apparently content to stand outside and get soaked. When Kel asked Tristan something, Tristan shook his head, appearing both discouraged and worried. Even from this distance, Marilyn could see the tension settling in her husband. Her first thought was that Tristan had come to take Kel away from her for some mission. Then other realizations started to surface.

If Kel had brought her here to take a break from work, why would he have told anyone in his squad how to find them? And why hadn't he just called Kel on his cell phone? Surely, if they needed him back at work immediately, it would have been more time efficient to have her drive Kel back to Virginia Beach rather than sending someone to get him.

Puzzled, Marilyn watched the two men closely, looking for anything in their body language that might give her a clue. Finally, Tristan turned and headed back to his truck, and Kel walked back into the inn.

Now convinced that everything wasn't as it seemed, Marilyn left the balcony and went back into the hotel room. She stood facing the door, her arms crossed as she waited for Kel to come back.

The minute he walked in and closed the door behind him, she asked, "What's going on?"

"It's nothing. Just a little problem the guys ran into at work."

"Then why didn't they just call you?"

"I guess my phone must not be getting reception here."

"Don't lie to me." Marilyn shook her head, anger bubbling up inside her. "You used your phone last night to order pizza. What's going on?"

"It's nothing to worry about."

"Kel, don't start this again." The anger faded, replaced by the deep hurt that had been welling up inside her for the past five years. "Don't shut me out and try to protect me from every little thing."

Kel leaned heavily on the cane and then lowered himself into a chair. He rubbed his hands over his face and seemed to be considering what to tell her.

Marilyn sat on the chair opposite him. She shifted to face him and reached across the little table between them to lay her hand on his. "We've been married for five years. It's time you stop treating me like some china doll that can sit on a shelf until it's convenient for you to take it down," Marilyn insisted. "You need to learn to trust me."

He drew his hand away and pushed back up to a stand. "I'm going to go for a walk."

"It's raining."

"I need to get some things sorted out in my mind," Kel responded quietly. "I'll be back in a few minutes."

Marilyn simply stared as her world crumbled down around her once more.

* * *

Kel walked along the jogging trail, using his cane more than he would have liked. He didn't know what to do. Whoever had called the hospital asking about him had not shown up looking for him at either the hospital or his house. He trusted his men and their ability to run surveillance undetected, so if they hadn't *seen* anything suspicious, it was unlikely there *was* anything suspicious.

He had been racking his brain trying to figure out who could be looking for him, but he kept coming up with nothing. His life was simple—work and home. He realized that his professional life might be considered complex by some, but to him it was like breathing. He just did it. Orders came in, he took action, he completed missions.

The possibility that someone would come after him was so far-fetched he was beginning to wonder if perhaps the nurse who had taken the message might have been confused. Perhaps it had been someone on the admiral's staff or even some reporter looking for a story. If news had leaked out about an injured SEAL, the press would probably have jumped on it. Investigative reporters were notorious for digging up whatever information they needed to get their job done.

Still, doubt lingered, and Kel worried about letting Marilyn go home until he knew what they were up against. He had hoped their stay at the inn would give his squad time to identify and eliminate any threat. Since that hadn't worked, he was back to square one. How could he explain to Marilyn that their home might not be safe? And how would she react when she found out that his job, the one she hated, could very well be bringing them into harm's way?

With the rain still falling steadily around him, Kel prayed for answers. Then, slowly, he turned back toward the inn. His stomach was churning with nerves when he opened the door and saw Marilyn sitting at the little table in their room writing something in a notebook.

"You're back." She quickly put her pen down and slipped the notebook into her purse. She looked up at him now. "And you're soaked."

"It doesn't matter," Kel told her. When her eyebrows lifted, he pulled open a drawer, grabbed a change of clothes, and stripped out of his wet clothes. When he had replaced them with dry ones, he sat down on the edge of the bed so that he was knee to knee with Marilyn.

"Are you going to tell me what's going on?"

"I'm not sure what I can tell you."

Marilyn let out a sigh. "You hide too much from me." Her eyes were serious, hurt reflected there as she continued, "Everything I know about what you do, about your past missions, is because someone else talked to me and assumed I already knew things. You don't trust me with anything, even the part that you can talk about."

Kel stared at her. She was right. He had tried to protect her from the truth about what he did, hoping to keep her from worrying about the danger. Seeing the hurt in her eyes, he suddenly needed to understand what she was feeling. "Does it really bother you that much when I don't talk about my work?"

Her eyes widened; she had expected him to refuse as he normally did. Slowly, she nodded. "It does. Your work has always been so important to you. I want to share that part of your life, or at least understand it." She hesitated briefly and then added, "I want you to trust me."

Kel's eyebrows drew together. "What do you mean? I trust you. I've always trusted you."

"No, you haven't. If you trusted me, you wouldn't be trying to hide why Tristan came to see you." Another sigh escaped her. "I can see your mind working now. You're trying to figure out how little you can tell me without starting a fight."

New understanding dawned, the realization that each assignment had been driving a wedge between them. He leaned forward, resting his arms on his knees. "What do you want to know?"

"I want to know everything," she started and then held up a hand before he could protest, "but I'll settle for anything you can tell me. Maybe you could start with telling me about a certain hostage rescue of a senator's daughter."

Kel managed to smile. "That was quite a story, actually."

"The pieces I've heard have been pretty interesting."

Not wanting to hurt her anymore, he said, "First, I need to tell you why I brought you here." Kel took her hand now. He took a deep breath and slowly let it out. "Someone called the hospital a couple of weeks ago claiming to be my father."

"What?" Her eyes widened.

"I didn't find out about it until right before I was released from the hospital," he told her. "Whoever it was wanted to know when I was getting released."

"Did the hospital tell him?"

Kel nodded. "When they asked for some of my personal information, he was able to answer their questions. They didn't have any reason not to believe he was really my father." Kel hesitated now. "Marilyn, one of the questions the nurse asked him was where I lived."

"I still don't understand." She shook her head. "Why would someone pretend to be your father?"

"No one's quite sure, but I'm afraid someone might be targeting me for some reason."

Marilyn looked down at their joined hands for a moment and then pulled her hand free. When her gaze shifted to his face once more, he expected to see her concern reflected there. He hadn't been prepared for the hurt or the tears in her eyes. "This whole time we've been here was just your way of keeping me from going home."

Kel stared at her, suddenly unsure what emotions he was facing. "Do you understand what I'm saying? I can't be sure our house is safe right now."

"I see," Marilyn said quietly, her tone distant. She stood up and stared down at him with tears still swimming in her eyes. "I should have known these last few days were too perfect. I don't know why I let myself believe that you brought me here just because you wanted to be with me."

"I did want to be with you," Kel insisted, now feeling like he was standing in a minefield and couldn't find a safe spot to step.

"Be honest, Kel. Would you have brought me here if that man hadn't called the hospital?"

The truth was in his eyes as he looked at her, and he knew it. Slowly, he shook his head, and then he stood up and managed to close the distance between them. "And I'm sorry I didn't think of it before. I should have." He put a hand on her shoulder and stared down at her. "And I have loved this time we've had together. But I'm worried, too."

Marilyn swiped at the tears on her cheeks and gave him a little nod. "Maybe it's time we head home."

"Honey, I don't want you to be back at our house until we can be sure who it was that called the hospital looking for me."

"You don't want me to go home?" she asked now, as though logic were finally breaking through her emotions. "For how long?"

"I don't know," Kel admitted. "I was hoping my guys could take care of the problem while we were here, but they haven't seen anything suspicious."

"Maybe there isn't anything suspicious to be seen," Marilyn suggested. "I mean, who would come after you?"

"We think it might be someone from a past mission."

"Do you know who?"

Kel shook his head. "That's what we're trying to figure out. When we go on missions, no one knows who we are. None of this is making any sense."

"You don't really expect us to stay away from home until you figure out who this guy is, do you?"

"I don't know." Kel turned her hand over and linked his fingers with hers. "But I think we need to wait a bit longer before we go back."

"Kel, we can't afford to stay here for long."

"I know." Kel rubbed his thumb over the back of her hand. "The reason Tristan came to see me wasn't just to tell me what was going on. Brent set us up with temporary quarters at the base in Norfolk while I'm going through physical therapy."

"Kel, I know you're worried, but I really want to go home. Don't you?"

"Marilyn, home is wherever you are." Kel leaned forward and kissed her. "Please, do this for me."

She sighed and then stared at him a moment, considering. "One month. Promise me if this isn't all taken care of after a month, we'll go back home."

He hesitated. "I don't know if I can make that promise."

"You can put in whatever security system you want. I don't care, but I'm tired of living out of suitcases."

"Okay," Kel agreed reluctantly. "One month."

15

"I think I found something," Quinn said, tipping back in his chair. "There was an article about Kel printed right after he was shot."

"What?"

"In his hometown newspaper. There was a little blurb about him being injured and that said he had been transported to Bethesda for treatment."

Brent's dark eyes narrowed. "How did the story get into the paper?"

"Who knows? I checked with public affairs, and they said it definitely wasn't authorized," Quinn told him. "Some reporter must have caught wind of him getting injured and dug up some basic info."

"That would explain how someone would know he was there but not who it was that is looking for him." Brent considered for a moment. "Did it say where he was injured?"

"Said it was a training accident," Quinn answered. The date of the article was only three days after Kel was shot. His eyes lifted to meet Brent's. "You don't think Ramir could have figured out that we were the ones who came into Nicaragua for Seth and Vanessa, do you?"

"I don't know how." Brent shook his head. "Intel reports indicated that Ramir thought it was the drug lord, Morenta, who kidnapped his niece."

"That was then," Seth said. "Vanessa told me that intel picked up on another conversation between Ramir and Morenta. Apparently, Morenta admitted that he hadn't kidnapped Lina Ramir after all and told Ramir that she had been captured by Americans."

"And Akil Ramir believed him?"

"Apparently so. Besides, the CIA already leaked a story that Lina was arrested again and is back in prison here in the United States. That was the only way they could let Vanessa stop pretending to be Lina while still keeping the possibility open in the future."

"Now that would be interesting." Quinn shifted to look at Seth. "A Navy SEAL's wife playing with terrorists and drug lords." He gave Seth a little smirk. "Conversation around your dinner table will never be dull."

"I don't think the word *dull* is in Vanessa's vocabulary." Seth's features relaxed into a smile.

"Have you set the date?" Tristan asked now from the other side of the room.

"Four weeks from Saturday."

"That's quick."

Seth laughed. "I've known her for twelve years. I hardly think this is quick."

Seth's phone rang, effectively interrupting the conversation. His side of the conversation was a series of "okays" and "thank yous," but when he hung up, his face was serious. "That was Vanessa. Her old boss just called to tell her that one of Akil Ramir's men was spotted on an airport surveillance video."

Brent nodded to him. "Go check it out."

Without a word, Seth left the room.

* * *

Halim stared out the back window, impatience shimmering from him. They knew. Somehow the commander knew that he was waiting for him. Two days had passed since he was supposed to arrive home, and still there was no sign of life on the other side of the fence. At least, not the life he had expected.

Every night he saw them come. Or rather, he sensed them. He couldn't be sure exactly who the men were who moved through the darkness and checked out the commander's house. He only knew that they were quiet and thorough. Knowing that he was expected had caused him to alter his plans. An accident would have been so easy—a gas leak followed by an untimely explosion. But these men checked for that. He was sure of it.

As he stared into the darkness, he knew that it was time to call in some help.

* * *

"Home sweet home," Kel said lightly, as he pushed open the door of their temporary quarters. He knew it wasn't what Marilyn was accustomed to, but at least he knew she would be safe while his squad sorted things out.

Marilyn stepped through the door and shifted the suitcase she carried from one hand to the other. She wandered past the tiny living area where a couch was pushed against a wall across from the single desk with its matching chair. She then entered the bedroom and set the suitcase down before turning back to face him. That was when she noticed the stack of boxes on the desk.

"What's this?" She moved to the desk, her eyes narrowing as she read the labels. "Computer equipment?"

"I know you said you took off from work, but there probably won't be a lot for you to do here," Kel told her. He wasn't sure how she was going to feel when she found out how much money he had spent. Or rather how much money he had given Tristan to spend on his behalf. "It's a splurge, but I thought this would help us both stay sane over the next few weeks."

Marilyn looked up at him, still not understanding.

"I bought you a laptop."

"What?" Her eyes widened, and she put a hand on the box in front of her.

"I hope you're not mad," Kel said, hoping to ease the shock. "But it's such a hassle for you to pack up your computer every time we go anywhere. You really need a laptop, even if you don't realize it. Besides, you seemed to like using the one you borrowed from the Whitmores."

To his surprise, she didn't start her standard lecture about saving money. Instead, she asked, "What's in this other box?"

"A printer." Kel moved closer and pulled out a pocket knife to open it for her. "It was one of those package deals. You know, buy a laptop and get a printer for free."

Marilyn watched him cut open the box and pull the new laptop free. When he set it down, he was surprised to look up and see tears in her eyes. His surprise magnified when she stepped forward and wrapped her arms around his neck. "Thank you."

Kel's hands came up to rest on her waist, unsure what to think of her reaction. "You're welcome."

She leaned back so she could see his face and gave him a watery smile. "I almost went out and bought one for myself after you were injured, but I couldn't bring myself to spend the money." She reached up and kissed him.

Kel smiled at her now. "There's supposed to be Internet service here. I thought maybe you'd let me borrow it every once in a while."

Marilyn cocked her head to the side and considered. Then she grinned. "Maybe."

* * *

"We've already checked the house out a dozen times," Tristan said from the passenger seat of Seth's car.

"And I'm coming with you this time to make sure you didn't miss anything," Seth told him as he parked the car half a block away from Kel's house.

Jay Wellman leaned forward and stared out the window as the two men in front of him studied the darkness. He had made this trip at least once every day since Commander Bennett had been released from the hospital. Other than slicing his hand when he'd picked the lock to the commander's house, this duty had become routine. "What are we looking for?"

"Anything out of place," Seth said simply.

Jay stared out into the darkness, wondering how these men could tell what was supposed to be there on the dark street and what they would consider suspicious. A minivan was parked in front of the house next door to the commander's. A streetlight was shining brightly into the neighbor's yard. Several cars were parked on the street. Jay already knew from his previous visits that the little blue compact two houses down belonged to a neighbor's teenage daughter. The pickup truck in front of it hadn't been moved over the past week.

Many of the yards were adorned with mature trees and various shrubs. Ornamental pear trees and azaleas seemed to be the favorites, although their blooms had long since come and gone. A motorcycle approached them, causing a couple of dogs to bark as it passed.

"Anything?" Seth asked.

Jay knew the question was aimed at Tristan. He was still just the new guy they had brought along for the ride.

Tristan shook his head. "Nothing that we haven't seen before."

"Let's go." Seth pushed the door open and climbed out.

Jay got out, as well, and moved to stand beside him. Not for the first time, Jay considered that he wouldn't want be on Seth's bad side, especially in a dark alley.

As though talking were suddenly taboo, Seth signaled Tristan to circle to the front of the house. As soon as Tristan complied, Seth signaled Jay to go through the back gate. Jay took a few steps, glancing back to see if Seth was following. That's when he saw it. A movement in the shadow behind a neighbor's tree, followed by the reflection of the street light off of something metal.

The sight of a predator here in this sleepy neighborhood was so surreal that Jay almost didn't react. Then his instincts kicked in, and he dove for Seth.

"Get down!" Jay tackled him around the waist as the first gunshots whizzed through the air above them. Both men scrambled for cover. They only made it three steps before more gunfire sounded, this time coming from Tristan, who was now in the front yard of the commander's house.

Heart pounding and eyes wide, Jay ducked behind a large utility box. His breath came in quick gasps, and his eyes shifted from side to side until they landed on Seth, who was behind a mature oak tree. He was squatting down, his back pressed against the trunk, a pistol in his hand.

For a brief moment, Jay wondered if this was a training exercise. The day before, Seth had suggested that Jay start carrying a sidearm. Jay hadn't seen the need, at least not when they weren't on a mission. Getting the concealed weapon permit and dealing with the hassle didn't seem worth it. Could Seth and Tristan be trying to teach him a lesson?

Lesson or not, his heart was racing, and the adrenaline pumping through him was real. He took a steadying breath and tried to remember the intensive training he had gone through such a short time ago. *Relax,* he told himself. His senses were keen; he just had to remember to use them.

He took another breath, smelling the freshly cut grass, the neighbor's roses, and traces of his own aftershave. A siren was barely audible in the distance, and he could hear the slight rustling in the bushes across the street.

Focusing on Seth, he saw the signal. He also saw his eyes and knew. This wasn't a lesson they were trying to teach him. This was real.

Jay shifted to make room for Seth, and a moment later another burst of gunfire sparked as the intruder reacted too late to stop Seth from joining Jay behind the junction box. Seth pulled up his pant leg and took his spare weapon from the holster strapped to his calf.

"When I tell you, dive for cover that way." Seth motioned to the left. "I'll go to the right."

"Then what?"

"Tristan has our back," Seth assured him. "Whoever gets a clean shot, takes it."

Jay took a deep breath, nodding as he let it out. "Okay."

"Stay low," Seth reminded him. Then he whispered, "Go!"

Weapon in hand, Jay dove toward a nearby tree, crawling the last few yards. Gunfire sprayed in their direction once more. Before Jay could even shift to take aim, Tristan stepped out and fired two shots. Then the night was still, except for the approaching sound of sirens.

16

"What do you mean, it's not improving?" Kel asked the doctor, trying to stay calm. He had been going to physical therapy faithfully for two weeks and was convinced that he was getting stronger. Now the doctor was unraveling that belief. "I thought I was supposed to be in physical therapy for at least a month before I was evaluated."

"That was our initial plan, but when I realized that the swelling keeps recurring, I wanted to take another look," the doctor told him. "I don't want you to waste your time in physical therapy when you really need to be spending that time recovering from surgery."

"Surgery?"

"My diagnosis is that you have a torn ligament. If I'm right, you aren't going to recover completely without reconstructive surgery."

"How can we be sure that you're right?" Kel asked. "I haven't even had an MRI."

"We can't do an MRI because of the gunshot wound," the doctor reminded him. "It's too risky."

Kel considered this for a moment, "But you think I can fully recover with surgery?" Kel looked at him. "Enough to go back to my squad?"

"I can't give you any guarantees," he said. "The general rule of thumb is that the injured leg should regain 85 to 90 percent of its presurgical strength."

"But 90 percent might not be enough for me to do my job."

"SEALs tend to have more physical demands than other disciplines in the service, but you're also in better condition starting out." He gave a shrug. "It's possible."

Kel blew out a breath, processing the doctor's words.

The doctor waited for a moment as Kel absorbed the news. Then he continued. "We will go in and take a look using arthroscopic surgery. If there is a tear in the ACL, we would then take a graft from your patellar tendon and reconstruct."

"How long for recovery?"

"We'll keep you overnight in the hospital, and then you'll be on crutches for about a week," he told Kel. "As for complete rehab, you're looking at a minimum of four to six months, but it will probably be more like six to eight."

Kel closed his eyes for a long moment, his jaw tensing. Then he looked at the doctor once more. "How soon can you get me scheduled?"

"Next week." The doctor hesitated and then added, "But to get you in that soon, you'll have to go back to Bethesda."

Kel took a deep breath as he considered the implications. He had promised Marilyn he would take her home in two more weeks, one way or another. Now he would likely be just getting off of crutches when their month was up. Feeling cornered, Kel nodded. "Get me in as soon as you can."

"Report to Bethesda at 0800 Monday morning," the doctor told him. "The nurse will have your paperwork faxed up there for you."

Discouraged, Kel stood and headed for the lobby. His limp was nearly gone, and he had been hopeful that this meeting was to inform him that the doctor was lifting the restrictions on his activities so he could get back to work. A knot settled in his stomach like a rock that wouldn't go away.

When he stepped outside, he saw Brent parked at the edge of the parking lot leaning against a government car. "Are you waiting for me?"

Brent nodded. He opened the passenger door for Kel. "We need to talk."

Afraid that his already bad day was about to get worse, Kel let out a sigh. With a shake of his head, he limped forward and got into the car.

As soon as Brent slid behind the wheel, Kel asked, "What's going on?"

"Someone took a shot at Seth last night outside of your house."

"What? Is everyone okay?"

Brent gave a wry grin. "Except for the shooter."

"Do you have an ID?"

"Nothing official, but Seth recognized him," Brent told him. "He said he only knew him as Imran, but he remembered him from when he was undercover with Vanessa at Akil Ramir's fortress."

"Why would Ramir come after me?"

"I don't know," Brent answered. "We found an article in your hometown newspaper that mentioned your injury and that you were at

Bethesda Naval Hospital. Maybe Ramir found the article and figured out we were the ones who took Vanessa and Seth from his fortress."

"And since Ramir thinks Vanessa is his niece, you think he's out for revenge?"

"Stranger things have happened."

"Or maybe he's looking for some leverage to get her back."

"You think he would try to kidnap a naval officer?"

"Like you said, stranger things have happened." Kel rubbed a hand over his face. "If Ramir really is behind this, he's going to send someone else."

"I agree," Brent nodded. "I also think it's time we stop playing this defensive game and figure out a way to take care of Ramir once and for all."

"Brent, we both know it's too dangerous." Kel tapped the crutches in his lap as though demonstrating the obvious concerns.

"Kel, we may not have a choice," Brent insisted. "If Vanessa hadn't stumbled onto one of Ramir's moles the day they had planned the last terrorist attack, half of Arizona wouldn't be habitable right now. It's time we take some action and stop these threats, or at least slow them down."

"I agree with you, but you have to know that the bureaucrats aren't going to approve a strike on foreign soil."

"I guess I'll have to convince them."

"Good luck with that," Kel said, now not sure if he should be relieved or worried that their superiors were unlikely to approve such a mission. Shifting gears, he thought of his own security concerns. "I wanted to ask you for a favor."

"Name it."

Kel took a deep breath and relayed what the doctor said and then proceeded to explain what he needed Brent to do for him. Finally, when he was done, Brent asked, "Are you sure about this?"

"No, but I have to do something." Wearily, Kel shook his head. "Marilyn doesn't understand what we're up against."

"It may be time you make her understand."

"I will," Kel agreed. "After everything is ready."

* * *

Marilyn lifted two bags of groceries from her car and headed for the door of her current residence. She had put off doing any real shopping, hoping that Kel would finally decide they could go back home, but after two weeks, she realized they needed more than a gallon of milk and a few boxes of cereal.

Even though their temporary apartment was small, it wasn't as bad as she initially expected. Of course, that was largely due to the laptop Kel had given her and the predictability of her husband's routine.

Each morning she drove Kel over to the hospital for his physical therapy. He had made arrangements to get a ride each day from the hospital to the office building where he was currently working for some admiral. Then, at the end of the day, Marilyn went back to pick him up at his temporary office.

With Kel gone during regular office hours, Marilyn had slipped into her own routine. As soon as she returned home from dropping Kel off, she booted up her laptop and got to work. She was nearing the end of this novel that had taken on a life of its own. Most days she managed to write for three or four hours before taking a lunch break. Most of her afternoons were spent visiting Heather in Virginia Beach or going for a walk to help her thoughts settle before going back to her story. Then every day before she went to pick up Kel, she made sure she saved her file and turned off the laptop.

She wished she could print out her new pages to look over them on paper, but she didn't dare. It was bad enough to know that her previous version was still hidden in her sock drawer at home. And she knew this version was significantly better.

Marilyn was so pleased with her latest story she even considered submitting the manuscript to a publisher, under an alias, of course. The agent she had sent some writing samples to a few months before said she could use a pen name to protect her privacy. He also said that he wanted to see her novel when she finished it. She had read enough articles about writing to know that having an agent interested in her work was a huge accomplishment.

Part of her wanted to share the dream, the possibilities with Kel, but she couldn't bring herself to do it. Logically, she knew he was always supportive of everything she did, but this was different. Her writing was like a window to her deepest fears, her darkest secrets, and her biggest dreams. She wasn't sure she was prepared to open that door, even to her husband.

Juggling the groceries in her hand, she pushed open the door and stopped short. Kel was sitting at the desk reading something on the laptop. Her mind raced. Had she closed the file she had been working on? Could he be reading *her* writing? She mentally retraced her steps before she left the house. She thought she remembered closing down her manuscript file and turning off the computer, but doubt lingered as she closed the door behind her.

Kel looked up and forced a smile. And Marilyn's tension hiked up another notch.

"What are you doing home already?" she managed to ask.

"I got a ride home after I met with the doctor today."

"You met with the doctor?" Marilyn asked, her tension taking on a new focus. "What did he say?"

"I have to report back to Bethesda on Monday," Kel told her. "For surgery."

"What?"

"The doctors think I have a torn ligament." Kel swiveled the chair so he was facing her. Wearily, he shook his head. "If they're right, I'm looking at about six months of recovery time, give or take."

"Kel, I'm sorry." Marilyn set the groceries down on the coffee table and crossed to him. Leaning down, she touched her lips to his. "Is there anything I can do?"

"Tell me I'm not crazy for thinking I can make it back."

"Kel, people have this surgery all the time." Marilyn lowered herself down and sat on the couch so she was facing him. She didn't want to think about him going back, but she forced herself to say the right words. "I'm sure everything will be fine."

He was quiet for a moment now. "Fine as in 'I'll make it back to the teams,' or fine as in 'You'll finally get your wish that I'll have to leave the SEALs'"?

Marilyn sucked in a breath. "I don't know." She pushed up to stand. Letting out a sigh, she held her hands out to her side and let them drop. "I want you to get better, really I do."

"But . . ."

"But I love knowing that you're going to be here every night and that I don't have to worry that the phone will ring and you'll disappear for who knows how long."

"So it would be better for you if I didn't get better."

"It might be better for *us,*" Marilyn ventured.

"I can't believe you really think that."

Marilyn felt her eyes sting with tears. She hated seeing Kel hurting, but she didn't know if he could ever understand what a nightmare it was to live most of her life without him, always waiting, always wondering. Her voice was soft when she said, "Maybe this happened for a reason."

"Yes, it happened for a reason," Kel said now. "I was shot because I okayed a risky mission, a mission that ultimately saved thousands, if not millions, of lives." He moved toward the door. "But you don't have to worry about me going behind enemy lines again. If your prayers are answered, this surgery won't work well enough for me to have the chance."

"Kel . . ." Marilyn took a step toward him.

"I'm going for a walk." Kel pulled the door open and let it rattle closed behind him.

All Marilyn could do was let the tears fall.

17

Kel swiped at his eyes, willing back the tears that threatened. He didn't know how many hours he had been standing here, leaning on the railing of the pier and staring out at the James River. It had been daylight when he'd left the apartment. Now only the last remnants of sunlight remained.

Not for the first time, Kel wondered where he had gone wrong. He wasn't the only member of his squad who was married, yet Brent's and Tristan's wives appeared to fully support their husbands' careers. Their marriages seemed so much tighter than his, their relationships so much more in tune with their spouses. Kel didn't know if it was because Marilyn was the only one of the wives who wanted her husband to change careers or if perhaps the fault somehow was his.

If he tried hard enough, he could remember the fun, spontaneous days of his courtship with Marilyn. He could remember the way they laughed together, the way they had shared their dreams. She had wanted to see the world with him, to search for adventure, and someday share a family with him. Now she only wanted to stay home, with him by her side. Kel wished he understood why Marilyn rarely accompanied him anywhere, why she usually found an excuse to send him to social events alone.

Looking back, he knew he probably should have dated Marilyn longer before getting married, but he had been without family for so long. He had seen her as the answer to his prayers, the person who could help him rebuild his life and help him create a family of his own. He wasn't sure how he would describe his relationship with Marilyn now, but the word *family* no longer came to mind.

Did he love her? Yes. Did she complete him? No. She had once, or at least she had started to. Then the deployments had started bothering her, and the little disagreements had blown up into major fights. He knew he shouldn't be so hurt by her admitting that she didn't want him to go back to the teams. She had said those words so many times to him before. But this time it was different. This time she was willing to hope that he wouldn't become whole again in order to get what she wanted.

And what if she did get what she wanted? What if he was forced out of the navy, forced to take a disability discharge? What then? He couldn't imagine going to work in a regular job. He couldn't say why, but the thought of donning a suit, driving in rush hour every day, and going into an office from nine to five terrified him. Perhaps it was his irrational fear of how his parents died in just such an environment, or maybe it was the idea of being closed inside all day. Regardless, he hoped and prayed he wouldn't have to learn to conform to something he had been avoiding his entire adult life.

His thoughts were interrupted when he heard his cell phone ring. He nearly silenced it without looking, assuming that it was Marilyn calling him again. His training wouldn't allow that simple act of selfishness, and instead he pulled his phone out of his pocket to check caller ID. He blew out a breath when he saw that the call was coming from a Pentagon prefix.

Hoping his voice sounded professional, he hit the talk button. "Commander Bennett."

"Evening, Commander." Admiral Mantiquez's voice came over the line.

"Admiral," Kel said, in lieu of a greeting. "What can I do for you?"

"I'm heading your direction tomorrow. We need to meet."

"Yes, sir. When and where?"

"Oh eight hundred at the officer's club at Norfolk," Admiral Mantiquez told him. "Do you need me to send a car for you?"

"No, thanks. I think I can manage to get there on my own."

"Good. I'll see you in the morning."

"Yes, sir." Kel hung up the phone, his brow furrowing in confusion. Why would the admiral want to meet with him? Could he have already heard about his impending surgery? Kel took a deep breath as another thought invaded his mind. Could the admiral have already decided to drop him from the teams?

Kel pressed his fingers to his eyes, trying to will away the doubts. Letting out a sigh, he turned and started toward his temporary quarters and wondered if he would ever be able to get his life in order again.

* * *

The worry was back, gnawing at her stomach. She wanted to go out and look for Kel, but she didn't have a clue where he might have gone. Of course, she never really knew where he went when he left, but this time was different. Tonight she expected him to come home . . . eventually.

Marilyn paced to the window and looked out into the darkness. Seeing nothing outside but parked cars and the glow of her porch light, she lowered herself into a chair. She closed her eyes, replaying her earlier conversation with Kel. In many ways it had been so much like the arguments that had surfaced when Kel had to deploy. So often she had suggested he leave the SEALs, usually as he was about to walk out the door.

In the past, Kel had been insistent that his involvement was critical. Today had been different. His confidence was lagging, Marilyn realized now. He wasn't standing tall anymore. He was no longer ready to take on the world and anyone in it that might get in his way. Over the past few weeks, she had begun to see a vulnerability she had rarely seen, except when he spoke of his family. That vulnerability seemed to be deepening, creating insecurities in Kel that were completely out of character.

She wasn't helping, Marilyn realized. Her own needs, her own insecurities were crippling both of them.

Tears welled up again as she looked at her watch and a new realization dawned. In the past, she had always been terrified that a knock would come at the door, that someone would be standing on the other side to tell her that her husband had been killed. Even now, after nearly twenty-five years, she could remember the shock of having the policeman come to her door to tell her and her mother that her dad had died.

Tonight it wasn't the fear of having that moment repeated; there was a new fear. The understanding that for the first time, it wasn't the possibility that Kel would be *unable* to return home to her but rather that he might be *unwilling* to come home.

Her cell phone rang, and she quickly answered it without checking the caller ID. "Hello?"

The voice on the other end wasn't Kel's but rather her mother's. "Hi, sweetie. Is something wrong? You sound upset."

Marilyn took a deep breath and let it out as she tried to steady her voice. "Kel just found out he has to have surgery on his knee. He's pretty upset."

Her mother's voice turned hopeful. "Have they decided to give him a medical discharge?"

"No, nothing like that." Marilyn shook her head and stared blankly out the window. "He's praying he can still recover, but it's going to be at least six months before he can return to his unit."

"At least that will keep him home for a while," Barbara reminded her.

"I'm starting to think that isn't such a good thing," Marilyn admitted, regretting her words the moment they were out of her mouth.

Barbara's voice took on a cynical edge. "What do you mean? Of course it's a good thing."

"Mom, Kel's miserable being stuck at home all the time. He hates knowing that his squad is moving on without him," Marilyn reluctantly confided in her. "It's awful seeing him so miserable."

"At least he's alive."

"Yeah, he's alive." Marilyn sighed.

"Let me know how the surgery goes," Barbara told her.

"I will," Marilyn agreed, still struggling to keep her voice steady. "I'll talk to you later." Marilyn hung up the phone as the worry continued to gnaw at her.

A tear spilled over, followed by another. She took a deep breath and prayed for strength as she considered what she had to do. Somehow, she had to find the strength to support Kel the way he needed her to. The doorknob turned, and Marilyn quickly stood up and faced the door.

Kel stepped inside, flipped the lock, and turned out the porch light before glancing in her direction. When he did turn toward her, his expression was guarded, his eyes weary.

Marilyn didn't try to hide the tears this time. "Kel, I'm sorry."

"Yeah, me, too," he said without any real feeling. He waved a hand in the direction of the laptop. "Do you mind if I use the computer for a while? I have an early meeting tomorrow I need to get ready for."

"Of course you can use it."

Kel gave her a curt nod and pressed the power button. He then sat down and turned away from her.

Marilyn could only stare as the knots in her stomach tightened. He was home, but this time the loneliness didn't disappear the moment he walked through the door.

18

Kel stepped into the officers' club fifteen minutes early, but he wasn't there for more than a minute or two before Admiral Mantiquez walked in behind him.

"Good morning, Admiral," Kel greeted him and shook the older man's hand.

"Morning." Admiral Mantiquez motioned for Kel to follow their waiter and then nodded to Kel as he settled into his chair. "Have a seat."

Kel lowered himself into the chair opposite the admiral. Already certain that his future with the teams was on the line, Kel got right to the point. "I assume you've already heard that I'm scheduled for surgery on Monday."

Admiral Mantiquez nodded. "Yeah, I was sorry to hear that, but that's not why I'm here."

Kel blinked twice. "It's not?"

He shook his head. Rather than elaborate, he motioned to a waiter. "I think we're ready to order."

Kel hadn't even opened his menu yet; he opened it briefly and picked something at random.

After their orders were taken, the admiral leaned back in his chair. "What do you see as your future with the navy?"

"I'm going to get back," Kel said with a confidence that belied his insecurities. "I'll have this surgery, go through rehab, and then rejoin my squad in about six months."

"Then what?"

Kel straightened a bit, surprised both by the admiral's acceptance of his plan and by his question. "I'm not following you."

"Do you see yourself moving beyond commanding your squad?"

Kel's shoulders lifted slightly. "I guess I never really thought about it. Commanding the Saint Squad has always felt like the perfect fit for me."

"Up until now, I agree that it has been," Admiral Mantiquez agreed. "But you may be destined for more."

"What kind of 'more'?" Kel lifted his water glass and took a sip.

"Command of SEAL Team Eight more."

Kel set the glass down a little too quickly, and water sloshed over the edge onto the tablecloth. "Excuse me?"

"Commander Daugherty put in for retirement. He'll be stepping down in three months," the admiral told him. "Your name is on the short list for his replacement."

"I don't understand," Kel said. "There are dozens of candidates who have more command experience than me."

"That's true, but I don't think any of them are right for the job," Admiral Mantiquez told him bluntly. "You're a rare breed when it comes to your style of leadership. Your men trust you, and they'll follow where you lead, but you've also been teaching them how to be leaders themselves. Lieutenant Miller did an exceptional job under difficult circumstances after you were injured. If you can instill that kind of leadership in all of the men in SEAL Team Eight, you should be the man in charge."

"Thanks for the vote of confidence, but even if I did want the position, you said yourself I'm on the short list. I'm sure there are other candidates competing for it, candidates who aren't looking at six months of rehab."

"There are," Admiral Mantiquez agreed. "But my vote's for you."

* * *

Marilyn paced the apartment for nearly an hour, her mind and body numb as she thought of the events of the past twenty-four hours. Kel had left that morning without saying a word to her. Not his usual "Good morning" or "I love you." Not even "I'll see you later."

She had sought solace in her writing for several hours that morning and into the afternoon, but as the sun had lowered in the sky and Kel hadn't returned at the normal time, she had been unable to do anything but wonder. Where was he? And was he coming back?

Kel had been angry with her before—many times—but this was the first time she had ever seen him so hurt by her words. Normally, he fought back. He would insist, demand, and argue. He was always so sure of himself and his convictions that his presence on his missions was crucial.

Seeing him broken and lying in the hospital bed had been a relief—not that he was injured but that he was still breathing. The hurt she had caused him the night before had backfired in a way she had never anticipated. She hadn't meant to admit she didn't want him to get better. Those words hadn't even been entirely true. She did want him to recover. She just didn't want him going out on missions again.

Marilyn heard a car pull up outside and hurried to look out the window. Her hopes that Kel had returned were dashed when she saw the next-door neighbor climb out of his car and grab his duffel bag from the backseat. His face was streaked with camouflage paint, and he looked like he had just returned from some kind of mission or training exercise.

His wife had clearly been watching for him because she ran out to greet him as he slammed the car door shut. Marilyn watched as the couple embraced and then kissed. They looked so happy to see one another, pure joy radiating from both of them. Even though Marilyn watched them longer than she intended, not once did she see any signs of resentment or bitterness from the wife over her husband's absence.

Turning from the window, Marilyn wondered if she could ever be like that or if she even wanted to try. Her fears had dominated her thoughts for so long, and she had never really considered what it would be like if she simply accepted her husband's career without complaint. She dropped herself into the desk chair and let the alternatives consume her mind.

No more fights, no more arguments. Could she be the kind of wife who could kiss her husband good-bye and wish him well even though her insides were sick with worry?

She opened a computer file, glancing at the time. Seven o'clock, or 1900, as Kel would say. *He should have been home hours ago,* she thought to herself. And she knew. If she had to choose between watching Kel leave on dangerous missions or living life without him, she would choose staying married. She tried to fight against that little seed of hope that Kel wouldn't be able to go on those missions anymore. Somehow she was going to have to overcome the fear and learn to live with the career he had chosen. The career he loved.

* * *

Kel settled onto a stool at the bar in the officers' club, deep in thought. He had spent the better part of the day in his old office working with Brent and the rest of his team. Nothing had jumped out at him to explain why someone would be targeting him, but he hoped Seth's understanding of Ramir's organization would help him discover why the threat was aimed his way and what they should do about it.

Seth had left the office early to take his fiancée to dinner but had agreed to meet Kel afterward. Both men hoped that together they might figure out how to alleviate the threat so Kel could finally return home.

He glanced at his watch to see that Seth wasn't due to arrive for a few more minutes. The bartender moved to take his order and moments later set a soda in front of him. Kel took a sip and then turned to look around the room. A few tables were filled with larger parties, people who appeared to work together and had chosen to socialize during their off hours. Many, though, were couples enjoying a quiet dinner.

Kel couldn't remember the last time he had been able to convince Marilyn to have dinner with him at the officers' club. He supposed it was her aversion to his career that caused her to always choose going somewhere else when they went out to eat.

Rubbing a hand over his face, Kel fell prey to his doubts about his marriage. Marilyn's words had been so shocking that he still could hardly believe she would wish for him to remain crippled. Logically, he understood that she just didn't want him back with his squad, but logic wasn't making the hurt go away. For the first time since meeting Marilyn, he was seriously considering whether their relationship was meant to last.

His thoughts were interrupted by Seth's arrival. Kel nodded a greeting as Seth settled onto the stool beside him. "How are the wedding plans going?"

"Actually, I wanted to talk to you about that," Seth said, shifting to face Kel more fully. "Vanessa and I were talking over dinner . . ." He hesitated now, as though trying to gather the energy to speak once more. "Maybe we should postpone the wedding for a few weeks until we're sure this Ramir problem is under control."

"Seth, you know better than that." Kel shook his head. "You can't put your life on hold until the world is safe and everyone is happy. Otherwise, you'll spend your future planning for it instead of living it."

"Yeah, but Vanessa and I are the only two who have been inside his organization. We're more likely to identify a threat than anyone."

"And you're more likely to be a target than anyone."

Seth's eyes narrowed. "What do you mean?"

"You're the one Ramir's man took a shot at, not me."

"You think *I'm* the target?" Seth shook his head. "That's crazy."

"It makes sense." Kel kept his eyes on Seth's. "The only thing I offer Ramir is the chance at getting to a naval officer on American soil. If that's all he wanted, he could go for anyone." Kel shrugged. "Why me?"

"Maybe it has to do with the newspaper clipping in your hometown paper."

"So you think that Ramir saw the newspaper article and realized that my injury was really from the navy sending me into his fortress to kidnap the woman he thought was his niece." Kel stated the unlikely facts.

"I know it's a stretch, but it's possible."

"Possible," Kel agreed. "But it might be more likely that he would come after me if he somehow figured out that you work for me."

"I don't know how . . ." Seth's voice trailed off as his eyes lit with a sudden awareness. "The picture."

"What?"

"There was a cropped photo of you with the newspaper article," Seth told him. "It was one taken of our squad a couple of years ago."

"So?"

"I was standing right behind you. Part of my face was visible in the newspaper article." Seth ran a hand over his face and shook his head. "Ramir could be coming after Vanessa."

"All the more reason to go through with your wedding and get her out of here for a couple of weeks," Kel told him. "If we're right, the only reason Ramir is looking for me is so that he can find you."

"Great," Seth muttered.

"In a way, that's actually good news. At least this explains why someone was looking for me."

"Yeah, but you and Marilyn are still in danger, especially if your name is the only one Ramir has managed to uncover."

"We're only in danger if he can find us."

Slowly, Seth nodded. "You know Brent wants to go back in after Ramir."

"Yeah, I know." Kel shifted in his seat, ignoring the twinge of pain that shot through his thigh where the bullet had struck him. "I told him I don't think it's worth the risk right now."

"Until tonight, I agreed with you, especially after what happened to you." Seth hesitated, considering in his slow, thoughtful way. "Now I'm starting to think that we should strike before he has time to recover from the last time we were there."

"Maybe you should keep your focus on your fiancée for now."

"Don't worry. Vanessa will keep me out of trouble." Seth stood up and changed the subject. "Take care of that leg."

Kel wanted to insist that it was too dangerous and could immediately hear his wife's voice saying those same words echoing in his past. Though it pained him to consider the risks, he forced himself to give Seth an encouraging nod, and then he watched him leave the room.

19

"Kel, we need to talk about this," Marilyn insisted as Kel packed an overnight bag on Sunday evening. "You have been avoiding me for days, and now you don't even want me to come with you when you have your surgery?"

"What is there to say? You don't want me to get better, and I do. End of story."

"Of course I want you to get better." Marilyn let out an exasperated sigh. She put her hand on his shoulder, letting out another sigh when he kept his eyes on the clothes he was packing rather than turning to look at her. "I love you, and I worry about you when you're gone. That's all."

Kel turned now. His eyes were tired, and he gave a little shake of his head. "Marilyn, it's not like I wasn't a SEAL when you married me. You knew this was what my life was like."

"You were a SEAL, but you weren't commanding a squad when we first met," Marilyn pointed out. Then she shook her head. "That doesn't matter. What matters is you getting better." She put a hand on his cheek now. "All the way better."

His eyes narrowed. "You're just saying that because it's what you think I want to hear."

"No, I'm saying it because it's true." Marilyn let her hand drop, but she kept her eyes on his. "I've always wanted you to get better, Kel. I just worry about you."

"I know."

"Now, can I come with you to Bethesda?"

Kel shook his head. "No, I want you to stay here. It's safer."

"What do you mean, 'it's safer'?"

"Someone is targeting me and at least one other person in my squad. I don't want you anywhere that you might be in danger."

"You can't be serious." Marilyn looked at him skeptically. "No one would ever try to hurt me."

"Maybe not, but I'm not willing to risk it." Kel's voice softened. "Please, just stay here. I'll be back by tomorrow afternoon."

Marilyn let out another sigh. "If that's what you want, but please have Brent call me as soon as the surgery is over." Her eyebrows lifted, a touch of amusement tainting her voice. "You know how I worry."

A little smile crossed Kel's face, and he leaned forward to give her a brief kiss. "Yeah, I know."

* * *

Brent pulled up in front of the Whitmores' home and pushed the button on the garage door opener that his in-laws had given him shortly after he had married their daughter. He had volunteered to take Kel to Bethesda for his surgery, hoping to find the opportunity to speak with his father-in-law. When he noticed that Jim's car was already parked alongside Katherine's SUV, he smiled to himself and climbed out of his car.

After knocking on the back door, Brent pushed the door open and called out a greeting. He wasn't surprised to see Katherine standing in the kitchen fixing dinner.

"Hi there." Katherine turned and smiled. "I'm glad to see you made it. How is Kel doing?"

"The doctor said the surgery went well. Now we just have to wait and see how his rehab goes."

"Well, we'll certainly keep him in our prayers."

"I'm sure he appreciates that," Brent told her. "I saw Jim's car here. Is he in his office?"

"Yeah, go on in." Katherine nodded. "Tell him dinner will be ready in a half hour."

"Thanks." Brent moved through the house and found Jim inside his office, a phone to his ear. He hesitated outside the door until Jim noticed him and waved him inside. Brent took a seat and waited for Jim to finish his call.

Jim then turned his attention to his son-in-law. "Admiral Mantiquez called a few minutes ago and said that Kel's surgery went okay."

Brent nodded. "So far, so good."

"The admiral also told me that you're looking for some help to get a mission cleared."

"I am." Brent let out a sigh and leaned forward to rest his elbows on his knees. "You know I hate to ask for favors, but this one could be vital to national security."

"Akil Ramir?"

"Yeah." Brent nodded. "The situation in Arizona was way too close for comfort. We both know he's going to try again. If not there, then somewhere else."

"I agree, but I also don't know how we can justify going into Nicaragua."

"I realize you don't normally condone black ops, but this may be the time to make an exception," Brent told him, and then he offered a little smile. "Besides, our latest intel says Ramir is in Aruba."

"Aruba? I thought he felt safest at his fortress in Nicaragua."

"We think he was worried about retribution from his partner in the last attack. According to Seth, the drug lord Morenta was at the fortress, and everyone was worried about what would happen if everything didn't go the way it was planned."

"Do we know where Ramir is hiding in Aruba?"

"Yeah. Seth's fiancée said that's where she first met Akil Ramir when she went undercover as his long-lost niece. She's already sketched out a floor plan and a layout of the basic security. Compared to the fortress, this will be a piece of cake."

"It should make things easier on my end, too. Our relationship with the authorities in Aruba is a lot more amenable, especially since they are so reliant on American tourists to stimulate their economy."

"We might not get an opportunity like this again," Brent offered.

Jim let out a sigh. "I'm still not sure about this, though. You want me to send you in against someone we haven't been able to prove is a terrorist."

"That's exactly what I want." Brent kept his eyes on Jim's. "Seth has the inside information we need to make this work, and he and Vanessa have the knowledge necessary to tie Ramir to the last terrorist attack."

"Kel also just had surgery because of the last time you boys went up against him."

"Yeah, but we didn't know as much then as we know now," Brent reminded him. "Besides, we've already had one of Ramir's men take a shot at Seth. If we don't take Ramir out soon, my squad may be in more danger by doing nothing."

Still playing the devil's advocate, Jim pointed out the obvious. "Your squad also has a new kid who is still untested."

"I think he can handle it," Brent said. "Besides, I'd much rather go in before Seth goes on leave for his honeymoon. We need his inside knowledge of Ramir's organization."

Jim blew out a breath, clearly considering. "How soon do you want to strike?"

"Seth is already working out the details, but we could move as early as tomorrow night."

"Tomorrow?" Jim's eyes widened. "You won't even get back from taking Kel home until tomorrow afternoon."

"I know. We would catch our ride tomorrow night and then strike the following day," Brent told him. "If everything goes the way we plan, we'll be home before the weekend."

"Sounds pretty optimistic."

"Seems to me optimism is a good thing."

"Will Amy go along?"

Brent shook his head. "Not this time. She's gathering intel right now, but there's no reason for her to go into the hot zone."

"This plan is sounding better by the minute."

"I thought you'd like that part of it." Brent grinned. "Now, how do we get permission?"

Jim smiled now. "I have a few ideas."

"I'd hoped you would."

* * *

Kel stared out at the James River from the passenger seat of Brent's car. They were almost to Norfolk, and he could see several cruisers docked at the naval base. The blue sky over equally blue water only served to depress him. It was a perfect day to go out for a sail or for a swim or even for a walk. He could do none of those things.

After his surgery, Kel had listened to the doctor, not surprised by the prognosis. The surgery had indeed revealed a torn ligament, and the doctor had successfully repaired the damage. How strong the reconstructed knee would be was yet to be determined. As his doctor in Norfolk had already told him, he would be lucky to regain 85 to 90 percent of his previous strength. Everyone felt confident that he would be able to remain on active duty, despite the lingering nerve damage from the gunshot wound, but no one, including Kel, knew if he would still be able to stay with the SEALs.

Brent had taken it upon himself to call Marilyn after speaking to the doctor, so Kel hadn't spoken to her since he had left the day before. He thought of their last conversation, wondering if she was genuinely coming around to how important his career was to him. He also wondered if her change of heart was coming too late.

Brent's voice interrupted his thoughts. "I forgot to tell you that the real estate agent called this morning."

"What did he say?"

"He found several houses he thought you might like." Brent checked his mirrors and changed lanes before continuing. "I told him that you'd just had surgery, so it might be a few days before you and your wife would be up to house hunting."

Kel looked down at the bandaged knee, hating the way it was upending everything in his life. "I'm not sure I want Marilyn to know about this until after everything is settled."

Brent's jaw dropped, and he glanced over at Kel. "You're planning to buy a house without telling your wife?" He shook his head. "Kel, I don't think this is the kind of surprise most women would like. Picking out a house is kind of a woman thing."

"I know, but I'm afraid if I don't force the issue, she won't want to move," Kel admitted. "I tried talking her into buying one a couple of years ago, but she said she didn't want to buy something when I might get transferred any minute."

Brent's eyebrows lifted. "Kel, we're in the navy. That's always going to be the case."

"I know." Kel rolled his eyes. "You'd think after being married to me for five years, she would understand that."

"Still, this time is different. You're planning on moving for safety reasons."

Insecurity laced Kel's voice now. "Yeah, but what if I can't make her recognize the danger of going back to the old house?"

"Surely she understands what Ramir is capable of," Brent insisted.

"She doesn't know who Ramir is. How could she? It isn't like my wife works with our unit like yours does."

"I just figured she'd have some idea of the kinds of people we deal with." Brent's voice was insistent as he continued, "She has the right to know what we're up against."

Kel's lips pressed into a hard line. Reluctantly, he gave a curt nod as dread settled in his stomach.

* * *

Marilyn set a drink down on the end table next to where Kel was sitting on the couch, his injured leg propped up on a pillow on the coffee table, a bag of ice draped over his knee. "Is there anything else I can get you?"

"No, I'm fine." Kel patted the couch beside him. "Sit down. I've been wanting to talk to you."

A million possibilities of what he might say flashed into her mind, none of them good. "Is something wrong?"

"Not exactly." He let out a little sigh, waiting for her to lower herself onto the couch before speaking again. Then he seemed to draw up all of his energy as he shifted to face her. "I hope you know that I've always done everything I could think of to keep my career from affecting you."

Still unsure, Marilyn managed to nod.

"I think I know who called the hospital pretending to be my dad."

"Who?"

"Akil Ramir. He's an arms dealer I've had a run-in with before. Actually, it was probably one of his men." Kel waved away that detail, forcing himself to look at her. "Either way, they know who I am, and they know where we live."

Marilyn listened to his words, feeling like she was watching a movie rather than living the moment. The thought of a criminal knowing where they lived, even caring where they lived, was completely surreal. Slowly, she asked, "How can you be so sure?"

"Last week some of my guys stopped by to check out our house. Someone took a shot at them." Kel's eyes darkened. "They're sure that the shooter was an associate of Akil Ramir."

Marilyn's eyes widened. "There was a shooting in our neighborhood?"

"I know you haven't been crazy about moving, but I really think we're going to have to," Kel said gently. "It's too dangerous to go back to our old house."

"You're serious?" Marilyn shook her head. "Did your squad catch the guy? If they did, maybe it's safe now."

"They caught him, but that doesn't mean Ramir won't send someone else." Kel reached for her hand and gave it a squeeze. "Marilyn, Ramir is ruthless. He kills people without thinking twice. You have to understand how dangerous he is."

"But why? Why would he come after you?"

Kel took a deep breath and blew it out. "My last assignment involved him. We think he may have seen an article about me getting wounded and figured out that I was there."

"So he's trying to get even or something?"

Kel hesitated briefly before answering, "Something like that." Now he took another deep breath. "I set up a meeting with a real estate agent tomorrow to look at houses."

Marilyn's jaw dropped. "What?"

"Marilyn, we have to move." Kel's voice was persuasive. "I can put us on the waiting list for a place on base, but I thought you would rather live in town."

"But how did this Ramir guy find you? Won't he be able to track us down again if we buy a house?"

"He probably found us through our DMV records. When we move, we'll have to get a post office box, too, in order to protect our address," Kel informed her. "I was also planning on buying the house in the name of my dad's trust so that we can't be tracked that way."

Marilyn tried to absorb his words. "It all sounds so complicated."

"I know, but it's all going to work out," Kel insisted. "Are you okay with this? You'll come house hunting with me tomorrow?"

"Are you sure we can afford this?"

"I'm sure. We've been saving for this day for a long time."

Though her stomach was churning with nerves, Marilyn forced a smile. "I guess given the choice of having someone shooting at us or buying a new house, house hunting sounds like the better end of the deal."

Kel looked relieved as he smiled at her. "We'll find a great house. I promise."

20

The third house had charm and then some. From the backseat of the Realtor's car, Kel ignored the throbbing in his knee and looked around the quiet cul-de-sac with mixed emotions. The street only had about a dozen houses on it, and the one for sale was situated on the circle. A soccer ball was nestled against the curb nearby, and a kid's bike lay on its side in a neighbor's yard. It was the perfect place to raise kids.

Kel pushed that thought aside and concentrated on the house in front of him. A single cherry tree adorned the wide front yard, a small wooden bench situated beneath it. The front porch extended the full length of the house and then wrapped around one side. Kel already knew from the listing that the back yard sloped down to the water and had a private dock.

He slid out of the car, shifted his crutches, and pushed to a standing position. Marilyn stepped beside him, her eyes meeting his. He read the emotion there—wonder and excitement—and his heartbeat picked up a little. Kel took her hand and gave it a squeeze before gripping his crutches once more.

The real estate agent started up the driveway, giving them the details: two-car garage, like they couldn't see that for themselves; four bedrooms; unfinished basement; private dock. The Realtor opened the lockbox and unlocked the door. He then pushed the door open and stepped to the side to let Kel and Marilyn enter first.

Inside was even better than Kel expected. The house was vacant, which he hoped meant they would be able to move in right away. Large ceramic tile covered the wide entryway and the formal dining room and then continued into the back of the house. Across from the open dining room, French doors led to a small study. Kel took once glance at the stairs in front of them and opted to continue down the hall into the kitchen.

He wasn't much of a cook, but he approved of the white cabinets and dark countertops and the way the dinette area opened into a cozy family room. Windows were placed generously along the back wall, overlooking the yard, with another set of French doors leading to the deck.

Kel shifted to the window so he could see the whole yard through the window. And he smiled. The inlet was wide, the private docks for each house well spaced. The bumpy lawn sloped gently from the house down into the quiet inlet.

When Kel had told the Realtor he'd wanted a house on the water, he had expected to find a house on the beach. As he listened to the water quietly lapping against the dock, he realized that this was what he really wanted. Instead of the roar of the ocean, they would be able to wake up each morning in this peaceful setting, maybe even have a boat of their own to go out and enjoy on his days off.

Marilyn stepped beside him to look out the window, as well, and put a hand on his arm. "What do you think?"

His eyebrows lifted, and he nodded thoughtfully. "I think we should take a look upstairs."

"I think so, too." Marilyn smiled.

* * *

Jay studied the floor plan of their final objective, but he wasn't sure what to think. He had been trained to jump out of helicopters and to insert onto a beach in the middle of the night. He understood how to operate a variety of surveillance equipment and how to safely use explosives and any number of weapons. But he hadn't been trained for this.

Currently, he was sitting in a car on the side of the road in Aruba waiting to hijack a delivery truck. In broad daylight. When he had found out that he was going out on his first real mission, he had been both excited and nervous. Now he was mystified.

Over the past few weeks, he felt like he was steadily gaining ground with his new teammates. Other than a few practical jokes and some lighthearted teasing, they seemed to be okay guys. He still wasn't sure what to think about some of their idiosyncrasies, especially their routine of praying at the beginning of each day and before every training mission. Everyone else seemed comfortable enough about it, and Jay didn't really care one way or the other if they wanted to pray, as long as they didn't expect him to say it.

Seth had been the one to say the prayer before they'd headed out on this mission, and his words had been oddly reassuring. Jay was sure he was ready for anything. Then Brent had briefed them on the method they were using to infiltrate Ramir's compound, and Jay realized that all of his training hadn't prepared him for reality.

He understood the intelligence reports and the one weak spot the CIA had identified at Akil Ramir's house in Aruba: the food. So now he waited, his weapon in his lap, as he and the rest of his squad watched for the truck that would hopefully be their ticket inside.

Quinn's voice came over his combat headset. "Get ready. The truck just left the market."

Sitting beside him in the driver's seat, Tristan started the car and edged it out into the street, angling it so that the road was blocked. He then cut the engine and hopped out to put the hood up as though they were having car trouble.

Jay stayed in the car as he had been instructed earlier, his palms sweating. He looked down at the automatic weapon and hoped he wouldn't have to use it.

The rumble of the oncoming truck sounded through the hot, moist air. A trickle of sweat beaded on Jay's forehead. He swiped at it with the back of his hands and then rubbed his palms on the fabric of his pants.

As expected, the delivery truck driver slowed down and came to a stop after seeing the obstacle in the road. The driver put the truck in park, shoved open the door, and started speaking rapidly in Papiamento. Tristan casually pushed away from the car and approached the other man. He pointed back at the car where Jay was still sitting and appeared to be asking for help.

As soon as the driver turned away from Tristan to look at Jay, Tristan moved quickly. He grabbed the man from behind and immediately plunged a syringe into the man's arm. The driver only had time to turn his head in surprise before he dropped limply to the ground.

From their positions in the brush, Brent and Seth emerged and opened the back of the truck to make sure no one else was inside.

Jay had to remind himself to shift into action. He slid over into the driver's seat and proceeded to move the car back to the side of the road as Tristan pulled the now unconscious driver toward where he parked it in the shade.

"Now what?" Jay asked as he climbed out of the car. "We aren't really going to just leave him here, are we?"

"Yeah. It'll be too hot if we put him inside the car." Tristan pulled the man farther into the brush and propped him against a palm tree where he wouldn't be visible from the road. "He should be out for a couple of hours."

Another vehicle approached, sending Jay's heart into overdrive. He breathed a little sigh of relief when he saw it was Quinn approaching on a motorcycle. He was already dressed in a delivery uniform identical to that of the man Tristan had just drugged. Quinn parked the motorcycle behind their car and impatiently motioned to Jay and Tristan. "Come on."

Following Tristan, Jay rounded the back of the truck and climbed in where Brent and Seth were waiting. A moment later, Brent closed the back, leaving them all in darkness.

21

The truck lurched to a stop, and Seth opened the door to let Tristan and Brent out. They were half a mile from Ramir's compound, but Tristan and Brent would go the rest of the way on foot so they could cover them from the brush. Up front, Quinn kept the truck idling as he waited for Brent to give him the signal that they were ready.

Seth wished they would have had more time to analyze Ramir's defenses, but he agreed with Brent that they needed to strike while Akil Ramir was in Aruba. None of them wanted to go back into his home base in Nicaragua again.

With Vanessa's firsthand knowledge of Ramir's house in Aruba, he was a lot more confident that they could succeed. She had lived here for more than a year when she was first undercover in Ramir's organization. As a result, she had given them a lot of insight they would never have discovered for themselves, even if they had had the time to do adequate surveillance. Vanessa had helped the Saint Squad develop the mission plan and had even been relatively certain about how many people they could expect to encounter once they penetrated the main residence.

Sure enough, the surveillance Quinn and Tristan had conducted earlier that day suggested that there were approximately twenty people inside. They also confirmed that two sentries were posted on top of the roof. They all hoped to remain invisible until long after those guards realized anything was wrong.

A ten-foot-high wall ran the full length of the property except for the area that opened up to the beach. Logically, inserting from the water made the most sense, but their information suggested that Ramir was actually the strongest there. Using infrared imaging, Quinn had identified approximately fifty people inside the two guardhouses situated opposite each other near the edge of the beach.

Realizing that Ramir was prepared for intruders arriving by water, they had chosen to take a more direct and difficult route—right through the front door. Or close to it, anyway.

Seth took a steadying breath when he felt the truck slow to a stop. They were there. Any second the back was going to open up. He just didn't know who was going to be standing on the other side when it did.

Seth shifted forward, an unusual sense of anxiety coursing through him, one he hadn't experienced in years. The rush of adrenaline he always felt during a mission was there, but so was a new sense of uneasiness. The lack of Kel's presence was an oddity in itself, and Seth struggled to push aside the guilt that his former commander's injury had resulted when the squad had helped bring him home.

Brent's leadership style wasn't much different from Kel's. The inherent trust was there, an understanding that he knew everyone would do their job and that success would be the final outcome.

Despite Brent's unspoken confidence, they all knew there was an untested factor that could endanger all of them. So far Jay had demonstrated that he had learned the essentials in BUD/S, the basic SEAL training, but they all knew how quickly unexpected problems could arise in the field. No one was sure yet how the new kid would react under pressure.

Seth had surprised everyone when he had volunteered to be Jay's buddy for this mission. Jay was young and eager, but Seth sensed a strength there, one that hadn't been completely explored. He also knew that Jay had already saved his life once when Ramir's man had shown up at Kel's house. That action had laid a foundation of trust Seth expected they could build on.

Whether Jay was prepared to take an enemy life if necessary was still an unknown, and Seth hoped that test would wait for another day. If they all did their jobs as planned, no one would have to die today.

Glancing over at Jay, Seth saw the nerves there. He understood them. Over their communication headsets, they could hear Quinn talking to the guards. Then footsteps sounded at the back of the truck. Seth gave Jay a little nod of encouragement. Both men quietly pressed back against opposite sides of the truck, poised to strike. Each of them lifted their weapons, a refined version of a tranquilizer gun. The darts were tiny, designed to drug the victim on impact.

Light flooded the inside when the door opened. One man stood outside with his hand still on the door handle, and another man pointed his weapon toward them. Seth squeezed the trigger, dropping the man nearest him. A split second later, he heard the other man's weapon rattle to the ground. He turned in time to see Jay's target melt into unconsciousness.

Seth and Jay jumped to the ground and lifted the two men into the back of the truck. Then they climbed back inside and pulled the door closed.

"The back's clear," Seth said quietly into his lip microphone.

Brent's command sounded over their headsets, "Go."

The truck jerked forward, and less than a minute later, they stopped again.

This time when they heard Quinn's voice over their headsets, they could hear a woman's voice telling him to bring everything inside. Again Seth and Jay pressed themselves against opposite sides of the truck, this time waiting for Quinn to open the door. Without looking at them, Quinn reached in and slid a box of fresh produce to the edge of the truck. He then hefted it up and turned away, leaving the door hanging open.

Seth waited a few seconds before leaping to the ground. He then turned and signaled for Jay to follow. Together they moved to the door leading to the kitchen. They stepped into a wide, professional-style kitchen. The lingering smell of frying onions and some kind of meat wafted through the air. A stereo was on, salsa music pumping through the overhead speakers. A woman, presumably the one who had spoken to Quinn, was lying on the ground unconscious, along with a man who appeared to be one of the household guards.

Next to the door leading to the rest of the house, Quinn was waiting for them. He held up four fingers, signaling how many people were in the next room. Aware that each of them could only use eight tranquilizer darts before reloading, Seth used hand signals to indicate that he would take the middle two when the door opened. He then assigned Jay to the person on the left and Quinn to the one on the right.

Seth's heart beat a little faster as he considered that Akil Ramir could be one of the residents of the next room. He nodded at Quinn, who pushed open the door. Four shots were fired; four people dropped to the ground. None of them was Ramir.

The three SEALs spread out, Quinn heading for the arched opening that led farther into the house and the other two moving toward the stairs. Seth led the way upstairs, hoping to find Ramir in his room or his upstairs office. He had only taken two steps when he heard a burst of gunfire from outside.

His mind took a moment to process the sound, to recognize that the shots had come from Uzis rather than the HK MP5s Brent and Tristan were armed with. Seth hesitated a brief moment. He didn't want to get caught in the stairwell if people started heading outside armed with real weapons, but he knew from Vanessa that Ramir was probably on the second level.

He glanced over at Jay and motioned to him to go back down the stairs and take cover. Sure enough, they had barely stepped out of sight when rapid footsteps sounded in the upstairs hallway.

Brent's voice came over his headset. "We've been spotted. We'll try to keep their attention."

Seth clicked into his microphone to signal that he'd heard Brent as he quickly positioned himself where he couldn't be seen by the men coming down the stairs. Out of the corner of his eye, he could see Jay take cover in the opposite direction.

Footsteps pounded louder as some of Ramir's men bounded down the stairway. Seth couldn't tell how many people were headed their way, but he knew there had to be at least three. Pressing himself back against the wall, he could see the front doorway. He waited for two men to pass the wall he was hiding behind before he took aim and tranquilized the next man to pass him.

The man let out a little squeak of surprise, causing the other two men to turn. Seth fired off two more shots, dropping both of the men before they could aim their weapons in his direction. A fourth man rushed forward, his gun at the ready.

Seth reached for his pistol knowing the man might get a shot off before a tranquilizer dart would take effect, but he heard the swish of a dart being fired before he could fully react. Then the man's weapon fell to the ground a split second before he did.

Abandoning his hiding place, Seth stepped out to see Jay with his tranquilizer gun in hand, two men sprawled at his feet.

Over their communications headsets, both men could hear Brent and Tristan communicating with one another as they tried to keep the guards near the beach from reaching the main house. Then came Brent's voice once more, "We're only going to be able to hold them off for a few more minutes. Hurry up."

"I've neutralized seven so far," Quinn responded. "The main level is clear, but there's no sign of Ramir."

Seth converged with Jay at the bottom of the stairwell. He then motioned for Jay to follow him up the stairs. Seth did the math, both for the number of occupants that should still be in the house as well as for how many tranquilizer darts they each had left. Jay had the most with three, but Quinn only had one left, assuming he hadn't missed, and Seth still had two.

With a total of sixteen people neutralized so far, Seth guessed that upstairs they would find Akil Ramir and his right-hand man, Halim Karel, probably with two guards. Sure enough, when Seth and Jay emerged at the top of the stairs, they could see two guards in the hallway, one outside the door that led to Ramir's office and the other down the hall outside a room that hadn't been identified on Vanessa's drawing of the floor plan.

Both guards were poised and ready for them. The one closest to Seth got a shot off as Seth squeezed his trigger and missed. He ducked back to take cover in the stairwell as he dropped his weapon and drew his pistol free. This time when he leaned forward to fire, he hit his target.

Beside him, Jay took aim and tranquilized the other guard. Jay then headed down the hall to clear the rooms on the eastern side of the house. Knowing that his superiors wanted Ramir alive, Seth holstered his handgun and picked up the tranquilizer gun once more. Then he made a beeline for Ramir's office.

He could hear Jay behind him open a door and clear a room, but Seth's focus was on finding Ramir. Convinced that the man was inside, he pushed the door open and immediately shot the dark-haired man inside. After scanning the room to make sure no one else was present, he hurried over to identify the man, only to find that he had never seen him before.

Frustrated, Seth turned just as a familiar voice spoke in French, "Well, well, well. If it isn't Seth Billaud."

Seth dropped the weapon and turned slowly. In the corner of his mind, he wondered how he could have missed seeing someone in the room. Then he saw it, an opening in the wall that had been concealed by a piece of wooden paneling. In front of it was Akil Ramir, holding a pistol.

"Monsieur."

"I wondered if I would see you again." Ramir's smile spread slowly. "The Navy SEAL who fooled my own niece."

"I don't think you have all of the facts," Seth said in French, his voice deceptively calm as he sized up the man before him. He was relatively confident he could strike and likely come out of the scuffle alive, but he couldn't be sure they both would. Seth knew Ramir had information they needed to ensure both national security as well as the safety of his own squad.

Ramir's dark eyes went cold, but his hand remained relaxed on his weapon. "I know that Lina trusted you, and she ended up in prison because of it."

Seth's voice remained steady. "I heard those rumors, as well."

"You don't really expect me to believe that you worked for my brother."

"Lina told you so herself," Seth reminded him. "Don't tell me you can't trust your own niece."

"And I'm sure you came here for a friendly visit."

"I need your help," Seth improvised. "To get Lina out of prison."

Ramir laughed now, a short expulsion of breath. "And the gunfire outside?"

"I was followed."

"And you were photographed with the injured Navy SEAL." Ramir's jaw clenched, and he flexed his hand on the gun.

"Is that why you sent Imran? Because you were looking for me?"

"You can imagine how upset Halim was when he found out Lina had been fooled by an American," Ramir said now. "If nothing else, he's extremely tenacious. If you hadn't come here, I imagine he would have stayed in America for years, if needed, in order to find you and exact his revenge."

Seth felt a chill run through him. He shifted his weight slightly, half wondering to himself why Ramir didn't shoot him the moment he saw him. "Halim is jealous. He would tell you anything to get me out of the way."

The corner of Ramir's mouth twitched up. "Jealous he is, but he is also loyal."

"Perhaps." Seth held his hands out and nodded at Ramir's weapon. "What now? Once again, you have me at a disadvantage."

"You're going to lead the way downstairs. Once I'm sure my guards have taken care of the problem outside, we'll decide how you will die." Ramir motioned with the gun for Seth to move through the door.

Seth stepped forward slowly, his eyes remaining on Ramir's. He moved through the door, listening for any sign of Jay or Quinn. At first glance the hallway was empty. Then Seth reached the top of the stairs, saw the figure in black, and ducked. The tranquilizer dart shot over his head to plunge into Akil Ramir's neck. Seth looked down to see Jay standing at the bottom of the stairs, his weapon now lowered to his side.

Turning back to where Ramir had fallen, Seth grabbed his arm, shifted his body, and then lifted him into a fireman's hold to carry him down the stairs.

"Where's Quinn?"

"In the truck. He said to tell you we're out of time."

"Then let's go."

Jay turned and headed for the kitchen exit with Seth right behind him. They reached the back of the truck, loaded the now unconscious Akil Ramir inside, and hopped in the back with him as gunfire continued to sound around them.

Seth slammed the door closed, turned to thank Jay for his help, and felt a little stick puncture his arm.

22

Kel read through the report and shook his head, struggling not to laugh at the absurdity of the situation. The mission Brent had launched without his knowledge had nearly gone down without a hitch. Sure, they had drawn some enemy fire when three of the SEALs were inside searching for Ramir, but that was an expected possibility in the mission plan.

They had even succeeded in capturing Akil Ramir alive, a huge feat that had never been attempted before. Jay Wellman had performed as efficiently as the other SEALs in the squad . . . right up until he had accidentally shot Seth with a tranquilizer dart.

Kel could hardly wait to hear what Seth had to say about the incident and to see if his squad would ever let Jay live his first mission down. With a shake of his head, Kel's smile faded, and he reminded himself that this wasn't his squad anymore. At least not for now.

He flipped to the next page of the report, and his eyes narrowed. Seth's conversation with Akil Ramir was summarized in front of him, along with the information that Halim Karel was still at large and presumably in the United States. With a new determination, Kel grabbed his keys and his crutches. It was time to get his wife safely into their new house.

* * *

"Are you ready for lunch?"

Marilyn nodded at Heather and closed her front door behind her. "Thanks for driving up here. I know you must have a ton of things to do to get ready for your move."

"It's all done. The movers came yesterday, and we fly out tomorrow." Heather headed for her car.

Marilyn followed behind her, wishing for the thousandth time that this wouldn't be their last afternoon together. Their friendship had given her a lifeline many times over the past five years, especially since Heather shared many of the same struggles. Like herself, Heather was often at home while her husband was deployed. Heather was also childless, a sometimes difficult position to be in, both as a military wife and as a Mormon.

Marilyn slid into the passenger seat and looked over at her friend. "I am really going to miss you."

"I'm going to miss you, too," Heather responded sympathetically. Then a slow smile spread across her face. "But I have news I just have to tell you about."

"What?"

"We got the call last night." Heather's face lit with excitement. "We're adopting a baby girl."

"What?" Marilyn's eyes widened. "I thought you said the waiting list was too long for infants."

"It is." Heather managed to laugh. "We've been waiting for three years, but it looks like the wait is finally paying off. The baby isn't due for another three months, but the adoption agency said that everything looks good."

"I'm so happy for you."

"Thanks." Heather gave Marilyn's hand a squeeze. "But keep us in your prayers that the birth mother doesn't change her mind."

"I will."

Heather shifted in her seat and started the car. "Come on. Let's go out and celebrate, and you can tell me what else has been going on since I saw you last."

"Actually, I have some interesting news of my own."

* * *

"This is all happening so fast." Marilyn finished making Kel a sandwich and put it on one of the plates she had picked up at Walmart a week earlier. She looked over her shoulder at Kel, who was sitting at the kitchen table. "Are you sure we can afford this? The mortgage is going to be way more than your housing allowance."

"I was planning on using some of my parents' life insurance money for a big down payment," he said matter-of-factly. When she continued to stare at him, he added, "It will be fine."

"I just can't believe you want to move in tomorrow. I mean, you just got out of the hospital two days ago."

"There's no reason to stay here, especially since we can occupy the new house," Kel told her.

Marilyn managed to smile at him as she set his plate in front of him. She turned back to fix herself some lunch, wondering how she had gotten caught in this whirlwind of change. As soon as they had decided they wanted to buy the house, Kel had immediately sat down with the real estate agent to write the contract. When she returned home from lunch with Heather, Kel announced that he wanted to move the next day.

She joined him at the table, finally thinking to ask, "Are we going to be able to get movers by tomorrow?"

"No." Kel shook his head. "But all of our stuff is going to have to go straight to a storage unit anyway."

"What do you mean?"

"If we have movers bring our stuff from our old house to the new one, we'll be announcing where we live," Kel explained.

Her mouth dropped open. "I can't have my old furniture?"

"Marilyn, it's just stuff," Kel said gently.

"Stuff that we've been accumulating for years. Stuff that has a lot of sentimental value," Marilyn argued. "You're seriously planning to have movers come pack up our entire house and then expect me to pretend that none of that stuff exists anymore?"

Kel stared at her for a moment and then nodded. "Yeah." He reached for her hand, sympathy in his eyes. "We have to."

"But . . . but what about the quilt my grandmother gave me? And the keepsakes you kept that belonged to your parents and your sister?"

Kel tensed briefly, but his voice remained calm. "We aren't getting rid of any of those things. They're just going to be in storage."

"For how long? Weeks? Months? Years?"

"I'm sorry, but it will probably be months or years," Kel said with a touch of regret. "We basically have to start from scratch."

Marilyn remained silent as she tried to dismiss the emotional ties to her things for now and focus on the practical. Finally she asked, "Do you have any idea how much money it will take to buy all new furniture?"

Kel shrugged. "A lot." He took a deep breath and then let out a sigh. "I told you I had money stashed away for a rainy day. That day has come."

Bewildered, Marilyn asked, "Exactly how much money do you have saved?"

"I still have almost all of the life insurance money from when my folks died and a lot of the inheritance Dad left me," Kel told her. "I haven't looked lately, but it's probably still over half a million."

Her eyes widened. Her jaw dropped. "You have more than five hundred thousand dollars in the bank?" She swallowed hard. "And you never mentioned it?"

Kel let out a sigh. "I don't know why this is such a huge shock to you. You know that I've been renting out Dad's old house, and I told you that they had life insurance when they died."

"Kel, I just assumed you had a few thousand dollars stashed. Not half a *million.*"

"Does it matter how much we have in the bank?" Kel asked now. "It's not like either of us is the type that wants to just go out and spend money."

"I'm sorry." She pressed her fingers against her temples as though fighting against the beginnings of a headache. "I don't know whether I should feel like I just won the lottery or if I should be furious at you for not telling me about this before."

"Marilyn, I wasn't trying to keep a secret from you. You never asked how much I had in my savings account, just like I don't ask you how much is in yours."

"Kel, I'm your wife. I'm not some roommate you have to worry about keeping out of your things." Marilyn's voice rose slightly.

"Look, I'm sorry. I just never thought about it before."

"Like you never thought about who Amy's father was or that your missions might affect me someday." Marilyn blinked hard against tears that threatened. She started to push away from the table, but Kel reached for her hand.

"Marilyn, please don't be upset." Kel's voice was soft, persuasive. "I'm sorry I never thought to tell you about the money, or Amy's dad, or even more about my job. Some things I tried to keep from you because I didn't want them to affect you. The money was just something that I've had for so long, I don't really think about it. Kind of like how I assume that everyone knows who Amy's dad is."

"How do you expect me to feel? Every time I turn around, I find out you're keeping another secret from me." Irritation, hurt, and anger all vibrated through her voice.

"Marilyn, I'm sorry." Kel kept his hand on hers, his eyes dark with emotion. "I'm really sorry."

Marilyn studied him for a moment, resigned that Kel had yet to learn how to confide in her. "Is there anything else you aren't telling me? Any secrets that I should know about or assumptions that you think I know about? I mean, you aren't some world-famous pie-eating champion or something, are you?"

"I don't think so." Kel lifted his eyebrows. Then he gave her a cautious smile. "I was thinking about buying a boat though, once we get settled at the new house."

"You're assuming that I won't spend all of your money on furniture," Marilyn said with a straight face.

When she saw the alarm in Kel's eyes, she only lasted ten seconds before a giggle escaped along with most of her tension. "I'm kidding."

Kel blew out a breath. "I think I'd better go shopping with you."

Marilyn nodded. "Probably not a bad idea."

23

Tristan walked into the restaurant and immediately noticed his wife sitting at a table with Amy. He also noticed the look in her eyes. Glancing back at Brent, who had followed him inside, he asked, "Do you know what they're up to?"

Brent shook his head. "No, but it always worries me when our wives spend too much time together."

"I know what you mean." Tristan nodded. He crossed to where his wife was sitting and leaned down to kiss her before taking the seat beside her. "So what's going on?"

"What do you mean?" Riley blinked innocently, even though her blue eyes sparked with mischief.

"Sometimes I don't think they trust us," Amy said now, grinning at Brent before looking back at Riley.

"That's because we're very perceptive," Tristan drawled.

Brent nodded. "Tell us what you're up to, and maybe we'll consider playing along."

"Well," Amy began. "You said that Kel and Marilyn would be moving into their new house tomorrow but that they have to get new furniture and everything."

"That's right." Brent nodded. "They're out shopping for furniture right now."

"What about their clothes and personal stuff?" Amy asked.

"They had a lot of their clothes with them since they were up in Bethesda for so long," Brent told her. Then he gave her a sheepish grin. "And we already retrieved all of their photos from their house. I mean, we couldn't leave pictures of them around in case someone broke into the house looking for more information on them."

Amy and Riley looked at each other. Both women smiled.

Tristan looked suspiciously from Riley to Amy and then back to Riley. "What?"

"If you've already sneaked things out, you shouldn't have any trouble getting the rest of their things for them."

"Why?" Tristan asked. "There isn't anything in there they can't replace."

"That's what you think." Riley shook her head and gave her husband a knowing look. "No woman should have to replace all of her clothes and books, not to mention all of the little knickknacks you collect over the years."

Amy nodded in agreement. "Besides, Marilyn isn't much of a shopper. It's going to be hard enough for her just to find new furniture."

"You can't seriously want us to plan a mission to go rescue their *clothes.*" Tristan stared at both women with disbelief.

"Not just clothes." Riley shifted closer to him and gave him that smile of hers, and he knew he was toast. "Honey, this should be easy for a couple of big, strong Navy SEALs."

"Surely you two aren't afraid of rescuing shoes and underwear," Amy added. "It's not like they're going to shoot at you."

"No, but the guys after Kel and Seth might," Brent reminded her.

"Then I guess you'd better take the rest of your squad with you to watch your backs." Amy gave a little shrug. "You said yourself that you think Ramir still has someone in play here. This is the perfect opportunity to see if one of his men is still watching Kel's house. Besides, Jay can always use another training exercise."

Brent looked at Amy, suddenly suspicious. "You already put this on the training schedule, didn't you?"

"Helping with the training schedule is part of my job." Amy grinned. "Just think of this as a housewarming gift for Kel and Marilyn. Trust me. They'll love it."

Brent looked at Tristan, who simply shrugged and said, "I told you they were up to something."

* * *

"I can't believe we're doing this," Tristan whispered to Quinn as they crouched together behind an ornamental pear tree in Kel's yard.

"I can't believe your wife planned this," Quinn retorted, slipping a handgun out of his shoulder holster.

"Amy started it."

"Yeah, like that makes it all better." Quinn rolled his eyes.

Tristan ignored him, instead staring at his watch as he counted off the seconds. "Let's go."

"You'd better pray we don't get arrested," Quinn mumbled, but he moved forward into the darkness.

They slipped around the side of the house, opting to enter through the back door. Tristan checked the door for booby traps while Quinn studied the yard for any movement, any sound. Once Tristan was sure the door was clear, he unlocked it and moved inside.

"Have you got the list?" Tristan asked as soon as Quinn shut the door.

"Yeah." Quinn holstered his weapon and pulled a mini flashlight free from his pocket to illuminate the piece of paper he held, one written in Riley's handwriting. "I'll start in the office."

"Then I'll start in their closet."

"What about the dressers?" Quinn asked. "I'm not going through Marilyn's underwear drawer!"

"*I'm* not doing it," Tristan insisted, turning to look at Quinn.

Then both men grinned and spoke in unison. "Jay can do it."

With grins still on their faces, they split up to pack what they could in the limited time they had. Items were loaded into trash bags and what few boxes and suitcases they could find. They then stacked everything in the garage.

"How much time is left?" Tristan asked.

Quinn glanced at his watch. "Jay should be here any minute."

An instant later, they could hear the garage door opening, followed by the sound of an engine, followed by the garage door closing. Both men waited silently until Jay emerged into the room.

"Are you ready to load up?" Jay asked.

Quinn nodded. "I'll start loading. There's still some stuff to pack in the dressers."

"What?" Jay looked uncomfortably from one man to another. "I thought you would be all done by now."

"We didn't want you to miss out on all the fun," Tristan said innocently. "Marilyn's dresser still needs to be taken care of."

Jay looked at him with a combination of horror and disbelief. "You've got to be kidding me."

Tristan shook his head and handed him two trash bags. "Two ought to do it."

"Thanks a lot." Jay let out a sigh, but he didn't bother to argue. Instead he headed down the hall to the bedroom.

Taking pity on him, Tristan followed. "Just pull out the drawers and dump everything into the bag. That way we don't have to look at what's inside," Tristan suggested.

Jay nodded hastily. "You hold the bag, and I'll dump."

"You got it." Tristan accommodated him, stretching open the large plastic bag. When the first bag was full, he tied it up and opened up the second. When Jay turned over the final drawer, the clothing fell into the bag, but a folder dropped down and bounced onto the floor.

"What's that?"

"Who cares?" Tristan quickly scooped up the folder and a few papers that had fallen free. "Let's go."

Jay set down the dresser drawer and lifted the bag Tristan had left for him. They walked outside just in time to see flashing lights outside.

Tristan looked over at Jay. "Let's hope that's someone we know."

Before Jay could respond, Quinn stepped into the doorway leading to the garage. "Just put the stuff in the van. Come on."

Tristan and Jay both rushed into the garage and tossed the trash bags into the back of the van. Tristan dropped the folder he was holding into an open box as the front door opened; footsteps echoed, and a figure followed them into the garage.

Then they heard a voice. "Let me see those hands."

All three men turned, and all three men let out a sigh of relief. Brent grinned at them and lowered the weapon he held.

"Where did you get the police car?"

"One of Riley's friends downtown," Brent said. "Seth intercepted a 911 call. We don't have much time."

"Great," Quinn muttered.

Brent pulled a wadded-up police shirt from his pocket and tossed it at Quinn. "Put this on. Here's what we're going to do."

Everyone listened to Brent's quick explanation and watched him hit the button to raise the garage door. Moments later Jay and Tristan were handcuffed and being escorted out to the police car by Brent. The moment they were safely in the backseat, Quinn pulled out of the garage in the van and started down the road.

Seeing the van leave, a neighbor rushed outside and across the street. "Hey! What's going on here?"

Brent turned to face the man coming toward him. "Sir, the situation is under control."

"Then why did that van just pull out of here full of stuff?"

"Evidence." Brent motioned to the backseat. "We have some suspects in custody. I need to ask you to please go back to your house. Another officer should be by any minute to take witness statements."

The man looked at Brent with uncertainty, but then he nodded slowly. "Okay."

"Thank you." Brent pulled open the driver's side door. "I need to take these men downtown."

"Thanks, officer."

Brent gave him a curt nod, slipped the key in the ignition, and backed out of the driveway. They were three blocks away before the men let out a collective sigh of relief and Brent let out a snort of laughter.

24

Halim Karel had hardly moved from his seat since the shooting ten days before. Impatience, anger, and frustration pulsed through him as he waited. He still couldn't believe the man he had trusted to help him move to the next stage of his plan had screwed up so completely.

Still staring out the window into Commander Bennett's backyard, Halim reached for an apple. The floor was littered with dishes the neighbors had brought, crumbs, orange peels, and apple cores that had been dropped into a pile beside his chair. He took a bite, finding no enjoyment in the crisp apple. He was hardly aware of what he was eating beyond knowing that he was giving his body the basic sustenance it needed to continue.

Knowing that his time was running out, Halim gritted his teeth. As much as Akil Ramir wanted retribution against the man who had stolen his niece from him, Halim knew that Akil wasn't going to give him a second chance at Seth. If he didn't achieve his goals while in the United States, Akil would insist on moving forward with one of his other plans, one that would affect more than one or two Navy SEALs.

Halim reasoned out his objectives and wondered why everything hadn't fallen into place. His instructions had been simple. The man didn't have to do anything except engage the men protecting the commander's house in battle. Theoretically, once they killed or captured the man they believed to be the threat, the commander would consider his home safe once more and return to it.

For whatever reason, the plan hadn't worked. Imran had died in battle, but these men who had killed him knew. Somehow they knew that the threat still existed. The nightly patrols that had taken place since his arrival had ceased since the shooting, and now the house appeared to be abandoned. At first, Halim had hoped that the patrols had stopped because they believed the threat really had been neutralized and that it was safe for the commander to return to his home.

But as the days had passed, he came to believe that the shooting had resulted in the opposite effect of what he had wanted. The commander wasn't coming back. Neither were the men who had been determined to protect him. Even worse was the knowledge that Seth had been there the night of the shooting and had survived the encounter.

Halim had only caught a brief glance of the big black man talking to the police after the shooting, but he was sure that it was the man he was determined to kill. Knowing that his accomplice had failed to capitalize on the unexpected opportunity infuriated him. And that fury had been building with each hour that passed.

The cell phone that lay on the windowsill beside him remained blessedly quiet, but he knew that Akil Ramir would call eventually. He estimated that he only had three or four days at most before he would face Ramir's wrath. Undoubtedly, Ramir would ultimately insist that he abandon his post so they could move on to something else.

When a police car pulled up in front of the commander's house, Halim stood and stepped closer to the window. He could see the flash of lights, but the house prevented him from seeing anything else. He debated for a moment whether to go outside to see if he could get a better look. Then he slipped his shoes on and hurried out his front door. He walked to the end of his street and turned the corner in time to see the police car driving in the opposite direction.

The rest of the street was quiet, the commander's house was dark, and a "For Rent" sign was posted in the front yard. Seething, Halim stared at the sign for several long minutes. Then he turned back toward his temporary shelter, a new plan already forming in his mind.

* * *

As far as Marilyn was concerned, moving day hadn't come soon enough. She and Kel had gone furniture shopping the day before, and she was surprised that they'd had any success, considering that Kel had been hobbling around on crutches. The few things they had bought, including a new bedroom set, were scheduled to be delivered today. They had also managed to find a few good deals at a thrift store that were even now being loaded into Tristan's pickup truck.

Kel had already started stretching his knee the way the doctor had told him to, mostly trying to bend and straighten it. The swelling was almost gone, although Marilyn didn't know if that was because he was healing well or because he still iced it frequently.

Hoping to show her support, Marilyn had suggested turning their dining room into a workout room for the first few weeks of his recovery so he wouldn't have to spend so much time dealing with stairs. Kel had already ordered an exercise bike and a treadmill, both of which were supposed to be delivered in a matter of hours.

While Kel focused on the practical things he would need to help with his recovery, Marilyn had turned her attention to the basics. Although she missed her old house, she couldn't help but feel the thrill of her upcoming move. She couldn't remember the last time she had been excited about buying a new mop bucket or a broom, but those little butterflies fluttering in her stomach seemed to be a constant since she and Kel had signed the contract for the house. Now she couldn't wait to start putting her new house in order.

Marilyn took another look around the apartment to make sure she had gotten everything. Then she picked up her computer bag and walked outside.

Brent met her at the door and motioned toward Tristan's truck parked out front. "Okay, you're all loaded up."

"Thanks." Marilyn smiled at him. "I guess we're ready then. I just need to swing the keys by the housing office."

"We'll meet you over there then," Brent said and moved to climb into the cab of the truck with Tristan.

"Thanks, Brent," Kel called to him from beside Marilyn's car where he was leaning on his crutches. Then he turned to his wife. "Are you ready?"

Marilyn grinned at him. "Yeah, let's go."

As soon as they were in the car, Kel shifted to look at her. "If I didn't know any better, I'd think you were excited about this move."

"It's a great house," she admitted.

"Yeah, it is."

After stopping by the housing office, Marilyn continued off the naval base and got onto I-64 toward Virginia Beach. They had barely driven two miles before they got stuck in bumper-to-bumper traffic.

Marilyn let out a heavy sigh. "I hate beach traffic."

"Me, too," Kel agreed. "Seeing this makes me grateful that the navy is letting me do my physical therapy in Virginia Beach."

Marilyn let out a sigh. "That makes two of us."

* * *

"What a great spot," Amy said, as she pulled up in front of Kel and Marilyn's new house. She turned to Riley, who was sitting in the passenger seat. "Come on. Let's see how much of this we can unload before everyone else shows up."

"Do you think Marilyn will mind us being in her house without her here?" Riley asked tentatively.

"With Marilyn, you can never tell." Amy shrugged and climbed out of her SUV.

Riley shifted the casserole dish she held on her lap and got out of the car, stepping beside Amy on the sidewalk. "I thought you knew her pretty well."

Amy shook her head. "No one knows Marilyn well, except maybe her husband."

"Really?"

"Marilyn is pretty quiet, and she doesn't come out much when the squad all gets together." Amy crossed the lawn to the front door and pulled out the key that Brent had gotten from Kel. "But Kel said it was okay for us to start taking things inside, so we might as well get started."

"Okay." Riley waited for Amy to push open the door, and together both women crossed the threshold.

Amy pointed at the food Riley was carrying. "Go ahead and put that in the refrigerator. Then we can get started on the other stuff."

Riley walked into the kitchen as the cell phone in her pocket chimed. She slid the dish into the empty refrigerator and then pulled the phone free to read her new text message.

Amy followed her into the kitchen. "Who was that?"

"Tristan just texted me. He said they're stuck in traffic."

"In that case, we should have plenty of time."

* * *

The first thing Marilyn noticed when she pulled up in front of her new house was Riley Crowther and Amy Miller standing on her front porch. "What are they doing here?"

"They offered to come over in case the delivery men showed up early," Kel told her as Marilyn pulled up in the driveway beside Tristan's truck.

She had barely put the car in park before he opened the door and shifted his crutches so he could maneuver himself to stand. He turned back to Marilyn and grinned. "Come on."

Marilyn grabbed her laptop case and moved to his side.

As they headed up the front walk, Amy grinned at them. "Welcome home! You really picked out a great house."

"Thanks," Kel said as Brent and Tristan emerged from inside the house.

Tristan came down the stairs and met them halfway. "Riley brought some lunch for us. I say we eat first. Then we can unload."

"That works for me," Kel agreed. "Did any of the deliveries come yet?"

"Not yet." Tristan shook his head. He waited until Marilyn passed by him and walked up onto the porch before he lowered his voice and added, "The security alarm company dropped by, though. The guy took a look around and said he would be back at two."

Kel looked wary. "Did you check the guy's ID?"

Tristan laughed now. "Oh yeah. The guy was pretty surprised that I asked for it. I also called the company like you asked and made sure he was the one they sent."

"Good." Kel nodded his approval.

"You know, if I hadn't been at your house the other night, I would think you were starting to get paranoid."

Kel's eyebrows lifted, his expression serious as his eyes shifted to the porch where Marilyn now stood with the other two women.

Tristan glanced back at Riley and then turned back to face him. His voice held understanding as he added, "I wish you didn't have to take so many precautions in your private life."

"Me, too," Kel agreed. "Come on. Let's eat."

As they moved into the kitchen, Marilyn was surprised to see a wide chair and a half in the living room. The color was a shade darker than the butter-cream walls, and the tags were still attached to the arm of the chair.

"Where did that come from?"

"It's a housewarming present." Amy joined her. "If you don't like it, we can exchange it, but it just looked like it belonged in this house."

Marilyn's eyes widened, and her voice was incredulous as she turned to Amy and asked, "You bought this for us?"

Amy nodded sheepishly. "I was in this furniture store yesterday checking out the sale items. I was debating on whether or not you would like this when a sales guy came in and told me that everything in the clearance room was an additional 50 percent off." Her shoulders lifted, and a little grin crossed her face. "I couldn't help it."

"In other words," Brent began, as he put a hand on Amy's shoulder, "my wife can't be trusted with a credit card in a furniture store."

"Now that isn't true," Amy insisted. She tried to look offended, and then she laughed. "I just can't be trusted with a credit card in a furniture store when I have an SUV parked outside."

Marilyn ran a hand over the soft fabric and then lowered herself into the chair. The cushions sank comfortably beneath her. Then she leaned back and sighed. "Oh, my gosh. I could sleep in this thing."

"You see why I got it?" Amy's eyebrows lifted as Marilyn looked up at her.

"Oh yeah." She laughed now and pushed herself out of the chair. Surprise showed on Amy's face when Marilyn crossed the room and gave her a hug. "Thank you."

"You're welcome." Amy grinned. Then she slung an arm around Marylin's shoulder. "Come on. Let's go something to eat, and then we can help you unpack."

"That sounds great."

25

Kel watched Marilyn as she made him another sandwich. Everyone was standing around their new kitchen eating off of paper plates, and for once, his wife looked like she belonged. Even though the other two men in the room had been in his life for most of their marriage, Marilyn had rarely spent any time with them unless they happened to go to church together. She had always shied away from their wives, as well.

Marilyn finished making the sandwich and handed it to him. "Here you go."

"Thanks." Kel shifted his weight so he could take it from her. Then he turned to Riley and said, "This was really great of you to bring over stuff for lunch."

"That's what friends are for." Riley smiled and motioned to the refrigerator. "There's also a casserole in the fridge for you for dinner. The baking instructions are taped on top."

"You didn't have to do that," Marilyn said as her relaxed stance became a little guarded.

"I wanted to," Riley told her. "Besides, by the time we get everything unpacked, we may end up inviting ourselves to join you for dinner."

"We don't really have that much stuff." Marilyn seemed to relax again as she leaned against the counter. "Just a couple of suitcases and a few pieces of furniture we picked up this week."

"Actually, you have a bit more than that," Tristan drawled, his eyes lighting with mischief.

"What do you mean?" Marilyn asked.

"These two instigated a little covert operation at your house." Brent pointed at Amy and Riley.

Marilyn looked at Amy and Riley, her brow furrowed. "Covert operation? I don't understand."

Kel shifted closer and put a hand on Marilyn's shoulder. "What they're saying is that they sneaked into our house and smuggled a bunch of our stuff out when no one was looking."

"You did what?" Marilyn's jaw dropped open. Then she shifted away so she could look at Kel. "I thought it was too dangerous to go back to our house."

"It is," Kel started, not sure how to explain that his men had taken risks that he wouldn't have approved of had he been consulted.

"I guess you could call this a rogue operation—" Amy commented as she gave Kel a perceptive smile. "One where we didn't ask for our commanding officer's approval because we knew he would say no."

"You know the old saying," Riley said knowingly. "'It's easier to ask for forgiveness than permission.'"

"Sometimes I think that saying should be our motto." Tristan laughed. He wiped his mouth with a napkin and then tossed it and his paper plate into the trash bag Riley had set next to the kitchen counter. "Are you all ready to unload?"

"I am." Brent turned toward the front door as the doorbell rang. "It looks like your furniture made it."

Kel turned to Marilyn. "I'll let you tell them where you want it."

"Are you saying you don't care how our bedroom furniture is set up or that you don't want to go up the stairs?"

"Both." Kel winked at her. "Don't worry. I trust your judgment."

Marilyn hesitated a moment and looked at Kel. Then, with a shy smile, she nodded and headed for the front door.

* * *

Marilyn finished putting a new comforter on her new bed and took a step back. Then she smiled. The oak bedroom set was exactly what she had wanted for years but had never dared spend the money on. She cringed a little inwardly as she thought of the price they had paid for it, but for once, she refused to let her buyer's remorse overshadow the enjoyment of having something new.

The headboard was an intricate crisscross pattern, a pattern that was duplicated on the drawer handles of both dressers. Several trash bags full of clothing still lay on the floor even though Amy and Riley had offered to help her put everything away. Not sure if everything in their dressers had been packed, Marilyn had decided to save that task for herself.

Instead, Marilyn had identified the bags containing their hanging clothes and had let the other two women help her get her closet in order. After unpacking what they could, all three women had then gone to the store to pick up a few more essentials Marilyn hadn't gotten to yet. Together they had picked out her new bedding along with new towels and trash cans for the bathrooms, a handful of decorating items, and some basic groceries.

Not knowing the other women well, Marilyn had been a bit intimidated at first as Amy and Riley had offered suggestions and opinions. She had felt herself withdrawing, afraid to express her opinion around them. Then Amy had picked up a ridiculous bright purple stuffed rhino. Marilyn couldn't help it. She'd laughed right along with Amy and Riley as they wondered who would buy such an item.

While Marilyn was bonding with her new friends, the men had made a trip to the hardware store to make some purchases of their own, including a new grill and patio set for the deck. Together they had all eaten dinner outside as the sun dropped down over the quiet water. Marilyn couldn't remember ever having a better day.

She looked around the bedroom once more, deciding that the rest of their clothes could wait until morning to be unpacked. She wandered into the other bedrooms, wondering if Kel would want to furnish them anytime soon.

The one nearest the master bedroom was the smallest and looked like it would be perfect for a baby's room. Marilyn pushed that thought away, along with the ache that never quite faded. She leaned on the doorjamb of the next room, a little smile crossing her face as she visualized white sheer curtains billowing in the breeze against the two windows that overlooked the front yard. She could picture the walls a pretty blue with a bed done all in white in the center of the room for any guests who might visit.

The room across the hall had wide windows that overlooked the sloping backyard. She wandered into the room and crossed to the windows so she could get a better look at the water. This would be the perfect place to put a desk, a place for her to set up her laptop and escape from reality as she found time to write.

She turned and looked around the room, letting herself dream of what she wanted the room to look like. A wide, open desk would stretch along the wall in front of the windows, with bookshelves on the far wall. What would it be like, she wondered, to have stacks of writing and reference books along with some of her favorite novels? Maybe even a comfortable chair where she could enjoy a book or read her own work.

Of course, it would never happen. With the little office downstairs, Kel would expect that they would put a desk in there, along with a bookshelf or two they could share. He couldn't possibly understand what it would mean to her to have her own space to indulge her love of writing. How could he? She couldn't imagine trying to explain her dreams to him.

Turning, she left the room and her dreams behind and made her way downstairs. She walked past the dining room where Kel's new treadmill and exercise bike were now set up and ready to use. She then entered the kitchen where Kel was unpacking their new dishes and loading them into the dishwasher.

Marilyn crossed to him and smiled when he leaned toward her for a kiss.

"I assumed that you would want these washed before we used them," Kel told her. "They were pretty dusty."

"You assumed correctly." Marilyn nodded. "You've got to be exhausted."

"Me?" Kel shook his head. "I've hardly done anything. You're the one who must be tired."

"A little," Marilyn admitted as she slid onto one of the wooden bar stools she had found at the thrift store. "I still can't believe your squad went into our house and got so many of our things."

"They still haven't told me exactly how they managed to get a vanload of stuff out of there without any of the neighbors calling the cops on them."

"I have a feeling it might be better if we don't ask."

Kel laughed. "Trust that feeling."

The corners of her mouth curved up. Then she looked around the kitchen and let out a little laugh. "I keep feeling like someone is going to walk in here and tell me that there's been some huge misunderstanding and that this isn't really our house."

Kel grinned at her. "I was thinking the same thing while I was doing the dishes."

Marilyn's eyes met his. Then she slid off of the stool and skirted around the counter so she could wrap her arms around his waist. "I really love this house."

"Me, too," Kel said. Then he shifted so he could see her face. "I hope you're happy here."

"I hope we're both happy here." She reached up to kiss him, drawing him closer. Then she looked up at him. "I think you've been on your feet for too long today."

"I am feeling a bit tired," Kel agreed. "I might consider going to bed if you come with me. I mean, I wouldn't feel right about turning in for the night if you were still up working."

Amused, Marilyn's eyebrows lifted. "Oh, really?"

"Yeah." Kel nodded and pulled her closer for another kiss. Then his voice dropped to a whisper. "Really."

26

Kel shifted his weight on his crutches, making his way into the dining room where his exercise equipment was currently stored. He had read an article online about a doctor who said he tried to get his patients on an exercise bike as soon as possible after Kel's type of surgery to help with strength and motion. After dealing with crutches for five days, Kel was ready to start moving beyond simple stretches.

Lowering his crutches to the ground, he eased himself onto the bicycle and positioned the pedals so that he could start with his injured leg in a relatively straight position. He shifted his weight, using his good leg to move the pedals forward. He winced in pain just as he heard Marilyn's voice.

"What are you doing?"

"Exercising." Kel looked down at his knee before looking back at her. "I hope."

Marilyn put her hands on her hips, disapproval obvious in her voice. "You know you shouldn't be on that bike already."

Insecurities rippled through him, and his own tone took on an edge. "I thought you said you wanted me to get better."

"Yes, and part of you getting better is to not push so fast that you cause even more damage," Marilyn insisted matter-of-factly. Then she let out a sigh. "Kel, it hasn't even been a week."

Kel pointed at the crutches. "Marilyn, I don't think I can stand being on these things anymore."

He wasn't sure what he expected when he looked at her, but the complete understanding surprised him. She took a step closer and leaned forward to give him a gentle kiss. "How about a compromise?"

"What kind of compromise?" Kel asked warily.

"I'll take you in to meet with the physical therapist first thing on Monday morning if you will promise to use those crutches for the rest of the weekend and stay off of the exercise equipment."

"That doesn't sound like much of a compromise," Kel told her. "I already have an appointment with the physical therapist on Thursday."

"Which means you might be able to start your rehab three days earlier," Marilyn said, looking pointedly at the bike before looking back at him. "Without guessing if starting too soon might cause your knee even more damage than is already there."

Kel let out a sigh. "Okay. You win."

"Good. Now, if you really want some exercise, there's a yard sale a few blocks over. We still have a lot of furniture to replace."

"You know we can just go to the furniture store if you want," Kel reminded her.

"Just because you have money in the bank doesn't mean I need to spend it," Marilyn said. "Besides, we can go to the furniture store after we check out the yard sale."

Kel laughed and nodded. "Deal."

* * *

"You really don't have to help me with all of this," Marilyn told Riley as she pulled open a trash bag full of clothes. "You did so much for us yesterday."

"Don't be silly." Riley brushed aside Marilyn's concerns. "I had fun yesterday. Besides, I really didn't want to go with the guys to pick up your stuff from the yard sale. I much prefer helping organize things once they're already moved in."

"I can't believe how much stuff we found today," Marilyn admitted, excitement humming through her voice. "The kitchen table and the entertainment unit looked like they were brand new."

"Have you found a couch yet?"

Marilyn shook her head. "Nothing that we both like. Kel did pick out a new recliner, though. I figure we can live with just that and the chair Amy got us until we find what we really want."

Riley nodded and then let out a little laugh. "Amy was so funny about that chair."

"What do you mean?"

"It was a total impulse buy for her, but then she was so worried you wouldn't like it."

"Really? Amy doesn't look like she ever worries about anything."

"I know. She hides it well." Riley nodded in agreement. Then she motioned to the trash bags stacked against a wall in the bedroom. "Okay, tell me what goes where."

Marilyn stepped beside her and pulled open a trash bag. Together they started unpacking all of the clothes and sorting them into the new dressers. Marilyn tried not to think about the fact that a bunch of men had packed her things. Seeing that there was no order to the contents, she guessed that they hadn't been any more comfortable about the prospect of packing her clothes than she was. It looked like they had simply dumped the contents of the drawer without even looking inside.

A sense of anticipation shot through her when she found the contents of her underwear drawer. Marilyn quickly started emptying the bag. When she reached the bottom without finding the folder she kept her writing in, she felt a little sense of panic. She knew it was possible that it might still be in her old house, but she had hoped that it was somewhere in her things, somewhere where she would find it before anyone else might.

Suddenly uneasy, she glanced over at Riley. Then she forced herself to relax. If Riley came across the old red folder, she would simply ask her where to put it. One thing she liked about Riley was that she wasn't nosy.

Still hopeful, Marilyn grabbed another bag, but her sense of unease began to grow as each bag was emptied. She tried to remind herself that she had been writing for weeks now without having her old work, but she dreaded the possibility of someone finding her file and reading her words.

Riley's voice broke into her thoughts, "Okay, I think that's the last one."

"Are you sure?" Marilyn asked, hoping that the panic in her voice wasn't noticeable.

"I think so." Riley's eyebrows drew together. "Why? Are you missing something?"

"Nothing really," Marilyn managed. "There are just a few things that I thought would have been here."

The rumble of Tristan's truck sounded outside. "Looks like the guys are here. Should we go help them unload?"

"I'll be right down. I'm going to finish up this last bag."

"Okay. I'll see you downstairs." Riley headed out of the room, and Marilyn quickly finished putting away the contents of her pajama drawer. When she reached the bottom of the last bag, she pushed it aside and then pulled open one of the drawers Riley had unpacked for her. She searched through it and then proceeded to the next drawer. After checking the contents of her dresser, she moved to Kel's and riffled through all of his clothes.

Finally, she shut the last dresser drawer and let out a long sigh. It wasn't here. The pages she had poured her heart and soul onto were missing, and she had no idea where they were.

27

Marilyn parked in front of the physical therapy office and shifted to look at her husband. He had been unusually quiet as they drove the few miles, and now she contemplated why. "You look worried."

"I'm afraid that I'll go in there and they'll tell me I'm not ready and that I shouldn't push it," Kel told her. "I don't know if I can wait another week."

Marilyn considered his concerns and tried to suppress her own. "You've never been very good at taking no for an answer. Why start now?"

Kel stared at her for a moment, and then the corner of his mouth lifted. He opened the car door and mumbled, "Here goes nothing."

Marilyn waited for him to balance on his good leg before handing him his crutches. Then they went inside together.

The waiting room wasn't terribly large, and the receptionist's desk was currently empty. Kel looked over at her and said, "You did say we were supposed to be here at nine, right?"

She nodded, glancing down at her watch to see that they were only five minutes early. "Yeah. You're supposed to be the first appointment of the day."

Before he could respond, a young woman emerged from a short hallway. "You must be the Bennetts. Come on back."

Remembering the one time she had seen Kel in rehab in Bethesda, Marilyn hesitated. "Maybe I should wait here."

"Actually, Adam wants to meet with both of you."

"Okay." Marilyn relented and followed the woman and Kel into the hall and then into an examining room where they were quickly met by a slender man holding a clipboard.

Adam introduced himself and then had Kel sit on the examining table. Marilyn watched on as Adam poked and prodded. He moved Kel's knee one way and then another, constantly asking how it felt and if there was any pain. Finally, he stepped back and nodded. "Okay, it looks like you're healing as expected, and your mobility isn't too bad. Let's go ahead and take you into the back, and we'll do some exercises."

Kel nodded, looking visibly relieved. "Okay." He stood and then picked up the crutches. "Do I have to keep using these?"

"For now." Adam nodded. "Let's keep you on the crutches until tomorrow. I'd like to see how your knee holds up after we stretch it out. If it looks okay tomorrow, we can have you use a cane for extra support for a couple more days. By the end of the week, you should be able to get around without any extra help as long as you take it slow."

"Sounds good," Kel agreed.

"I'll go ahead and wait for you in the waiting room." Marilyn watched Adam lead Kel out of the room, and then she went out to the car and retrieved her laptop. She had missed spending time with her characters since all of her time had recently been spent unpacking and shopping. Ideas had been brewing in her head, and she hoped to at least jot a few down while Kel underwent his first physical therapy session.

She sat down in the corner of the waiting room, booted up the computer, and opened the correct file. The ideas started flowing the moment the document flashed in front of her, and her fingers could barely keep up.

The door opening didn't break into her chain of thoughts, but Kel's voice abruptly brought her back to reality. "Are you ready?"

"Yeah." Marilyn swiftly hit the save button and then exited the document. She slipped the laptop into its case and then stood and headed for the door.

Then Kel asked the dreaded question, "What were you writing?"

"Oh, nothing," Marilyn said a little too quickly. "Just a letter to my mom."

Though he looked a little puzzled, Kel seemed to accept her answer.

Before he could question her further, Marilyn asked, "How did it go?"

"Good, I think. Adam said I can use the bike at home for a few minutes a couple of times a day, at least to start with."

Marilyn gave him a knowing smile. "I guess compromising works sometimes after all."

"Maybe." Kel considered for a moment before leaning forward to give her a quick kiss. "Thanks for moving up my appointment."

Marilyn simply nodded. "You're welcome."

* * *

Desks, bookshelves, end tables, and filing cabinets filled the far corner of the store. Kel looked at their choices and wished he never had to go shopping again. They had selected the shelves they wanted, but now they needed to find a desk. Kel glanced over at Marilyn, noticing that she looked as exhausted as he felt. "Are you getting tired of looking at furniture?"

Her shoulders lifted noncommittally. "It will just be nice to have the house all put together. It kind of feels like we haven't had time to enjoy living in our new house because we're always busy trying to get it ready to live in."

"I know what you mean," Kel agreed. "Just think, though. Once we get a desk and some bookshelves, we'll be able to get the rest of our stuff put away, and we won't have any more boxes or bags lying around."

"That's true." Marilyn ran a fingertip along a long, sleek desk. She looked at it a little wistfully before moving on.

"Did you like this one?"

"It's great, but it's too big for the study." She turned and pointed at a more traditional desk. "Something like that would probably be better."

"You're probably right." Kel moved closer to the one she had motioned to. Then another desk caught his eye. It was an old-style rolltop desk in honey oak. A little smile crept over his face as he thought of the desk his father had owned when he was growing up that was very much like this one. "What about this?"

"It's nice," Marilyn said hesitantly.

"What?"

"Nothing," she started. Then she gave a little shrug. "It's just that it isn't very functional—it won't really hold a computer."

"I know, but we weren't really planning on having a desktop computer anymore, and a laptop would fit fine on it," Kel reminded her. Then he pointed at a small hutch in the same honey oak. "We could put the desk along the wall by the window and then put this behind it to put a computer on."

"I think the hutch would make the room too crowded." Marilyn shook her head. "If you really want that desk, why don't we get it and the bookshelves today? Once we get all of that set up we can decide if there's room for the hutch, too."

"That's a good idea," Kel agreed. Then he grinned. "Do you think I can talk Tristan into coming and picking this stuff up today so we don't have to wait for it to be delivered?"

Marilyn gave another shrug. "You are his commanding officer."

Kel laughed now. "I think he's going to regret owning a pickup truck before this week is over."

* * *

The research had been time consuming and tedious, but after days upon days of looking for the proverbial needle in the haystack, Halim had found his first breakthrough. His list of possibilities wasn't as long as he would have liked, but he was determined to make this new information work for him.

Four days had passed since the SEALs had visited the commander's house. Four days since he had received the news that Akil Ramir had been kidnapped by the Americans and thrown into one of their prisons.

The news of his employer's capture had brought out mixed emotions. His first reaction had been complete outrage. Then the realization settled over him that as Ramir's second-in-command, the Americans had in effect promoted him. They had also relieved him of the concern that Ramir would call him back before he completed his objective.

He felt a new sense of urgency to free Lina. His feelings for her aside, he needed her now. Or at least he needed her last name if he was going to be successful in accessing many of Ramir's key assets. If he could convince her to join forces with him, one way or another, his takeover of the Ramir empire would be complete.

Surely, Lina already knew that Seth wasn't who he claimed to be. With him no longer in her life, Halim was certain that she would finally return his affections, especially once he succeeded in liberating her.

Halim saw Ramir's capture in a new light now. He was taking charge of Ramir's empire using phone calls and cryptic e-mails. His plans for his time in the US had changed, but, finally, everything was falling into place. A little more time, a little more research, and all of his dreams would become reality.

28

Finally, everything was coming together. Marilyn knew that there were still a lot of things she needed for the house to help make it feel more like a home, but at least now she felt like it was functional.

Kel's new desk was already in the study, and she had to admit that it looked great. Even though she knew it was more suited for his needs than hers, she was glad she hadn't insisted on a more traditional computer desk. All of the bags and boxes were now unpacked except for the few books and files Kel's squad had rescued from their house.

Marilyn was hoping to finish putting all of those away as soon as Kel finished putting the bookshelves together.

"Hey, Marilyn," Kel called out to her.

"Yeah?" Marilyn answered as she walked into the front entryway and looked into the study. "What do you need?"

"Can you get me a regular screwdriver?"

"Is this one of those requests that requires me to get in the car and go buy what you need, or do we already have one here at this house?"

Kel chuckled and grinned at her. "We already have one. It should be in the junk drawer in the kitchen."

"In that case, I'd be happy to get you a screwdriver." Marilyn retrieved the tool and handed it to him. "Did you have any preferences for what I fix for dinner?"

"Anything is fine," Kel assured her. "I should be done with these in about an hour."

"Okay." Marilyn headed for the kitchen and busied herself with fixing dinner and working in the kitchen. An hour and a half later, she called out, "Kel, dinner's ready." When she didn't hear any movement in the office, she called out again. "Kel?"

When he still didn't answer, she walked down the hall. Her brows drew together when she saw that the French doors leading to the study were closed. Through the glass she could see Kel sitting at the desk reading something.

Behind him the bookcases were all assembled and lined up against the wall, a box filled with books sitting on the floor beside them.

Marilyn pushed open the door, surprised that Kel didn't react to the sound. "Honey, dinner's ready."

Kel looked up now, an unreadable expression on his face.

"Is something wrong?" Marilyn took a step forward.

Then Kel held up the ragged folder Marilyn knew so well. He seemed to draw up his energy, and then he asked, "What's this?"

She could feel her cheeks heat as an overwhelming wave of embarrassment welled up inside her. At first she couldn't even speak. Then she managed to ask, "Where did you find that? Why were you going through my things?"

"I wasn't going through your things," Kel said now, his voice tight. "It was in one of the boxes I was unpacking."

"And you read it?" Marilyn asked, horrified.

"I just wanted to know what it was." Kel's voice was low and even. "Imagine my surprise to find the better part of a novel hidden with our books, and I never even knew my wife liked to write."

Rather than answer the underlying accusation, Marilyn took another step forward and held out her trembling hand. She hated that her voice shook, and she wished desperately that she could just disappear. "May I have it back?"

Kel picked up the pages he had apparently already read—over a hundred of them—and stacked them with the others. Marilyn could feel her cheeks heating. He had been in here reading her words, her private thoughts, for the past hour while she was cooking for him.

After putting the papers back into the folder, he held it up and stared at her. "Why didn't you ever tell me about this? This is part of who you are. I can't believe you would keep something like this secret from me."

"Secret? Don't you *dare* talk to *me* about what secrets I am keeping from you." She swallowed hard, staring at him with a combination of anger and embarrassment. "You don't tell me anything, even when I beg you to share your life with me. Now you're going to criticize me for having something I want to keep private?" She took a steadying breath before speaking again, her voice now flat. "Dinner is on the table. Help yourself." She then stepped out of the study and turned away from the kitchen.

* * *

Kel sat on the deck and stared out at the water. The smell of meat grilling tingled his senses and stirred his stomach. He hadn't bothered to eat dinner. After Marilyn had stormed out, he had come outside, staying in the kitchen just long enough to put the casserole in the refrigerator. That had been over an hour ago, and he had yet to hear any movement in the kitchen since then.

He imagined Marilyn was hiding up in their room, probably using her laptop to create some other fictional account of why his career was ruining someone's life. He still couldn't get over what he had read. The characters' emotions had been so *real.* Within the lines, he could see the woman's struggles. He found himself feeling sorry for her. At times he even caught himself rooting for her husband to change careers.

Kel shook his head as he wondered how his wife had found the time to write and then realized that he didn't have to ask that question. Obviously, she had to do something when he was away. Except for an occasional comment about work or going out with Heather, Marilyn rarely talked about how she spent her days. A wave of guilt washed over him as he considered that he had never before thought to wonder what she did with her time while he was gone. He could see now how her anger and frustration about each assignment had poured into the words she had written.

He also began to understand just how deeply seeded her resentment really was. Even though he was now making an effort to be more open with Marilyn about his life as a SEAL, after tonight, he was beginning to realize just how hard his career had been on her.

A back door opened a couple of houses down, and Kel watched a boy of about seven race outside and bound down the back steps holding a baseball glove in his hand. Following more slowly was his father. Something twisted inside Kel as he watched the father cross the lawn and then turn to toss the ball to his son. He might never have that, Kel realized.

Then another thought invaded his mind with a swift vengeance. Did Marilyn really want children? In the early days of their marriage, they had talked about starting a family. Nearly three years had passed since they had started trying for a baby. As the months had passed into years without any success, Marilyn could barely talk about children without tears filling her eyes. What should have been a joyous discussion had become a topic he had learned to avoid.

Even though he continually hoped and prayed that they would be able to start a family of their own, Kel now wondered if Marilyn still shared that desire. After reading her unfinished novel, he wondered if everything about her was just an illusion.

As he watched the neighbors throwing the ball around, he stretched his leg out in front of him and then slowly lowered it. The exercise was a simple one, one that had become a habit every time he found himself sitting for more than a few minutes. He repeated the motions ten times and then switched to his stronger leg.

A woman's voice called out that dinner was ready, effectively ending the ball practice down the street. Minutes stretched out unnoticed as darkness fell and the sounds of the neighborhood faded until only the lapping of the water and an occasional dog barking could be heard.

The door behind him opened, but instead of Marilyn's voice, it was Seth's Southern drawl that broke into the silence. "Hey, Kel."

Kel shifted enough to see the big man standing behind him. "Hey. I didn't think I would see you until the wedding. It's getting close."

"I know." Seth was grinning as he moved forward so that he was standing in front of Kel. "Believe me, Saturday can't come soon enough."

Kel tried to muster up some enthusiasm for his friend. "So what brings you by?"

"I was in the neighborhood and thought I would stop by," Seth told him. "I just dropped Vanessa off for her last meeting with the caterer."

Kel's eyebrows lifted, and he motioned for Seth to sit down. "She didn't make you go with her?"

"I guess you could say she took pity on me." Seth let out a soft laugh and lowered himself into a chair. "I hate dealing with those kinds of things. Besides, she knows what I like."

"Really?" Kel asked, a touch of the bitterness coursing through him, seeping into the word before he could stop it.

"Yeah." Seth's dark eyes sharpened, but his body remained relaxed. "Is something wrong?"

Kel jerked one shoulder up and avoided the question. "Just a lot going on, I guess."

"Like?"

Kel let out a sigh and shook his head. Then he asked a question that surprised both of them. "Do you think you really know Vanessa?"

"Well, yeah." Seth shrugged. "I've known her since we were in high school."

"Yeah, but do you really know her?" Kel continued. "Do you know what she hopes for in the future? What her biggest dreams are?"

"I don't know. I guess I never really thought of it that way," Seth said now, sounding a bit less certain. "We've talked about getting a house and having kids. I know she wants to keep working at least for the next couple of years, but after that she hasn't really decided."

"Are you okay with it if she wants to keep working after you have kids?"

"Yeah. I don't know why not." Seth shrugged. "Personally, I doubt she would want to stay full time for long after starting a family." Then he leaned forward and grinned. "And I did tell her that I was putting my foot down about undercover assignments once we have kids. It's one thing to have to lie to your neighbors about where your wife is, but there's no way I want to try that with a two-year-old."

Kel laughed, despite the hollowness that still filled him. "I can see your point."

Seth shifted in his chair and stretched one long leg out in front of him. "So are you going to tell me what's bothering you?"

Kel started to shake his head and then reconsidered. Though he knew he could trust all of the men in the unit to keep a secret, Seth was the one who could have taught a class on the meaning of confidentiality. "I guess I'm starting to realize that I don't know my wife as well as I thought I did."

"I'm sure being together so much has to be a huge adjustment for both of you," Seth said. "When was the last time you were home for longer than a long weekend? Even when we're not on assignment, you still go to work every day, and she has the house to herself."

"Yeah, but it's more than that," Kel admitted. "I was putting away the books that you guys got from my house, and I came across a manuscript Marilyn had written."

"I didn't know Marilyn was a writer." Seth's eyebrows lifted slightly.

"Neither did I."

Seth was quiet for a brief moment, and then he nodded. "And therein lies the problem."

"I can't believe I've been married to her for five years, and not once did she ever tell me that she liked to write."

"That is pretty odd," Seth agreed cautiously.

"What's even worse is that her story parallels our lives. It's like everything that she doesn't like about the SEALs and the navy is woven into those pages."

Seth considered for a minute. "So, what bothers you more? The fact that she didn't tell you about her writing or that you didn't like what she wrote?"

"I don't know." Kel shook his head. "I guess I already knew how she felt about my career, but reading about it that way really hit home."

"Sounds like she's a pretty good writer."

Kel considered for a moment and then let out a half laugh. "You know, I didn't even think about it, but yeah, I guess she is."

"I wonder if she knows that."

"Knows what?"

"That she's a good writer." Seth shrugged. "Why do you think she hid it from you?"

"I've been wondering the same thing."

"A lot of those creative types get funny when it comes to their art," Seth commented. "And Marilyn's always struck me as being a bit shy. Maybe she was afraid to show her writing to anyone for fear that she'd find out it wasn't any good."

"I don't know. Maybe, but I didn't think I was just anyone." Kel considered Seth's opinion. "The real question is what do I do now?"

Seth paused for a moment. "Seems to me that you've got two choices. You can support her writing, or you can go back to the way things were and pretend you don't know anything about it."

"And if I decide to try to support this hobby of hers, then what?"

"Like I'm such an expert on women." Seth laughed now. "All I know for sure is that the women I've known all seem to expect us to read their minds."

"Maybe you know more about women than I gave you credit for."

"I don't know about that, but I have known Vanessa a long time, and she's definitely made me work through a few of those mind-reading expectations." He stood up and tapped Kel on the shoulder. "If nothing comes to mind, pray about it. I'm sure you'll figure something out."

"Thanks, Seth." Kel stood up. "Thanks for stopping by."

"Anytime."

29

Marilyn watched Kel and Seth on the deck below, embarrassment still burning deep inside her. She could only imagine what they were saying, talking and laughing about the words she had written.

For so long she had worried that this day would come, that Kel would find out about her writing, that he would patronize it as a simple hobby or that he would hate what she had written. The look on his face when she had found him reading her work had been even worse than she had imagined it would be. He had looked so disappointed, so betrayed.

She had thought that if Kel found her writing that he might ask her what it was or where it had come from. She had never truly thought that he would read it or at least not much of it. With a sigh, she tried to slow down her thoughts, forcing herself to consider what she should have expected. Did she really think that he would find her half-written novel and say, "Here, honey, I think this is yours"? Even more unrealistic was the absurd idea that he would have pretended he had never seen it in the first place.

After leaving Kel in the office, she had gone upstairs and locked herself in the spare bedroom that overlooked the water. Hoping to escape from reality, she had turned on her laptop and tried to bury herself in her story. For once she hadn't been able to write through her insecurities and frustrations. Instead, she had sat down by the window and opened the pages Kel had read. Thinking of him, she began reading them herself.

Each word was painful to read, especially since the new version on her computer was so vastly altered from what was in front of her now. These characters were bitter, much more so than their revised selves. Their anger and resentment, even their hopes and dreams, seemed so much different than how she thought of them now.

Although she hadn't been able to spend much time writing over the past two weeks, she felt the story slowly moving forward. With Kel at home, her only time writing had been during his physical therapy appointments, but even those few minutes had given her hope that she was nearing the end of the story. Now she didn't know if she would ever be able to explore where the characters were destined to go.

Marilyn heard the door close below her, and she looked outside to see that Kel and Seth were no longer sitting there. She rested one hand on the windowsill and stared out into the darkening sky. She imagined Kel would come look for her eventually. Then again, maybe he wouldn't. Marilyn wasn't sure she was ready to face him yet.

Then she heard Kel call her name, and she couldn't move. She could hear him looking briefly in their room, and then a knock came on the door.

"Marilyn, open the door."

She couldn't answer. She couldn't find any words.

Then she heard the lock turning, followed by the doorknob, and the door swung open.

"We need to talk," Kel began.

Marilyn's embarrassment crested, and her silence was broken. "You were talking to Seth about me. You told him what you found."

"Yeah, I talked to Seth. He's a friend, one I can confide in," Kel said defensively.

"How could you? How could you tell him about what I wrote, what you read?" Marilyn felt tears sting her eyes. "Did it ever occur to you that I might not want your friends to know how I spend my free time?"

"Do your friends know how you spend your free time?" Kel asked now, a fresh wave of frustration cresting.

"I only have one friend, but no, Heather doesn't know about any of this."

Kel considered her words, oddly satisfied that Marilyn's secret hadn't been kept only from him. His next thought was the realization of how much Heather's move would affect her. Focusing back on the issue at hand, he blew out a breath. "If you don't want people to know you're a writer, that's your business."

"I'm not a writer," Marilyn said, interrupting him.

Kel looked at her completely perplexed. "Then what do you call the manuscript I found downstairs?"

"It's just something I was playing around with," Marilyn muttered. "It's nothing."

"Marilyn, don't shut me out. I may not do a lot of reading, but even I can recognize when someone knows how to write," Kel said. "And you know how to write."

She didn't know what to say. For years she had barely admitted to anyone that she wanted to write, always wondering if she was good enough to share her words. Kel's offhanded comment evoked both hope and fear.

He limped forward until he was standing beside her. Then he looked out the window as though gathering his thoughts. "I didn't mean to invade your privacy or anything. I was just so surprised when I came across that folder. I had no idea that you liked to write." Kel shifted to look at her now. "And I thought I knew you."

"You do know me."

"No, I don't." Kel shook his head, a sadness reflecting in his eyes. "I only thought I did."

Her embarrassment slowly faded as she considered Kel's feelings. She hated seeing that wounded look on his face. "Kel, I'm sorry. I've just never felt comfortable sharing this with anyone." She stood a little straighter, hoping to explain in a way he could understand. "I guess it's a little like when you go on a mission and you aren't allowed to talk about it. You don't see it as keeping anything from me because you know you aren't allowed to."

"Yeah, but that's stuff that's classified, not something that I'm choosing to keep from you."

Her eyebrows lifted. "Some of what you keep from me is classified, and some of it is private. You don't feel comfortable sharing that part of your life with me, just like I didn't feel comfortable sharing this with you."

He looked at her for several long seconds. Then he took a step back. "I guess we both have secrets we feel like we need to keep."

Marilyn watched him limp back to the door, her stomach feeling like it was filled with lead. She wanted to say something to wipe away that hurt look, but she didn't know how.

Then Kel turned back to look at her. "You must be hungry. Maybe we should go downstairs and get some dinner."

"Okay." Marilyn nodded meekly. She followed him out of the room and wondered how life would ever be able to return to normal.

* * *

Phones were ringing as Halim stepped off the elevator and walked toward his new office—if it could even be considered an office. The whole floor of the office building was open except for the cubicles that divided the space into tiny compartments, compartments the people at the electric company called offices.

Halim had spent several days exploring his options of how to locate where Commander Kelan Bennett was currently hiding. He could admit now that the commander had been relatively thorough when he'd pulled his disappearing act. The DMV didn't have a change of address for him, and the forwarding address listed at the post office was to a post office box, one that no one ever checked.

It hadn't taken long to figure out that the commander was using a series of forwarding addresses to get his mail and that the post office staff wasn't about to give him enough information to find the final location.

Realizing that he was going to have to dig deeper, Halim had started hacking into credit card companies until he found the information he was looking for, or at least part of it. The activity on the commander's cards had been practically nonexistent until several days before. Then the charges had started popping up, all within the Virginia Beach area.

Hoping that the Bennetts had relocated to somewhere nearby, Halim had taken a job in the customer service department at the electric company in hopes of finding them.

Someone called out a greeting as he passed by, and Halim gave the man a nod and a forced smile. He couldn't understand these people or their ignorance. Didn't they understand that they were at war? One thing was certain. They definitely didn't know what the enemy looked like; Halim had found one of the Americans' biggest downfalls.

The job had been easier to get than he had expected, but hiding his contempt for his co-workers was a constant challenge. They didn't seem to care what the person sitting beside them looked like or what they believed. Halim only hoped he didn't have to keep the job for long. Unfortunately, his search so far seemed endless.

His first two days working had been spent learning how to access the information he needed. The next day he had learned how to appear as though he were helping customers when he was really doing the work he had come here for.

Each day he sorted through the list of new and transferred service connections and then mapped them on the Internet to narrow down which ones were the most likely based on their proximity to where charge card purchases had occurred.

The credit card activity had only lasted for about a week, and then it appeared as though the commander had figured out that someone might track him that way. Still, the dates of the charges helped Halim select his targets with care. Already he was spending his off hours observing the various locations on his list to see if he had finally found his target, or, rather, the means to find it.

His list of possible locations was nearly complete, which would allow him to abandon this tedious job and the annoying friendly co-workers. Once he could begin searching full time, he knew he would be one step closer to finding the Bennetts . . . and the prize they could bring him.

30

"How much time do we have?" Kel asked Tristan, as he lowered the tailgate of his truck.

"Riley said she was taking Marilyn to lunch across town, and then they were going to stop by a thrift store on their way back," Tristan told him. "That should give us at least two or three hours."

"I really appreciate you guys helping me with this."

"No problem." Seth climbed up into the truck and grabbed the end of the new desk they had picked up for Kel. "Marilyn is going to be so surprised."

"That's the idea." Kel nodded.

Tristan lifted the bottom part of the desk. "Okay, slide it forward."

Kel moved closer and grabbed the center, supporting some of the weight as Seth and Tristan tilted it and slowly lowered it to the ground. Ignoring the cane he was supposed to use for the next few days, Kel leaned into the truck and grabbed the new office chair and moved it closer so he could pull it out of the truck bed.

As Tristan and Seth maneuvered the desk through the front door, Kel put the chair down on the driveway and began rolling it forward. With a quick glance at his watch, he prayed they would have enough time.

* * *

"Thanks again for lunch," Marilyn said as she climbed out of Riley's car.

"I'm glad you could come," Riley told her. "Sorry we didn't find anything good at the thrift store."

"That's okay. You know how those stores are. Sometimes they have great stuff, and sometimes it's all junk."

"So true," Riley agreed. She leaned forward and added, "Give me a call if you want to hit the yard sales on Saturday."

"I will." Marilyn stepped back. "Thanks again."

Riley put the vehicle in gear and waved as she pulled out of the driveway. Marilyn turned and walked up the front steps, wondering if Kel's mood had improved at all since that morning.

Everything had been so different when they had finally eaten dinner two nights before, and all day yesterday he had been uncomfortably quiet. She was starting to wish he would fight with her so she would at least know what he was thinking. Then again, she wasn't sure she wanted to know what he was thinking.

She still dreaded finding out what he thought of her writing. He seemed to think she had at least some talent, but she was afraid to know what he thought of the story she had created and the parallels it had to their lives. She also wished she could explain that her characters' emotions were exaggerations of what she sometimes felt, that she often channeled her feelings into her story as a way to keep her problems in perspective.

Her tension rose as she pushed the door open and saw Kel sitting in the study at his desk. She immediately saw the changes he had made to the room. A narrow table was pushed into the corner behind his desk. Atop the table was a desktop computer.

"You got a new computer?"

Kel turned to face her, his expression guarded as he nodded. "I splurged."

Her practical streak surfaced, pushing aside her other concerns. "Do you really think we should be spending so much money?"

"We needed to upgrade our computer anyway," Kel told her.

Marilyn nodded automatically, but she couldn't quite shake the unsettled feeling she had been living with over the past two days. She forced herself to look at him, forced herself to start the conversation she didn't really want to have. "Kel, we need to talk about what happened the other night."

"I don't know what else there is to say," Kel said, his expression unreadable.

"There's a lot to say," Marilyn said, pushing forward. "We've both been keeping secrets from each other." She hesitated briefly as she stepped farther into the room. "I don't want it to be that way anymore."

Kel's eyebrows lifted. "Does this mean you're going to let me read what you write?"

Marilyn struggled with that idea for a moment, her insecurities rushing through her. Slowly, she nodded. "As long as you let me edit my stuff first." Then she tilted her head and ventured, "And as long as you stop hiding everything about your work from me."

"You do understand that I can't tell you everything." Kel's voice was serious. "A lot of my work is classified, even now that I'm working a desk."

"I know, but I need you to share your life with me—more than you used to."

Kel nodded slowly. Then, before she could say anything else, he stood up and motioned to the stairs. "Come on. I want to show you something."

"What?"

A smile crossed his face, giving Marilyn some hope that things were starting to settle down between them. "You'll see."

Kel headed for the stairs and motioned for her to follow him. Curious, Marilyn followed him up the stairs and then into the hallway. Then she stopped when he put a hand on the doorknob to her favorite spare room.

"What are you up to?"

"I have a little present for you." Kel pushed the door open and stepped inside.

Marilyn took a step forward, and her jaw dropped open. The desk she had been eyeing at the furniture store was stretched out in front of the windows, exactly where she would have put it had she designed the room. A tall office chair faced the window, and her laptop was already on the desk, along with her printer. Two tall bookcases graced one wall, and on the opposite wall a loveseat was positioned beside an end table in the same maple as the desk. On top of the table were a white ceramic lamp and a candy dish filled with chocolate kisses.

She moved farther into the room and turned in a complete circle before looking back at Kel. "I don't understand. Where did all of this come from?"

"Tristan and Seth helped me put it together." Kel gave a little shrug as he attempted to look nonchalant, but Marilyn could see the eagerness on his face. "Do you like it?"

"Do I like it?" Marilyn repeated, her eyes wide. Then she moved closer to him and threw her arms around his neck. "It's perfect. It's exactly what I wanted."

"Really?" Kel shifted so he could see her face.

"Yeah." Marilyn laughed now. "I imagined that desk right there, with bookcases and somewhere I could read." She reached up and touched her lips to his. "I absolutely love it."

"Just make sure you still remember me when you're a famous author."

Her eyes narrowed for a moment, and her voice grew serious. "I doubt that will ever happen, but even if it did, it would never change the fact that I love you."

Kel smiled now. "Good, because I love you, too."

* * *

"Did you see this?" Seth dropped a file marked "Top Secret" on Brent's desk.

"Is that the report on Ramir?"

"No." Seth shook his head. "No one has gotten anything out of him so far, and I don't know that they will be able to. Ramir isn't ever going to admit that he was involved in anything here in the US."

Brent picked up the report. "Then what's this?"

"I wanted to see if I could track Kel's location to see if he's still vulnerable."

"Yeah?" Brent looked up at him. "Is there a problem?"

Seth shrugged. "He had some credit card activity during the days before and after he moved into his new house."

"I know." Brent nodded as he slid the papers out of the file. "He didn't have enough cash on him when they started buying furniture, so he had to use credit." Brent looked down at the top sheet in the file and noted that it was a list of Kel's credit card activity. "I don't think this should be much of a problem, though. The charges were pretty spread out, and none of them is close to where the new house is."

"No, but they do place him here in the Virginia Beach area."

"Halim Karel, or whoever is looking for him, already knows that Kel's here."

"I guess." Seth shook his head. "It still worries me, though."

"Are you worried that this Halim guy is going to find Kel or that Kel won't be able to handle it if he does?"

"Both," Seth admitted. "And I'm worried that he might figure out where Vanessa and I are living. Halim isn't someone I would want to meet in a dark alley, and that's somewhere that I'd be prepared for someone to jump out at me. If he manages to track Kel to his new house, I don't know if Kel will be ready for it."

"I think Kel was worried about the same thing. That's why he put an alarm system in," Brent said. "If it would make you feel better, though, we can tie into the security system's readings. That way if there's any sign of a breach, we'll know as soon as the cops do."

Seth nodded, a little of the tension in his stomach easing. "Better safe than sorry."

"Go ahead and set it up then," Brent said. He waited until Seth took a step toward the door before he added, "And, Seth, after you finish that, give all of the information to Tristan. It's time you start shifting into vacation mode. You're getting married in two days."

Seth managed a little grin. "I'll try."

31

"Are you really sure I need to come with you to the temple ceremony?" Marilyn asked as she watched Kel pack his suit in a hanging bag. The Whitmores had invited them, along with the rest of the Saint Squad, to stay the night at their house in northern Virginia so they wouldn't have to get up at four in the morning to make it to the Washington D.C. Temple in time for Seth and Vanessa's wedding.

As much as Marilyn enjoyed her time staying with Jim and Katherine, she wasn't sure she was ready to stay with them in a house with so many people there all at one time. She ventured, "I don't know Seth that well. Maybe I should stay here and only go to the reception."

"Of course you should come." Kel turned to look at her. "If you want, bring your laptop. You might find some time to write while we're there."

"Maybe," Marilyn said doubtfully.

"Don't you want to go?"

She shrugged. "I just always feel out of place with your squad."

"Marilyn, right now they aren't my squad," Kel said softly, a touch of sadness in his eyes.

A sigh escaped her. The familiar panic and nerves tangled in her stomach, feelings that she didn't think she could ever explain to Kel, but now along with them was compassion and concern for his feelings and his needs.

She was still wavering when he stepped closer and took her hand. "Please come with me."

Even though everything in her wanted to say no, she felt herself nodding. Before she could reconsider, he slipped his arms around her waist and drew her close. "Thank you. I really want to be there for Seth, but I don't know if I could handle going on my own. Seth still feels responsible for my injury, and it can get awkward sometimes."

Marilyn let out a little sigh. "I guess I'd better go pack."

* * *

"Are you all ready for the big day?" Kel asked as he sat beside Seth in the Whitmores' living room.

"More than ready," Seth answered without hesitation. "When we first got engaged, we had planned to get married around Memorial Day. Waiting these extra few weeks has been tough."

Kel's eyes narrowed. "You didn't push off your wedding because of me, did you?"

"No, it was her grandparents who threw the dates off. Neither one of us realized that they were going to be visiting some of their family in Morocco during the month of June," Seth told him. Then he grinned. "They only got back on Wednesday."

"As in two days ago?" Kel let out a little laugh. "They're probably not even on our time zone yet." He glanced over at the older couple who were currently talking to Brent in Arabic. "They speak English, don't they?"

Before Seth could answer, Vanessa plopped down beside Seth and answered for him. "Only when they absolutely have to."

"I assume you learned Arabic from them," Kel said now.

Vanessa nodded. "I never realized how useful that skill would be when I was younger. Then again, I hadn't planned to work for the CIA back then, either."

"How is the new job going?"

"So far, so good." Vanessa smiled. "It's hard being out of the loop on Ramir's organization, but I can't tell you how good it feels to go to sleep and know that I don't need to keep a gun under my pillow."

Kel and Seth exchanged knowing glances, and Vanessa immediately sat a little straighter. "What's going on?"

"It's nothing to worry about," Seth said a little too quickly.

Both elegant eyebrows lifted, but now instead of looking relaxed, Vanessa looked like she was poised for a fight. "Don't give me that. What happened?"

Seth glanced over at Kel, apparently considering how much to tell Vanessa. "We think Ramir still has someone in play here in the US."

She looked from Seth to Kel, concerned. "You think someone is still after you?"

"Not me, exactly." Kel looked at Seth apologetically.

A myriad of emotions crossed Vanessa's face, ranging from her initial surprise to understanding. "Halim is here, isn't he?"

"We think so." Seth took her hand, lacing his fingers through hers.

Understanding dawned in her eyes. "That's why you didn't want to put a picture in the newspaper with our wedding announcement."

Seth gave her a wry smile. "That and the fact that we both sometimes work undercover." He lifted her hand to his lips and kissed the back of it. "Look at this as the perfect time to go on a secluded vacation."

Vanessa rolled right over his suggestion, her posture still tense. "Seth, we know more about Halim than anyone. We should be involved."

"And Halim knows more about us than anyone. We need to lie low for a while and see what happens."

Before Vanessa could respond, Kel spoke, "I know how hard it is to be out of the loop, but I'm sure your friends at CIA will turn up something. Besides, you know the Saint Squad won't stop digging for information until they find him."

"I hope they find him before he finds one of you," Vanessa said, a combination of compassion and fear in her eyes. "He's an evil man, one who doesn't understand boundaries."

"Neither do Navy SEALs." Kel used his cane to push to a stand. "I think I'd better go rescue my wife from kitchen duty."

Vanessa stood, as well. "And I'd better round up my family so we can get some rest."

"I'll let Katherine know you're leaving," Kel said. He then headed for the kitchen, where Marilyn was helping Katherine wash the last of the dinner dishes. "You two should be out enjoying your guests, not doing dishes," Kel told them. "I think Vanessa and her family are about to leave."

"I'd better go say good-bye," Katherine said and closed the dishwasher. She glanced over at Marilyn and grinned. "Why don't you go grab the Boggle game out of the closet, and we'll challenge the men to a game."

"Wait a minute." Kel held up a hand in protest. "If we're playing on teams, I get Marilyn on mine."

"You sound like Brent when we play Pictionary." Katherine laughed. "Come on. Let's go say good-bye, and we'll figure out the teams."

"As long as Marilyn is on mine," Kel repeated as he took his wife's hand. "I know where the talent lies in my family."

Marilyn glanced up at him, her cheeks reddening with pleasure. Then she gave him a little shrug and followed him in to talk to his friends.

32

The past few days had been like living in a fairy tale. Marilyn felt as if there were a huge weight off her shoulders, several weights, in fact. No longer did she have to hide why she wanted to spend time on her computer, and she was amazed at how supportive Kel was about her writing.

Their time together at the temple for Seth and Vanessa's wedding had been wonderful, and Marilyn had even surprised herself by having fun at the reception. She was awed by the friendships she was forging, especially with Tristan's wife, Riley. Their time at the Whitmores' home had been surprisingly comfortable, and for once, she hadn't felt awkward with Kel's friends.

Kel's physical therapy was progressing steadily, and other than carrying a cane with him in case he needed a little extra help going up and down stairs, he was able to get around well. He was even expecting the doctor to clear him to drive at his next appointment.

The physical therapist seemed pleased with Kel's progress, and Kel finally seemed to be overcoming the negative thoughts that had plagued him in the days before his surgery. Marilyn had fallen into a comfortable routine of using her laptop in the waiting room every day when Kel was in therapy. Today was no exception.

She was deep into her story when Kel tapped her on the shoulder to let her know that he was finished. Marilyn quickly finished the sentence she was typing and then saved her file before closing the laptop. "Did we have any errands to run today, or are we going straight home?"

"Actually, we need to stop at the bank." Kel pushed the door open and led the way out to the car.

As soon as they were both seated inside, Marilyn said, "I thought we weren't closing on the house until next week."

"We aren't, but I have a couple of things to take care of."

"Okay." Marilyn put the car in gear and drove the few blocks to the bank. She pulled into the parking lot and then shifted to face him. "Did you want me to wait here?"

"Actually, I need you to come inside with me," Kel told her. "I thought it was about time to put you on all of my bank accounts. Maybe you'll do a better job than I did of keeping track of how much we have."

Marilyn's eyebrows lifted. "Are you sure?"

Kel nodded. "I've always thought of it as our money." His voice grew serious as he added, "Marilyn, this is something I should have done years ago when we were first married. I'm sorry I never got around to it before."

"You really trust me with all of that money?" Marilyn asked now, her eyes lighting with mischief.

"I hope I can trust you." Kel let out a soft laugh. "Besides, if you're still willing to buy furniture at yard sales and thrift stores, I think it's a safe bet that you won't go blow it all in one place."

"You don't mind that I like yard sales, do you?" Marilyn asked now, her face earnest.

"Of course not." Kel reached for her hand. "I don't want you to change how you do things. I just want to change how we are. You said yourself that I need to trust you. I hope this shows that I do."

"Kel, it doesn't matter if I'm on the accounts or not. I just don't want us to have any more secrets between us, especially now that you know all of mine."

"I know." Kel opened the car door and nodded toward the bank. "Come on. Let's go take care of the paperwork for this, and then we'll grab some lunch."

Marilyn smiled now. "Sounds good."

Together they walked inside and waited for one of the account managers to help them. Kel explained the changes they wanted to make, and then they signed in the necessary places. They stood to leave just as two men walked in the door—two men wearing ski masks and holding guns. Marilyn's mind didn't comprehend the reality at first. Then she gasped, and suddenly she could barely breathe.

She couldn't see the man holding the gun, but the gun itself filled her vision. The movement beside her didn't register in her brain as Kel shifted his cane so that he was no longer leaning on it but rather holding it as a weapon. She was blind to the energy pulsing through her husband as he analyzed and waited.

The man by the door spoke, his voice strained and anxious. "Everybody on the floor! On your stomachs!" Marilyn and several others didn't respond at first, still struggling through their shock. When he yelled, "Move!" they complied much more quickly. Except for Kel. He was moving more slowly. Much more slowly.

After dropping onto the floor, Marilyn shifted her head to look at her husband, only to see him spring forward. The cane was extended out toward the man closest to them, and Kel succeeded in knocking him and his gun to the ground in one fluid movement. In a matter of seconds, Kel scooped the weapon up as the man across the room shifted his gun to aim at Kel.

"No!" Marilyn heard herself scream, her single word interrupted by two quick gunshots. The man across the room dropped to the ground with a thud even as Marilyn tried to grasp the reality of it all. The reality that the man who had threatened her husband appeared to be dead and that his partner was now grappling with Kel.

The gun was knocked to the floor once more, but this time neither man attempted to retrieve it. Marilyn sat up as the scuffle moved in her direction, her eyes widening at the scene before her. Her husband, her *injured* husband, was using his fists and elbows in rapid succession, and he didn't even look like he was winded. The would-be bank robber made another aggressive move, but Kel swiftly moved out of the way and delivered a hard blow to the back of the man's head. A split second later, the man was on the floor, unconscious, and Kel was at her side.

"Are you okay?"

Marilyn's mouth dropped open. "Am I okay? You just . . . you just . . ." Marilyn pointed at the man in front of her with a helpless wave, her eyes filling with tears.

"Come here." Kel offered her a hand and pulled her up and into his arms. She trembled as she buried her face in his shoulder and the police burst through the door, only to find the two criminals sprawled out on the floor.

* * *

The questions dragged on, and Kel wondered if the police were ever going to let him go home. One of the officers had escorted Marilyn to one of the squad cars so that her statement could be taken, but now she was waiting by their car, her face still looking too pale.

When the officer interviewing him started to repeat the same questions yet again, Kel finally interrupted, "Look, I really need to get my wife home. You have my number if you need more information, but I've already told you everything that happened."

The officer looked over at Marilyn and seemed to accept Kel's request. "Okay, Commander."

Kel gave him a nod and then limped toward his car. When he reached Marilyn's side, he asked, "Why don't you let me drive?"

Marilyn didn't question him. She simply handed him the keys.

Kel took her by the arm and walked her to the passenger side of the car. Then he climbed behind the wheel and glanced over at her. "Let's get you home."

Marilyn remained quiet all the way back to the house. He parked in the garage, but he had barely turned off the car when Marilyn pushed her way out of the car and hurried into the house.

Not sure what to think, Kel hurried after her and found her in the kitchen with a cup of water in her hand. "Are you okay?"

Marilyn shook her head, still clearly in shock.

"Why don't you sit down?" Kel suggested.

Again, Marilyn shook her head, but now she looked up at Kel with an odd expression. She drew a slow breath and then spoke in an even tone that edged toward accusatory, "You killed a man."

Kel felt like he'd taken a bullet to the heart. He took a deep breath of his own. "Yeah, I killed a man. I killed a man who was threatening my wife and dozens of innocent civilians, a man who was trying to kill me."

"You didn't have to kill him," Marilyn said now. "I mean, aren't you a sharp shooter? Couldn't you have just wounded him?"

Kel felt his chest tighten as he drew another breath and slowly let it out. He searched for the right words, wondering if they even existed. "In my line of work, I shoot to kill. If I had wounded him, he might have still been able to shoot back. I couldn't take the chance that he would hurt you."

He could see in her face the way her world blurred and then refocused in the blink of an eye. "You've killed before."

Slowly, Kel nodded. "Yes, I've killed before."

"How . . . ?" Marilyn began, apparently struggling against this reality now that she could visualize what her husband did when he was away from her. "How can you do this for a living? How can you go to church on Sunday knowing that you've taken someone's life?"

Kel paced across the room and stared out the window. The pain in his leg was fading fast, but a new ache was quickly taking over. He turned back to face his wife, hoping he could somehow explain what he did, why he did it. "When your dad was killed, would it have been okay if he'd shot and killed the man shooting at him?"

"That's different," Marilyn said immediately.

"No, it's not. I don't kill people who aren't trying to kill me or someone I've sworn to protect," Kel insisted as he prayed for guidance. "Every time I take a life, a part of me dies inside. And every time, I pray that my actions are justified."

Marilyn's voice was incredulous. "You pray after killing someone?"

"Yes, I do. There have even been times when I've gone in to talk to the bishop after a really difficult situation," Kel said, recognizing how odd his admission must sound. "It's not easy to take a life, even when I know that killing someone is ultimately going to save lives."

Kel paused for a moment, gathering his thoughts. "That bank robber today had every intention of killing someone. If he had succeeded in shooting me, you might have been next." Kel sat beside her, reached for her hand, his heart breaking a little as he watched the tears streaming down her face. "Don't you understand? You are everything to me. I don't think I could live with myself if something happened to you, especially knowing I could have done something to stop it."

"I don't understand anything anymore," she said through her tears. "I feel like you're two people—the man I married and a complete stranger, both sharing the same body."

"Marilyn, I'm still the same," Kel insisted. He wondered if it were even possible to explain what he was feeling or to understand her emotions. He reached over and touched her cheek, waiting for her eyes to meet his. "Every day I pray that I won't have to shoot anyone, that I won't be forced to make that choice. I hate that there are people in this world who make it necessary for men like me to carry guns and sometimes use them."

"But you do it," Marilyn said now. "You carry a gun, knowing that you might have to use it."

Kel nodded. "Yes."

"Maybe it was better when I didn't understand what you did," she said softly. Then she pulled her hand free, stood up, and left the room.

33

Kel rocked gently on his front porch as he watched the neighborhood kids at play. The scene before him was what he always imagined life should be like in middle-class America. Kids on bicycles, skateboards, and scooters, a couple more playing fetch with a dog. He wanted to be part of the scene in front of him so badly it hurt.

He ached for children of his own, a dog in the backyard. He wanted to be hanging out with the other dads who were standing across the street watching over their kids. He wished Marilyn had a reason to hang out on the neighbor's porch with the other moms as they visited before calling their families in for dinner.

Instead, Marilyn was locked in her office upstairs, undoubtedly working on her computer. He wondered if she ever looked out and saw what he saw, wished for the same things he prayed for. He had thought that they shared the same dreams, but the words she had written still haunted him. That window to her inner thoughts and feelings had opened his eyes, proving that he didn't really know his wife. Today had apparently shown her that she didn't really know him, either.

Kel continued to rock, thinking that his house probably looked normal to those walking by. The lawn was neatly mowed, thanks to the lawn service Kel had hired to help out until he was able to take care of it himself. The "For Sale" sign was no longer in the yard, and the front porch was now equipped with two wooden rocking chairs Marilyn had found the week before at a yard sale.

He thought of Marilyn once more. Everything had being going so great up until that morning at the bank. Sure Ramir had someone out there who might be trying to kill him, but the most important thing in his life, his relationship with his wife, had improved significantly over the past few weeks. Not that they hadn't fought through some struggles, but they were finally pushing through so many of the obstacles they had created over the years that had been interfering with their happiness.

Now he could only wonder if a single event could unravel everything.

He still couldn't quite get past the randomness of his presence at the bank that morning. *What are the chances . . .* he thought to himself once more. What were the chances that he would choose that exact moment to stop by the bank? That he would be there to stop the robbery before it happened? And what were the chances that it would all take place in front of Marilyn, where she would be forced to see him for who he really was? What he really was?

A car turned onto his street, moving slowly as it waited for the sea of kids to move out of the way so it could continue forward. Moments later it parked in front of Kel's house, and Brent got out and crossed the lawn in long easy strides.

"I heard you had some excitement today," Brent said as he climbed the porch steps and lowered himself into the other rocking chair.

"You could say that." Kel's voice was flat.

Brent looked at him sympathetically. "How is Marilyn doing?"

"I don't know."

"Still in shock?" Brent asked, continuing before Kel could respond. "I'm sure seeing someone point a gun at her had to be traumatic."

"You would think so." Kel nodded. "But she seems more focused on the fact that I killed someone in front of her."

Brent's voice softened. "How are you doing with that?"

"What do you mean, how am I doing with that?" Kel asked edgily. "I shot and killed a man in front of my wife and a dozen civilians."

"A man threatening you with a gun," Brent reminded him. Then he shook his head. "I thought you would have worked through this crisis of conscience years ago."

"Crisis of conscience?" Kel shifted now to look at Brent. "You've got to be kidding me."

"What would you call it?" Brent asked evenly. "You've admitted that you don't like to talk to Marilyn about work. Maybe you were just afraid of what she'd think if she knew that we sometimes have to kill the bad guy. If you haven't come to terms with that part of our lives, there's no way you can make her understand."

"After what happened at the bank, I think it's pretty obvious how she feels about killing the enemy."

"She's still in shock," Brent insisted. "Come on, Kel. Look at it from her point of view for a minute. She's probably never seen a dead body in her life, and she certainly hasn't ever seen someone killed right in front of her. That would shake anyone."

"Yeah, anyone except those of us who kill for a living."

"She said that?"

"More or less."

"I hate to say it, but she probably just needs some more time." Brent hesitated and then added, "And she needs you to trust her enough to tell her what our life is like at work."

"What do you do?" Kel looked at Brent, his voice shimmering with anger. "Do you come home at the end of a mission and tell your wife, 'Hi honey; I'm home; I had to kill someone today; I'm not sure if it was the right thing to do, but I was under orders, so I guess it's okay'?" Then Kel waved a frustrated hand in the air and shook his head. "You don't even have to say anything to Amy. She can read the mission reports."

"She can," Brent conceded. "But I still talk to her about it, especially when things go bad."

"How?" Kel looked at him, trying to comprehend how anyone could possibly verbalize the pain, the conflict that came from taking another human life. "How can you make her understand what it's like? How can anyone really understand what it's like to pull the trigger and know that your actions ended a life?"

"I don't think anyone really can understand it unless they've experienced it themselves," Brent admitted. "But Amy does know what it does to me. She knows that I'm going to struggle sometimes with what we have to do, and she's there to remind me that we don't always have any other options." Brent leaned back in his chair, his eyes serious. "Wars have been around since biblical times. The Lord understands what's in our hearts."

"But Marilyn doesn't."

"Just talk to her," Brent insisted.

Kel glanced back at the house and let out a sigh. "I guess I don't have a choice."

* * *

Marilyn paced across the room for the hundredth time, her mind unable to settle down enough for her to write. She wanted to escape into her novel, to sort out her feelings, but her characters had become strangers to her. Her novel was nearly done, the story so close to finding its happily ever after, but every time she sat down at her desk, the desk Kel had bought for her, the words wouldn't come.

She dropped down onto the loveseat and looked around the room. It was a dream come true—her own private place to write, to create, to fantasize. How could Kel understand her so well and she know him so little? Kel had somehow worked past the shock of finding out her deepest secret and then had done everything he could to keep it from becoming a barrier between them.

Marilyn didn't know if she could ever overcome the barrier between them now that she understood some of Kel's secrets. She closed her eyes, fighting back the nausea that welled up when she let herself remember the events of that morning.

The man who had fought the bank robbers wasn't someone she knew, wasn't even someone she had ever seen before. She let out a sigh, other memories surfacing.

How many times had she seen Kel's gear in the garage? Or seen him cleaning his sidearm or sharpening a knife? How often had Brent stopped by to see if Kel wanted to spend some extra time on the shooting range?

Logically, she knew that this part of Kel's life wasn't really a mystery to her. Emotionally, she still couldn't quite move past the knowledge that her husband had killed a man. That it hadn't been the first time.

Had she been deluding herself all of this time? Perhaps she had gotten caught up in pretending that Kel was simply the handsome man in uniform, the one who made her feel beautiful. All of these years, she had never let herself think about why he spent so much time on weapons training or what his career required him to do.

Tears welled up in her eyes as a new realization washed over her. Could this be the reason Kel never talked to her about his work? Had he sensed that she didn't want to know the whole truth about what he did? Perhaps he knew that she couldn't handle his reality when he was away from home. Was he right?

An emptiness spread through her, a sensation she couldn't push away as she gave in to the tears. Suddenly chilled, she pulled the afghan from the back of the loveseat and curled up beneath it. Squeezing her eyes shut, she surrendered to the onslaught of emotions.

34

Kel crossed the hall to Marilyn's office and stared at the closed door for a moment. She hadn't ever come to bed last night, and he didn't know if he could stand the silence between them anymore. They had certainly had their share of difficulties before but never like this. Never had Marilyn been unwilling to face him and discuss the issues with him.

Determined to talk to her, he pushed the door open, his eyes immediately landing on the desk and the empty chair beside it. Then he noticed Marilyn sound asleep on the loveseat, despite the light that was streaming through the windows.

A sense of wonder and panic coursed through him. She was so beautiful—her light brown curls against porcelain skin, her long fingers curled into a fist and tucked under her chin. Her eyes were puffy, a bit of mascara smudged under them. He thought of the tears she must have shed and wondered what he would do if she couldn't come to terms with his past and his present.

Staring down at her, he didn't know what to think. He thought of his talk with Brent the night before. He had spent most of the night wondering what he could say, what he could do to help Marilyn comprehend who he really was and how much he needed her to accept and support him.

Could she even fathom his desire to protect and the way that desire often warred with the necessity to kill? More importantly, did she understand that his desire to protect stemmed from his unwillingness to lose her as he had his parents and sister?

He reached down and softly brushed a curl from her cheek. She stirred slightly but didn't wake. He could only wonder if her tears had come because of the trauma she had suffered the day before or if they had stemmed from his part in stopping the bank robbers.

Though he wished he could stay and watch over her, Kel straightened and left the room. He quietly closed the door behind him and started to head downstairs. Then he stopped and reversed course, going into his bedroom instead. Slowly, he dropped to his knees beside the bed and poured out his fears to the Lord. As he prayed, he asked for Marilyn to find comfort and understanding and that somehow she would be able to accept who he was. Though he hesitated to say the words, he finally added a request that the Lord would also help him find peace with the violence of his past and that he might gain understanding of what he should do in his future.

When he finally closed his prayer, Kel felt as though he had more questions than answers. His heart still heavy, he grabbed his car keys and headed out the door. As he pulled out of the garage and drove to his physical therapy session, Kel mentally adjusted his plans for work that day. Certain that his obligations in the office could wait, he decided he would let his wife sleep for the next hour. Then somehow he was going to break down these walls that had been built between them.

* * *

Halim crossed off another address, gritting his teeth as he looked at the remaining possibilities. Pages of crumpled paper littered the back of his car, a sign of his frustration as he eliminated one house after another. He hated the way he was living right now. He hated the mess, the chaos, the need to assimilate with these infidels.

He watched the tall blond load her two children into the car and pull away from the house he had been staking out. As soon as they disappeared around the corner, he started the rental car and put it into gear. Only one more page of addresses to check and he would be out of options. If the Bennetts didn't reside at one of them, he would have to start over.

Fury bubbled inside him as he considered having to start over again. He took a deep breath, trying to calm himself as he remembered that he needed to blend in. Slowly, he pulled away from the curb and started for the next address on the list.

* * *

Marilyn started to roll over, nearly falling off the narrow loveseat. Reaching back to rub at the kink in her neck, she let her feet drop to the floor and shifted into a sitting position. Blinking slowly, she looked around the room, feeling it come into focus. She started to smile, remembering this gift Kel had given her. Then the expression faded as other memories surfaced.

For a moment she didn't move, listening for any sound that would indicate that Kel was still home. When she heard nothing but the hum of her computer, she stood slowly and crossed the room. She moved the mouse to deactivate the screen saver and looked at the time in the lower right-hand corner. Nine fifteen.

Kel would be at physical therapy by now.

She could feel the puffiness under her eyes and immediately knew that no amount of makeup was going to hide the fact that she had given into a long crying spree the night before. She was a little surprised that Kel hadn't come in and woken her when she hadn't come to bed the night before. He typically wasn't the type to let a fight last past bedtime, except, of course, when an argument was caused by the phone calls that took him away for duty and he wasn't home to make things right.

She walked into the master bedroom, noticing that the sheets were all twisted and the bed unmade. Turning into the bathroom, she reached for a washcloth and then turned the faucet on cold. After wetting the washcloth, she pressed it against her eyes, even as she felt tears trying to surface once more.

An image of the bank robbers invaded her thoughts. She had been so shocked to see the guns they held that she couldn't remember much of anything else until Kel had refused to let them succeed. She stared at herself in the mirror and let herself analyze the day before. What would have happened had they not stopped at the bank? What would have happened if Kel hadn't been there?

The outcome certainly would have been different, both for them and for everyone at the bank. The bank robber Kel had shot would still be alive, and he would have likely gotten away with who knows how much money. The customers would have been traumatized, certainly, but they probably would have been safe if they had done what the robbers had asked. Or would they?

Marilyn blew out a breath, reliving the moment when the one robber had aimed his gun at Kel. He looked like he was ready to shoot, ready to kill. If Kel hadn't stepped forward, would everyone have really remained safe? Suddenly, Marilyn wasn't so sure. She also found herself considering the odds that they had been in the bank at the exact time the robbery had been attempted. Had the Lord allowed this to happen so that she would see what her husband was capable of?

Hoping to wash away her doubts, she showered and changed, knowing that Kel would likely come home for lunch. She just didn't know what she was going to say to him when he did arrive.

Through the open window, she heard something rustle in the bushes in the backyard. Kel must have decided to come home after physical therapy. Marilyn garnered her energy and made her way downstairs. She couldn't stand this hollow feeling inside her anymore. One way or another, she had to face her husband.

She pulled the back door open before she thought to disengage the alarm. When it sounded, she turned toward the control panel, wondering why Kel hadn't turned it off before he went outside. Instinctively, she stepped closer to the panel and punched in the access code. Then she heard rapid footsteps behind her and felt a hand grab her from behind.

Before she thought to struggle free, someone's hand pressed a cloth firmly over her mouth. She whimpered as she tried to push the cloth away from her mouth. She felt the hand holding the cloth in place just as she took a breath. Then all she could think of was the sickly sweet smell and the tingling sensation that swept through her. Gasping once more, her eyelids became heavy, and slowly, she sank into the darkness.

35

Kel walked inside, went to deactivate the alarm, and noticed that Marilyn had already turned it off. He didn't hear her on the main level, so he headed for the stairs and called out her name, "Marilyn?"

When she didn't respond, he headed for her office first and then the bedroom. When he didn't find her anywhere, he walked back into her office and looked out the window to see if she was in the backyard. He pushed open the window, and again he called her name. Again, there was no response.

Sliding the window closed once more, he considered where she could be. Her car was still in the garage, so he didn't think she had gone out. Then again, she had been spending a lot of time with Riley lately.

He reached for the phone to call her, stopping when he noticed that her computer was on. He glanced over his shoulder, hesitated for a brief moment, and then he sat down in the office chair. He couldn't help it. Kel knew that Marilyn didn't want him reading her novel, but he needed to see if he could find a clue to what she was feeling, what he could do to make her understand.

He opened up the word processor and clicked on the button to display the most current files. Guessing that the most recent was Marilyn's novel in progress, Kel clicked on the file only to discover that she had put a password on it.

A little surprised and hurt that she had taken such a precaution, Kel typed in a couple of passwords he had known her to use in the past. When those didn't work, he typed in her birthday. Again, the password wasn't accepted.

Kel rubbed his chin as he considered other possibilities. He typed in a few more variations of old passwords. Then he considered the password he used the most for his own files, that of his younger sister Maggie's birthday. He typed Marilyn's mom's birthday, then tried reversing Marilyn's birthday. It wasn't until he typed in his own birthday that the file opened.

The corners of his mouth lifted. Then he started reading, quickly absorbed in the fictional world his wife had created.

* * *

Tristan stared at the computer screen in front of him, not sure exactly what he was looking at. Seth was usually the one on their squad who took care of any computer surveillance, but with him on leave, Tristan had been tasked with finishing up a project Seth had started. The data in front of him didn't look right, and he wasn't sure why.

The idea of trying to track down Kel's residence seemed like such an odd thing to do when he knew exactly where his former commander lived. Still, if going through the process would help find Halim Karel, Tristan was willing to go through the motions.

He hacked his way into the credit card system the way Seth had taught him and then continued working through the checklist of other places to search. It wasn't until he logged in to the security company's system that he saw it. The alarm system at Kel's house had been activated for a few seconds that morning. It had been brief—short-lived enough that the security company would not have checked in.

Marilyn or Kel had probably forgotten to turn it off when they got home that morning, but Tristan felt a sense of unease settle over him. Tristan stared at his monitor a moment longer before reaching for his phone. It wouldn't hurt to be safe.

He dialed Kel's cell phone number, a little surprised that it rang four times before Kel picked up with a simple hello.

"Hey, Kel. It's Tristan," he began. "I just wanted to make sure everything is okay at your house."

"Yeah, why?"

"I was checking out your alarm system this morning and noticed that it had gone off for a few seconds," Tristan said a little sheepishly. "I know someone probably just forgot to turn it off, but I thought I'd better check."

"Let me call you right back."

Tristan's sense of unease doubled as he clicked off his phone and waited. Less than two minutes later, it rang again.

Kel didn't mince words. "Is there any chance Marilyn is with Riley right now?"

"No," Tristan told him. "Riley is teaching a class today."

"Get everyone over to my house. Now."

"Kel, what's going on?"

"I don't know, but Marilyn isn't here." Kel's voice was clipped, but panic ran through it. "Her car is here. Her purse and cell phone are here, but there's no sign of her."

"Could she have gone out for a walk?"

"I doubt it. I've been home for almost an hour," Kel said tensely. "I need you guys to come help me find her."

"We'll be right there," Tristan promised.

* * *

Kel hung up the phone and started to search the house again. The garage door had been closed when he arrived home, but he hadn't noticed that the front door was locked until after Tristan called. Nor had he realized that Marilyn's purse and cell phone were still sitting neatly on the kitchen counter.

He had been deep into Marilyn's story when Tristan had called, completely caught up in her land of make-believe. Now he wished he could go back there.

The panic rushing through him wasn't an emotion he was accustomed to. Adrenaline and fear he could handle, but panic was an emotion he had been trained to defeat. An emotion that seemed to be winning right now.

Kel had gone out onto the deck after Tristan had called and had called out her name again. He had checked the front porch and the garage. Now he walked out on the back deck again. He would be embarrassed if his squad showed up only to find that Marilyn had been there the whole time and just hadn't heard him or had chosen not to respond. He did a more thorough search of the backyard, but there was no sign of her.

Where could she be? Kel asked himself for the thousandth time. Constant prayers were running through his mind, prayers that Marilyn would walk through their door to prove his concerns unwarranted. No matter how hard he prayed, he couldn't dismiss the two disturbing thoughts that continued to pop up. One was that she had left because of what had happened at the bank the day before. The other even more frightening possibility was that somehow Halim Karel had found his home. Surely, there had to be a third option. At least, Kel prayed there was.

He wanted to believe that she was just out for a walk like Tristan suggested, but he couldn't picture it. Marilyn was a creature of habit. She always took her cell phone with her everywhere. And why would she have left through the back door?

"Kel?" Brent's voice called out as the gate to the backyard swung open.

"I'm back here." Kel put a hand on the deck railing. He couldn't bring himself to look Brent in the eye, fighting back the tears stinging his own. "I don't know where she is."

"We'll find her," Brent insisted.

Kel took a deep breath and rubbed his temples. "I'm going to feel pretty stupid when she walks in here with a bunch of shopping bags."

Brent walked up the steps, put a hand on Kel's shoulder, and motioned to the door. "Have you found any clues as to where she might be?"

Kel shook his head as he walked through the back door into the kitchen. He pointed at the kitchen counter. "I don't know where she would have gone without taking her cell phone." Kel looked around the room, searching for any clues. "Her car is in the garage; her purse is still here."

"Did you check the call history on her cell phone?"

Kel shook his head, annoyed that he hadn't thought of it himself. He crossed to the counter and picked up her phone. After hitting a few buttons he looked back up at Brent. "Nothing. She hasn't even used her phone since before we went to the bank yesterday."

Quinn walked in from the garage. "There isn't anything unusual out there, and her car is cold."

"I just don't get it. She should be here. Even her laptop is upstairs . . ." Kel trailed off, his mind wrapping around that detail for the first time. "Her laptop is upstairs," he repeated.

Brent looked at him confused. "I'm not following you."

"She takes that thing with her everywhere. It's like a security blanket." Kel turned and went onto the back deck to look around again, this time his mind searching for any sign of who might have been there besides his wife.

Quinn's voice sounded behind him. "I'll go talk to the neighbors. Someone may have seen something."

"Take Jay with you," Brent told him before following Kel outside once more. "Now what? Do you want me to call NCIS?" he asked, referring to the Naval Criminal Investigative Service.

Kel looked down at the ground at the base of the steps. A couple of footprints were visible where the grass was thin, but he couldn't tell if they were his, one of his friend's, or if they belonged to someone who had invaded his home. He looked up, stared out at the quiet water that edged his property, and blew out a breath. Then he nodded. "Call NCIS. I think I'm going to need all the help I can get."

36

Special Agent Larry Steinert from the Naval Criminal Investigative Service looked around the living room, recognizing its barely lived-in feel. The couch looked new, the end table old, and the carpets appeared to have been cleaned recently. Added up, he guessed the Bennetts had just moved in. And, apparently, they were already having a spat about something if the missus had run off without a word.

Still, he had been the lucky one to take the call when some higher up had decided that the commander's concern about his runaway wife was worth looking into. It was strange, he could admit to himself, that the woman had walked off without her purse or cell phone. Even stranger was the fact that a US Navy SEAL and his squad couldn't find Mrs. Bennett themselves.

"Commander, I don't know that there's much we can do." Larry typed a few observations into his Blackberry and looked up at Kel. "You said yourself that you saw your wife when you left the house at nine. That was only three hours ago. And you admit that she was upset about the bank robbery yesterday. There's nothing here suggesting that she didn't just go out for a walk to clear her head."

Kel's eyes hardened. "Are you saying you won't help me?"

"I'm sorry, but, generally, we don't investigate this kind of case until someone's been missing for at least twenty-four hours."

"I don't think we can afford to wait twenty-four hours to start an investigation." Kel's voice was controlled, but a hint of fury mixed with panic hummed through his words. "My wife isn't prone to leaving the house without taking her car, and I can't think of a reason she would choose to go somewhere without her cell phone, even if she was just out for a walk."

Larry's eyebrows lifted. "You're saying someone abducted her?"

"That's exactly what I'm saying."

"Any idea who?"

"Halim Karel."

"Who is this Mr. Karel? How do you know him?"

Kel's jaw clenched for a moment. "I don't know him. He knows me."

Brent interrupted before Steinert could continue asking questions, "Before we continue with this, can you at least make sure that your boys at headquarters are set up to trace any calls that come into the commander's phone?"

"What makes you think you're going to hear from this Halim fellow?"

Kel spoke with conviction. "He'll call. He wants something."

"What?"

"I don't know." Kel's eyes flashed with fury and impatience. "I guess he'll tell me when he calls."

"Tell you what. I'll set everything up to track down anyone who calls you, if you'll give me the rest of the story. I want to know why you're so convinced Halim Karel has abducted your wife."

Kel nodded. "Deal."

* * *

She was living a dream, her dream. Her characters were living out the fantasy she had created on her little laptop, the hero looking so much like Kel, the heroine a prettier version of herself. And so much stronger. Isabella, as she was called in the fantasy, didn't hide from danger. She didn't fear the unknown. Isabella knew she could accomplish anything she set her mind to.

The sound of children's laughter sounded outside, altering the dream. Groggy and still half asleep, Marilyn struggled to open her eyes. She tried to cover her eyes with her hand. Then she felt the metal bracelet and the resistance.

Her eyes flew open then, and she gasped. She was lying on a bed, one hand handcuffed to the brass headboard. She struggled unsuccessfully against the restraint, twisting her wrist one way and then the other.

One panicked breath followed another as she struggled, both against the handcuff and against the confusion. Where was she? Why was she here? And how did she get here? Questions tumbled over one another, but her brain wouldn't slow down long enough for her to find the answers.

She vaguely remembered waking up late that morning. She remembered going downstairs and hearing Kel outside. Then reality crashed over her. It hadn't been Kel in the backyard. Someone had grabbed her from behind. But why?

Then she remembered her conversation with Kel and her comment that no one would ever want to kidnap her. But someone had. Kel had been right. He had known she was in danger.

Several minutes passed before her panic eased enough to let her vision expand beyond the bed and the fact that she was chained to it. The room wasn't terribly large. It was stylishly decorated with an underlying impersonal feel, as though no one really lived here. Someone's guest room or a rental house, perhaps?

There were plenty of rentals in the area, especially near the beaches. She shifted, trying to let logic surface through the underlying terror. She wondered how Kel would handle a situation like this. The only thing she could be sure of was that he would do everything he could to get free. She didn't have his skills with picking locks, but maybe she could find something to help her escape or at least some clue about where she was.

Her eyes swept over the room. A plush chair was nestled in the corner, and an elegant mirror graced the wall above a cherry dresser. There was a matching table beside the bed, greenery spilling out of the brass urn situated on top of it.

Daylight streamed through the sheer white curtains that were drawn across a sliding glass door leading to a small balcony. She pushed up onto her knees so she could get a clearer view. She could see a fenced backyard with a small storage shed situated in the far corner.

When she heard children's laughter again, she shifted as close to the door as she could, finally able to see the edge of a playground in the yard next door. Then her gaze shifted to the simple, one-story house with a sign. What had once apparently been a residence appeared to have been converted into a day care center.

Marilyn saw a couple of preschoolers run into her view. She leaned forward, but the handcuff kept her in place.

Then she heard the footsteps in the hall. A new wave of terror crashed over her as she scooted back on the bed, putting as much distance between herself and the bedroom door as she could. She held her breath and silently prayed for help as she heard the doorknob turn.

Then the door swung open, and she forced herself to look at her captor. He looked so . . . normal. The dark-haired man was dressed casually in a collared shirt and khaki pants. His eyes were direct, his presence commanding.

The corner of his mouth lifted as though he were amused at the way Marilyn had positioned herself on the bed. "Good to see that you're awake."

Marilyn could only stare. "Who are you? Where am I?"

He ignored Marilyn's questions, instead retrieving a cell phone from the pocket of his slacks. "It's time for you to make a call." His eyes hardened now, giving Marilyn a glimpse of the evil lurking behind the polished surface. "Do exactly as I tell you and you won't get hurt."

Marilyn swallowed hard, and then she nodded. Slowly, she reached out and took the phone.

* * *

Kel stood on the back deck and stared out at the water without seeing it. The panic had settled deep within him, the illusion of calm glossing over it as the hours wore on. Prayers tumbled over one another in his head, prayers that Marilyn would be okay, prayers that somehow he was wrong about why she wasn't home. Silently, he prayed for the miracle that they would find the clue that would lead them to her.

The house behind him had turned into a hub of activity over the past few hours, especially after Jay had found a witness who had seen a man leaving their cul-de-sac shortly before Kel got home. The woman had apparently been in her yard at the top of the street watching her kids play when an unfamiliar car had driven past her. She hadn't noticed much except that a dark-haired man had been driving and that someone had been in the passenger seat.

Steinert from NCIS hadn't been terribly concerned with the witness's report until his own search had turned up some material fibers on the fence. Added to that little piece of physical evidence was the call Steinert had received from Admiral Mantiquez insisting that this case be given top priority.

Even though he didn't want to believe it, Kel knew it was Halim Karel who was responsible for Marilyn's disappearance. What he didn't know was whether Karel had been after him or if he had specifically targeted Marilyn.

How was it possible, he wondered, that he had taken so many precautions but still hadn't been able to protect his wife? Even more disheartening was the reality that the profession Marilyn had been begging him to abandon for so long had come back to threaten her in a way he had never thought possible.

He didn't try to fight the guilt that rushed through him. Since joining the SEAL teams, he had always thought of his involvement as a sacrifice he was willing to make for his country. Now, he could only see how selfish he had been to put a career he loved before his family.

The door behind him opened, but Kel didn't turn as Brent stepped beside him.

"Here's your phone back." Brent handed Kel his cell phone. "NCIS put some kind of transmitter inside your phone so they'll be able to hear any conversation you have on it."

"Assuming he calls."

"He'll call," Brent assured him. "He probably doesn't even know that we're already looking for him. Normally, you would just be getting home from work right now."

"I still can't believe this is happening." Kel shook his head. "I keep expecting to hear Marilyn walk in the front door and wonder why we have all of these people over."

Brent stood beside him in silence for a moment. Then he said, "I called Seth. He and Vanessa will be here in an hour."

Kel turned to look at him now. "You interrupted Seth's honeymoon?"

Brent nodded. "Seth knows more about Ramir's organization and the men inside it than all of us put together. Vanessa knows even more than Seth does."

"That may be true," Kel said, his voice tight. "But they aren't going to have any idea where Halim would be holding Marilyn."

"Kel, you taught me years ago that we should always take advantage of all of our resources. Besides, they volunteered to come back. Seth feels responsible for all of this. He insists that if he hadn't been in that photo with you, none of this would have happened."

"None of this is his fault."

"I know, but we'll never convince him of that. I only called to see if they had any ideas of where Halim might be hiding out."

Kel drew a steadying breath. "Did they?"

"Vanessa said that Halim doesn't like credit cards, so we're probably looking for someplace that's either abandoned or would accept cash or a wire transfer for payment," Brent told him. "She also said that in the few terrorist attacks she has seen him attempt, he normally has his men hide in well populated areas or where there are a lot of civilians nearby. Apparently, he figures that local law enforcement is less likely to strike if there are innocent civilians around."

"Still, there are hundreds of places that fit that description."

"I know." Brent nodded. "NCIS is trying to locate the car your neighbor described on the traffic cameras, and the locals are checking out the area hotels for anyone who may have rented a room and paid in cash."

"How'd they get the locals to help?"

"Apparently, they jumped at the chance when they found out it was your wife in trouble. You made quite an impression when you broke up that bank robbery yesterday," Brent told him. "Not to mention the fact that they don't like the idea of having terrorists operating here in their backyard."

Kel rubbed at the knot in his stomach as the memory of his last conversation with Marilyn crowded his mind. She had seen him use a gun to protect her, and his actions had driven a wedge between them. Yet, here he was, ready to kill again if it meant saving her life. He couldn't lose his family again, not this way.

Beside him, Brent put a hand on his shoulder. "I'll let you know when Seth and Vanessa get here."

Kel nodded. And then his phone rang.

37

Kel turned to face the house as he watched the men inside his living room spring into action. When Steinert nodded, Kel answered the call with a simple, "Hello."

"Kel?" The voice was shaky, but Kel recognized it immediately as Marilyn's. And the relief that she was still alive breathed strength and determination into him.

"Where are you?"

"I don't know." Marilyn hesitated, and Kel thought he could hear someone speaking to her in the background. "I'm supposed to tell you that I'll be okay if you can get the government to release Lina Ramir."

"Lina?" Kel's eyes widened with surprise. He didn't know what he expected in the way of a ransom demand, but the request for Akil Ramir's niece was definitely not it, especially since the woman Halim Karel believed to be Lina Ramir was really Seth's new bride, Vanessa.

"That's right. Lina Ramir," Marilyn repeated. "You're supposed to have her released from prison and then taken to La Guardia Airport, along with a man named Seth Billaud. As soon as they get there, Lina is supposed to call this number for more information."

"I'll do everything I can to make it happen," Kel promised. "It will take a few hours for me to find who can help me get Lina and Seth released."

"I'll tell him," Marilyn said tensely. Then she added, "Tell Dad and Maggie I love them."

Kel swallowed hard as the line went dead. Slowly, he turned and walked inside to face a wall of people staring at him.

Brent spoke first. "Who's Maggie?"

Kel felt the breath rush out of him. He forced himself to look at Brent and say the words, "My little sister."

Brent didn't mention that he had been unaware of Maggie's existence. Instead, he asked, "Why would she talk about your sister and her father?"

"I don't know." Kel rubbed a hand over his face. "Her father was a cop. He died in the line of duty when she was little. And all she knows about Maggie is that she was killed in the Oklahoma City bombing." Kel looked up at his men, felt their surprise and unspoken horror. He took a breath and added, "She was in the day care center in the Alfred P. Murrah building that day."

"Maybe she's at an office building or a day care center," Brent suggested. "Where was her father when he died?"

"It was an armed robbery that went bad."

"Where?" Brent pressed.

Kel shook his head, and his eyes lit with understanding. "It was at a single-family home."

"She must be telling us that she's being held in a house somewhere."

"Near a day care center," Tristan added as he shifted the laptop computer on the kitchen counter in front of him and rapidly tapped on his keyboard.

"There are dozens of day care centers around here, but how do we know that's what she's trying to tell us?"

"It's a place to start."

Steinert hung up his phone. "We triangulated the signal from the cell phone your wife called on. She wasn't on long enough to get an exact location, but we narrowed it down to a two-mile radius near the beach."

A little slice of hope cut through Kel. "Tristan, get me a list of all of the day care centers in that area."

"I'm on it."

Kel turned to Steinert now. "When the time comes, we'll be the ones going in to get my wife."

"You're out of your jurisdiction here."

"Right now, I'm having a hard time caring about jurisdiction," Kel said in a controlled voice.

Before Steinert could retaliate, Brent stepped forward. "Special Agent Steinert, I have to agree with the commander. No one knows Ramir's organization the way we do. Once Seth Johnson gets here, he and Vanessa will be the only ones who will even have a chance at identifying the kidnapper."

"If you know Ramir's men so well, tell me this. What are the chances that Halim will let Mrs. Bennett go if we cooperate?"

Kel lifted his eyes to meet Steinert's. "None."

* * *

He wasn't going to let her go. Marilyn didn't know how she knew it, but she knew. She was going to die. She had wasted so much time wishing her life were different, that things were easier. She had let herself fall into the same trap her mother had, always too afraid to really live life, instead always looking for the safest route in every situation.

Kel had stalled for at least a couple of hours. Did he know that she wasn't going to survive unless somehow he found her?

She thought of the way Maggie's name had popped into her head when she had been talking to Kel. Had she been inspired to mention Maggie and her father to give him that clue? It was a small one, but just maybe . . . Marilyn took a deep breath, and her eyes flooded with tears. She knew Kel's squad was good. They had to be with all of the medals they had received. But this wasn't just one of their missions. It was her life.

She didn't know how long Kel's squad usually had to prepare for a mission, but she was pretty sure it was normally more than the few hours Kel had mentioned. A few hours. Marilyn's breath caught as logic broke through her sobs. As soon as Lina Ramir called, as soon as her captor gave her the information to pass along, she would no longer have any value as a hostage.

Would Kel know that? Had he even known she was missing before she had called?

She swiped at the tears and recalled the phone call. The only question Kel had asked her was where she was. That would have been a normal question if he had come home to find her gone, but then he had taken everything else in stride so easily. Too easily?

She shifted on the bed she was still chained to and considered. He knew who Lina and Seth were. She was sure of it. It hadn't been until her captor had told her what to say that everything had started making sense. Kel had gone to such lengths to hide her from the terrorist he had told her about. The man's name hadn't been important to her when Kel had first tried to explain the dangers, dangers she hadn't truly understood.

Now she understood. The moment she heard Lina Ramir's name, she realized that Kel hadn't exaggerated the dangers they had been hiding from. Undoubtedly, Lina was somehow related to Akil Ramir. Marilyn didn't know how, and she didn't really care. She was still trying to work past the realization that she was in danger because of Kel's career.

For so long he had kept his secrets, and now one of them had marched right into their home and dropped her straight into an unimaginable nightmare. It would be easy enough to blame Kel for what she was going through, but for now, all she cared about was how she was going to get out of this place alive.

Swiping at her tears once more, she closed her eyes and began a litany of silent prayers.

* * *

Seth Johnson gave two quick raps on Kel's front door before he pushed it open and led Vanessa inside. Together, they hurried toward the back of the house where they could hear the movement, voices, and the underlying hum of electronic equipment. Seth looked past the men who were in various stages of planning in the family room and quickly honed in on Kel, who was standing by the kitchen counter with Brent.

"What have we got so far?"

"Thanks for coming." Kel put a hand on Seth's back and gave a brief nod to Vanessa. Then he motioned to the photos spread out on the counter. "It's a long shot, but we think Marilyn was trying to tell us that she is in a house near a day care center."

"How many day care centers are in the search grid?"

"Eight."

"That's too many."

"I know." Kel picked up a printout and held it out so Seth could see it. "NCIS is still analyzing their recording of the phone call, but they did say that they didn't hear any traffic in the background in their initial screening. That suggests the day care center is one of these two residential locations."

Brent quickly shifted two photos on the counter as Vanessa moved forward to study them.

Seth glanced down at them, but his voice was skeptical. "Are we sure they weren't just calling from a well-insulated room? You can't always hear traffic if you're inside a building."

"They could hear seagulls in the background, so we know the outside noise was audible."

"Okay." Seth nodded, relieved. He put his hand on Vanessa's back and nudged her forward so she was standing beside him. "What do we know about these two so far?"

"They are both single-family homes that were converted into day care centers." Kel shifted one photo forward. "This one is about four blocks from the beach. The other one is almost two miles inland. We're checking on rental properties Halim could be using nearby."

"How much more time do we have?" Vanessa asked.

"An hour. Maybe two." Kel glanced across the room and then motioned to Seth and Vanessa. "Come outside with me for a minute. Maybe one of you will see something we missed."

"I doubt that," Seth started. Then he noticed something in Kel's eyes and found himself nodding. "But we'll certainly give it a try."

Kel opened the back door and led the way onto the deck and then down to the porch. "We know Marilyn was taken out through here . . ." he started, pointing at the gate. Then he turned as Vanessa closed the door behind them and joined them on the lawn. As soon as she stepped beside Seth, Kel spoke once more, "NCIS hasn't said anything yet, but I got a call from Admiral Mantiquez a little while ago. They're going to try to negotiate, or at least pretend to."

"What do you mean, 'pretend to'?" Seth's eyes narrowed.

"NCIS found out that Halim believes Vanessa is Lina Ramir," Kel told them. "Since we've narrowed the search area significantly, they think that when she calls, they'll be able to track the call and move in before Marilyn gets hurt."

"Are they optimistic or just stupid?"

"Both." Kel shook his head. The muscle in his jaw twitched before he added, "We all know that the second Marilyn hangs up the phone, Halim is going to pull the trigger. And we both know that there is only one reason Halim would ask for you to be released along with Lina."

"He's looking for revenge. He wants me dead." Seth nodded. "What do you want me to do?"

"NCIS doesn't know that Halim uses cash when he travels. Tristan checked with all of the rental companies in the area. Two houses near the day care centers were rented using cash, one beginning on Saturday and the other two weeks ago."

"What do we know about them?"

"One is across the street from a day care. The other is a couple of houses down from one," Kel told them. "Jay is out right now doing a drive-by of both of them."

Seth's eyebrows lifted. "Jay?"

Kel shrugged. "He's the only one of us Halim wouldn't recognize."

Vanessa stepped forward and asked Kel, "Are you sure it's a good idea to keep NCIS out of the loop?"

"I'm not sure of anything right now, but I know when it comes to my wife's safety, there isn't anyone I trust more than the Saint Squad."

Seth put a hand on Kel's shoulder and gave it a squeeze. "We won't let you down."

38

Jay navigated through the residential streets, going exactly the speed limit. He wanted to slow down, but he knew he couldn't afford to draw attention to himself. This was the first time his squad had trusted him to do a job without one of them looking over his shoulder, and he was determined to do it right. His car was the same one he had bought during his third year at the Naval Academy, and he was dressed casually in a pair of khaki shorts and a plain white T-shirt in the hopes of blending in.

He reached a stop sign and checked the house numbers as he started to pull forward. His eyes shifted to the fifth house up on the left and saw three blond kids playing out front. Surprised to see kids there, he glanced down at the paper beside him and double-checked the address Brent had given him. As he passed by the house, he saw another kid come bounding out. Then he saw the house number posted beside the door.

Satisfied that this house wasn't Halim Karel's hideout, Jay continued down the street and headed to the other location he was supposed to check out. Convinced that this had to be the one, Jay parked his car two blocks around the corner from his intended destination and chose to go out on foot so he could get a better look.

He kept his pace steady, strolling along the sidewalk as though he weren't in any particular hurry. He turned the corner and spotted the sign in a yard down the street that identified a boxy blue house as a day care center. Past the day care, only two houses were visible before the street curved out of sight right where the main outlet intersected it. The information Jay had been given indicated that the rental in question was four houses away.

Curious, Jay continued forward. He made the turn and identified the address of the rental property. The rental didn't have a garage, and no cars were visible in the driveway or on the street. Jay glanced back in the direction he had come, confirming that he could no longer see any sign of the day care center. Confused, he continued on and made his way around the block. After making a complete circle, Jay could only shake his head in confusion. If Marilyn Bennett was being held inside, he had no idea how she would have seen the day care center.

A bit deflated that he hadn't found any solid clues, Jay headed back to his car and called Brent.

"Did you see anything?" Brent asked in lieu of a greeting.

"Not really," Jay reported. "The first home had kids playing out in the yard, so I think we can rule that one out."

"And the other one?"

"It didn't look like anyone was home, but the day care center isn't visible from the house."

"I thought it was only a couple of houses down."

"It is, but the road bends, and you can't see it from the front or back yards."

Brent hesitated a moment. "Do you see any seagulls there?"

"Seagulls?" Jay asked, instinctively looking up. He was inland far enough that he could feel the sticky humidity but not have the relief of the breeze coming off of the water. He also didn't see any sign of seagulls. "No, why?"

"There were seagulls in the background when Marilyn called," Brent told him. "Come on back. Looks like we may have to explore some other options."

"Okay." Jay looked up at the sky once more. Then he climbed into his car and hoped Marilyn Bennett could last until they could uncover enough clues to find her.

* * *

Marilyn glanced out at the darkening sky and wondered if this would be her last sunset. She didn't have a watch on, but she knew time was growing short.

The man holding her hadn't appeared since he had told her to call Kel, but she had heard repeated movement in the hallway outside of her room over the past twenty minutes or so, as though someone were pacing there.

She pulled her knees up to her chin and started yet another prayer. "Heavenly Father, please help me get out of here. Help me be strong and have faith. And please help Kel find me." She closed her simple prayer as her own words repeated in her mind. Somewhere out there her husband was trying to find her. Somehow he was going to find her, she amended.

Footsteps sounded in the hallway once more. She held her breath when she heard them stop near the door. Then she heard them sound again, and she prayed Kel would find her before it was too late.

* * *

Brent stared down at the papers scattered on Kel's kitchen counter and shook his head. "We must be missing something."

"We're running out of time," Kel said, his voice tight. The NCIS team was out somewhere checking on a lead, but everyone knew that they would return soon and insist that Vanessa make the phone call to Marilyn to put their plans in motion.

Brent nodded and turned to Seth. "Let's expand the search at the rental companies to include all cash transactions."

Kel pointed to Tristan, who was still searching his computer for more clues. "Tristan, get me a list of all rentals near those two day care centers, no matter how they were paid for."

"I already have it," Tristan told him and reached for a paper on the coffee table. "I think NCIS is checking them out right now."

"Then we need to concentrate on the other cash rentals," Kel said, now ignoring the paper Tristan was holding. "We don't have time to duplicate what NCIS is working on."

"I agree," Brent said.

"Okay, here's what we've got," Seth interrupted. "Besides the two places Jay already checked out, there are three more that paid using wire transfers."

"We're going to have to split up to check them out." Kel stepped away from the counter, and the men quickly divided into three teams.

"What about me?" Vanessa asked as the men prepared to leave.

"Stay on top of what NCIS is doing. Call us if they get ready to move," Kel told her. Then his voice softened. "Please don't call Marilyn until we're in position."

"I'll wait for you to tell me when," Vanessa promised.

"Thanks." Kel nodded and headed for the front door.

Vanessa reached for Seth's hand and lowered her voice as the others left the room. "You know I'm not staying here, right?"

"I was afraid you were going to say that." Seth leaned down and kissed her. "I'll call you as soon as I have a location."

Vanessa nodded, even as her eyes narrowed. "You know that I'm going to be really annoyed at you if you're lying to me less than a week after our wedding."

Seth rolled his eyes. "I promise I will call you." Then he turned and followed the rest of his squad out the front door.

* * *

Tristan drove his battered truck down the street as dusk edged into darkness. He was ready to see this nightmare end for their commander.

Beside him, Quinn straightened and pointed down the street. "Look at that."

Tristan's gaze shifted, and he saw the object of Quinn's concern. A day care sign was hanging on the front of the house next door to the rental they had been sent to investigate. "That one wasn't on our list."

"Maybe it's new," Quinn said impatiently as he lifted his binoculars.

"I hope this is the place." Tristan slowed down as they passed by the house. "Can you see anything?"

"Not from here." Quinn pointed to the day care center. "Park over there. I'll climb up onto the roof and see if I can see in the upstairs windows."

Tristan circled around and pulled into the wide driveway of the currently vacant day care center. "Let's go. We're running out of time."

"Give me a boost," Quinn told him, lifting one foot up and waiting for Tristan to muscle him up onto the roof. Tristan waited impatiently for a minute, and then Quinn peeked over the edge. "This is it! Marilyn's on the bed in the corner room."

Tristan flipped open his phone. "I'll call and get everyone over here."

Quinn nodded as he eased himself off the roof and dropped to the ground. Then the two men climbed back into the truck and drove around the corner where they could stay out of sight until the rest of their team arrived.

39

Kel pushed himself out of Brent's car as Tristan strode toward him.

"What have we got?" Kel asked.

"The rental is two stories with a balcony running along the back of it," Tristan began. "Quinn was able to see Marilyn in the corner room on the far side of the house."

"That's where we need to go in," Quinn said confidently. "It's an easy shot to get onto the balcony, and we can put someone up on the roof or on top of that playground equipment next door to provide cover."

"Good work," Brent said. Then he turned to Kel. "How do you want to handle this?"

Kel considered for a moment. "I say we keep it simple. You and Tristan can go in through the balcony. Quinn can cover with a sniper's rifle from next door, and I'll go in the front. If Seth and Jay get here in time, they can take the back door."

"What if Marilyn calls again?" Brent asked. "If your phone rings in there, we're going to have a major problem."

"You want me to stay out here?" Kel asked incredulously.

"That's not what I said." Brent shook his head. "But we do need someone ready to answer in case Marilyn calls."

"How long until Jay and Seth get here?"

"They should be here any minute."

"Okay. We wait for Seth and Jay. Then I'll forward my calls."

"Should we call and tell them what's going on?"

"We'll clue them in as soon as Seth gets here," Kel said as he watched the glow of headlights coming toward them. "I think that's him."

The car parked down the street, and then Seth and Jay climbed out and crossed to them. Seth scanned the houses nearby and then shook his head as he approached Kel.

"Which one is it?" Seth asked.

"The white one with the balcony." Tristan pointed it out.

"Something doesn't feel right," Seth said as he studied the structure. The balcony was visible in the moonlight, and only one light was illuminated inside. "It feels like we're being set up."

"What do you mean?"

"One thing I learned about Halim when I was working with him undercover is that he's completely paranoid, just like Ramir," Seth told Kel. "He's not the type to leave a balcony unguarded."

Kel considered his words for a minute, trying to fight the impulse to charge in right then to take his wife back. "You think he's expecting us to come in that way?"

"Yeah." Seth nodded. "I think the reason there's only one light on in the whole house is to lure us up there."

"What do you suggest?"

"I say we go after Halim the same way we got Ramir," Seth told him. "Right through the front door. If there's going to be a weak spot, I think that's where it'll be."

Kel let out a sigh and gave a nod of approval. Then he noticed another car pull up. "That had better not be Steinert."

"It isn't," Seth said as he watched Vanessa step out of the car and start toward them.

"What's she doing here?"

"Halim is expecting us," Seth told him and then nodded at Vanessa. "Not her."

"It's too dangerous to have her here," Kel insisted. It was bad enough that his own wife was in harm's way, but putting Seth's new wife at risk was more than he had bargained for.

"Kel, she lived undercover in Ramir's organization for over a year," Seth reminded him. "She may be the extra edge we need to get Marilyn safely out of there. Besides, I have an idea of how we might be able to use Halim's feelings for her to our advantage."

"I don't like it," Kel said.

"You don't have to like it. Neither do I," Seth told him. "But you need to trust me, and we both need to trust Vanessa."

As soon as Vanessa joined them on the sidewalk, Brent stepped in. "Okay, everyone gear up." Then he added, "And let's try not to scare the neighbors."

* * *

Halim paced down the hall for the fortieth time, a cell phone in his hand. He hated waiting, but it would be over soon, he assured himself.

He wasn't sure he would get what he wanted this time around, but if he didn't, he had a backup plan. He always had a backup plan. He hoped that the commander's injury would play in his favor and that he would simply cooperate and deliver Lina and Seth to the airport as demanded. So far, this operation had been pathetically simple, and Halim's confidence rose another notch as he considered how clever he had been in planning everything out.

After seeing the tenacity of the commander's men at his house and the precautions he took to keep his wife safe, he knew that he had to be prepared for a rescue attempt. Glancing down at his watch, he wondered if the US military was even capable of planning a rescue in such a short period of time, especially since they would have to track him down first. He already knew that the cell phone call hadn't been long enough to trace with any accuracy, and the commander's wife still didn't have a clue where she was.

Besides, the pretty little Marilyn Bennett was still chained up inside her room. Except for letting her go to the bathroom once, she hadn't moved from the bed since he had carried her inside while she was still unconscious.

He had prepared the house for intruders days ago, long before he'd identified where the Bennetts were living. Both the front door and the door that led to the patio were wired with small explosives charges. Expecting the Navy SEALs to work as a team, he had wired the two explosives together. The minute one door opened, both blasts would go off. Neither explosion would cause significant structural damage to the house, but the nails embedded within the explosives would ensure that anyone near the doors wouldn't survive—and neither would Marilyn Bennett.

The way he figured it, if the commander was willing to deal, Lina would call and would likely tell him that the Americans had to talk to Marilyn Bennett before they released her. If a deal wasn't in the works, then, eventually, a rescue attempt would be made, one that would result in as much media coverage as a successful terrorist attack. After all, if he could kill a group of Navy SEALs, surely the Americans would realize that he could strike anywhere, anytime.

Glancing at his watch once more, he decided he could wait a few more minutes. Then he would have his guest make another call and issue an ultimatum.

* * *

Kel watched Brent and Tristan make their climb onto the dark balcony using the decking and drainpipes to aid their upward progress. Taking Seth's concerns into account, they had adapted their mission plan. Now, instead of having the two men enter through the balcony door like they had originally planned, they were heading for the windows in the darkest part of the house.

Quinn was already in place, lying on the roof of the day care center where he had a clear shot at the east side of the house. Jay had taken position on the side of the house where he could watch the door leading to the carport. Nearby Vanessa had concealed herself behind a line of azalea bushes.

With a prayer in his heart, Kel adjusted his night-vision goggles and signaled to Seth that it was time. The two men moved silently forward until they reached the front door.

Their timing was crucial, their goal simple: neutralize Halim and safely rescue Marilyn.

Kel looked down at his watch and then over at the bushes where he could barely make out the silhouette of Vanessa. He could see her with her cell phone to her ear and knew that she was making the call to the local authorities. Even though they were trained to be silent, they all knew that there was a good chance a neighbor would spot one of them and call 911. If Vanessa was successful, she would ensure that the cops wouldn't come in with their sirens blaring. She was also planning on letting them coordinate with NCIS.

They figured the locals wouldn't try to interfere, knowing what was at stake. NCIS was another story. They hoped they would have at least five minutes to get Marilyn out of the rental house before Steinert and his team showed up and decided to negotiate with a man that they all knew was beyond reason.

Kel shifted his attention back to the front entrance. Seth edged forward until he was right next to the door, but then he froze for several long seconds. He took a step back and signaled for Kel to do the same. Even though everything in him wanted to continue forward, Kel stepped back beside Seth.

Before Kel could ask Seth why he had backed off, Seth spoke quietly into his lip mike. "We've got a problem here. The front door shows signs of tampering."

Kel was the first to ask the obvious question. "What kind of tampering?"

"The explosive kind," Seth told him. "Kel, this guy is expecting us."

"You guys stand down," Kel ordered. "I'll take my chances going in through one of the windows."

Brent's voice came over the communications headset now. "Kel, you can't go in alone."

"I'm not going to risk the rest of you," Kel said firmly. "It's my wife in there. You can cover me from out here."

"Negative," Tristan's drawl sounded quietly. "I'm already in."

"Great," Kel muttered as he pressed against the side of the house and considered his options. "Everyone make sure you check for booby traps. And Jay, you stay outside."

"Yes, sir," Jay said obediently, making Kel wonder briefly what he had done to make the rest of the squad feel they could ignore his orders.

"The balcony door is set with an explosive charge, too," Brent informed them. "But the windows are clear."

"Copy that," Kel responded.

Kel saw Seth go to work on a main level window. Vanessa moved forward to squat beside her husband. Moments later, Seth slipped inside, followed by Kel and Vanessa. They all looked past the typical furnishings, Vanessa staying with Seth as he and Kel split up to check out the main level. When they were satisfied there wasn't anyone on the first floor, Kel ignored the stiffness in his knee and headed up the stairs. That's when he heard the footsteps.

He signaled Seth and gripped the weapon in his hand. Then the footsteps stopped, followed by the sound of a doorknob turning.

Seth edged beside him as a man's voice carried toward them. "It's time for you to call your husband again to make sure he hasn't forgotten about you."

Marilyn's voice sounded surprisingly calm. "Why are you doing this?"

Kel started forward only to have Seth grab his arm to hold him in place. Kel looked back to see Seth speak softly into his lip mike. It took him a minute to register the words that he was hearing through his earpiece, to readjust the plan in his mind.

Quietly, Kel took off the night-vision goggles, pushing them onto the top of his head. Then he crept forward, quickly closing the distance between the top of the stairs and the open door. He stopped just outside the door, first worried that he no longer heard voices and then surprised that he didn't see Halim still standing near the doorway. Vanessa moved beside him, pressing her back against the wall as Seth stepped beside her.

Then he heard a cell phone ring, followed by Halim's voice. "Put it on speaker."

Marilyn's voice sounded now as she answered the cell phone, "Kel?"

The words that came next were words Kel would have said, but it was Jay's voice that sounded in the room. "Marilyn, are you okay?"

She hesitated slightly, and then she spoke, "Yes, I'm okay. Were you able to get Lina Ramir released?"

Jay didn't answer now. Kel did. His gun ready, he stepped into the room, one hand on Vanessa as though he were holding her in front of him by force. "She's right here. Let my wife go, and you can have Lina."

Halim saw Kel, and his eyes widened when he saw Vanessa. Then, in a rapid movement, he turned his gun toward the bed where Marilyn was still handcuffed to the headboard.

"No!" Kel shouted, panic shooting through him as Halim fired one shot.

Marilyn screamed, and suddenly both of her hands were free. Halim's bullet hadn't been aimed at her, but rather at the chain of the handcuffs. In the space of two heartbeats, he grabbed Marilyn and pulled her in front of him.

Halim's eyes were dark as he held his ground, one hand aiming his gun at Kel, the other gripping Marilyn's arm as he held her in place as his human shield.

Kel didn't let himself look at his wife. He couldn't let himself think of what she was feeling right now. Instead he had to focus on what Halim was going to do next. Halim wasn't close enough to the balcony window for Quinn or Brent to take a shot through the glass, and he knew he couldn't attempt taking one himself as long as Marilyn was at risk.

Vanessa's voice cut into his thoughts, but she didn't speak in English. Instead, her words were in French. "Halim, they have a car waiting for us outside. Let's go."

Halim also spoke in French as his eyes shifted from Vanessa to Kel and then back again. "Do you really think they're going to let us walk out of here alive?"

"They're Americans. They don't like to kill," Lina told him. "Bring the woman with us for insurance. We can let her go once we get to Nicaragua."

Halim seemed to consider her suggestion for a moment. Then he turned the gun to aim it at Marilyn. "Let Lina go, or I will kill her."

Kel's voice vibrated with fury and a hint of fear. "You kill her, you're next. And Lina will die right beside you."

"Understood," Halim said simply.

Then Kel took a leap of faith, releasing Vanessa and taking a step away from her as he moved farther into the room.

"You made a wise decision," Halim said. "Perhaps I will let your wife live after all." An evil grin crossed his face as he took a step toward the door, still keeping Marilyn in place between them. "You, however, I don't trust to let us go."

The moment Vanessa was out of harm's way, Halim's intention became clear. He glanced at her and then shifted his attention back to Kel. His grip loosened on Marilyn as he took aim. Then the room exploded with activity. Seth dove through the door and knocked Kel to the ground. Marilyn screamed, glass shattered, and gunfire erupted.

"Marilyn!" Kel ignored the throbbing in his knee and scrambled to stand as Seth shifted beside him. Both men stood to find Brent standing outside the window and Tristan leaning over Halim to check for a pulse.

Logically, Kel understood that Brent had shot Halim from his position on the balcony. He knew Tristan must have entered the bedroom behind Seth. None of that mattered to him now. Instead, his only focus was on his wife and the blood splattered on her clothes. But she was still standing, and she was still breathing.

And an enormous wave of relief rushed through him as he realized that the blood was Halim's, not hers. As she struggled to catch her breath, Kel closed the distance between them and drew her into his arms.

"Are you hurt?" Kel managed to ask, one hand stroking her hair.

Marilyn shook her head as she took several deep breaths and her body trembled against him. They stood there for a moment in silence. Then she swallowed hard and shifted so she could see his face. "I was praying that you would come."

Kel leaned down and kissed her softly. "And I was praying that I would find you."

"I hate to break this up," Seth interrupted, "but I think we should get this handcuff off you."

Marilyn let out a shaky breath and held up her arm where part of the handcuff was still attached to her arm. "I'd like that."

Seth popped the lock and then looked at Kel. "Why don't you get her out of here? We'll deal with NCIS and the cops when they get here."

"Thanks," Kel said, his eyes meeting Seth's as he replayed the moment Seth had pushed him out of harm's way. "Thanks for everything."

Seth gave him a quick nod. "You're welcome."

40

She was home, and she was alive. The miracle she had prayed for had happened, and Kel had really been able to find her. Marilyn was still amazed that his squad had been able to rescue her only three hours after she had given them such a tiny hint.

Some navy cops had shown up to question her shortly after Kel had brought her home. They were still questioning Kel downstairs, but, finally, she was free to let those images go. Of course, she couldn't—at least not yet.

She had spent nearly an hour in the shower trying to erase that man's blood off of her, trying to wash away the nightmare she had witnessed. Even though it was after midnight, Marilyn had gone into her office instead of her bedroom. She couldn't sleep, and she hoped that by writing a little she might be able to organize her thoughts and find a way to release herself from the disturbing images that wouldn't go away.

She opened up a blank file on her computer and started typing. She described that deadly scene in the rental house, the way death scented the air, and her incredible relief that Kel hadn't been the one lying on the floor bleeding. She replayed the sound of the shattering glass and her scream piercing the air. Her memory shifted back further to the moment she heard Kel's voice, to the moment a shot rang out, to the moment the bullet had connected with the wall right behind where her husband had been standing.

Her fingers flew over the keyboard, her mind somehow processing the events and the emotions they evoked. She ended up with over eight typed pages by the time Kel came into the room, her stomach still sick with the emotions she had forced herself to relive.

"Hey. I thought you'd be in bed by now."

Marilyn turned to face him and rolled her shoulders, recognizing the stiffness there for the first time. "What time is it?"

"About two thirty." Kel crossed to her, put his hands on her shoulders, and started to rub them. "You should come to bed."

"I didn't want to go to bed without you, especially after being chained to a bed all day." Marilyn tried to force the muscles in her neck and shoulders to relax. She tipped her head back and looked up at him. "That feels good."

"It's supposed to." Kel leaned down and gave her a gentle kiss. "You have to be tired."

"I am, but . . ." Her voice trailed off. How could she explain to Kel that she was still afraid, even though she knew that she was supposed to feel safe now?

"But what?" Kel asked. When she didn't answer right away, he shifted so that he was in front of her. He stared at her a moment, as though trying to read her emotions. "You're still scared."

Marilyn nodded. "I know that must sound silly, especially to you."

"No, it doesn't." He shook his head. "Marilyn, I'm so sorry about what happened today," Kel said, his voice guilt ridden. "This was all my fault."

"Your fault?" Marilyn's eyebrows lifted. She didn't have to ask why he was saying the words. She understood his logic. She had shared it at one time. Now she hoped she knew better. "Kel, I don't blame you for what happened. You aren't responsible for the choices other people make. You didn't ask to be in the bank the day it was robbed any more than you expected that man to kidnap me."

"But if I had left the teams like you wanted me to, you wouldn't have been in danger."

"No, I wouldn't have," Marilyn agreed. "But if it hadn't been me, it would have been someone else."

Kel jerked a shoulder. "Probably."

"In a way, I guess it was a good thing that he decided to go after me. Not every woman's husband has your talents." Marilyn reached up and kissed him. "Come on. Let's go to bed."

Still looking unsure, he nodded. Then he took her hand and led her from the room.

* * *

Kel leaned down to tie his shoes and then looked back up at his wife. He had taken a couple of days off from work after Marilyn's kidnapping, but this afternoon he had a meeting he knew he couldn't miss. "Are you sure you're going to be okay here by yourself?"

"I'll be fine," Marilyn assured him. "I'll turn the alarm on as soon as you leave."

Kel stared over at her, a little surprised she wasn't more concerned about being home alone. Over the past several days, he had been by her side constantly, but he wasn't sure if that was more for her benefit or for his.

He had canceled all of his physical therapy appointments since the incident, instead exercising at home where he could be close to Marilyn. He knew working out on his own might slow down his recovery a bit, but for the first time since his injury, he didn't care. He had been putting his career first for too long, and he knew he couldn't do that anymore.

Marilyn was doing amazingly well working through the horrifying memories of her kidnapping. She still didn't like to go to bed by herself, but other than that and an occasional nightmare, she seemed to be recovering from the traumatic events of the past week.

Kel stood up and brushed a speck of lint off his uniform. Then he turned to look at her again. "Call my cell phone if you need anything. Even if I can't get away, I can send Amy or one of my men to keep an eye on things."

"I'll be fine," Marilyn repeated, more insistently this time. "Besides, I have a lot of writing I want to get done. It will be good for me to have a little quiet time to myself."

Kel looked at her suspiciously. "Are you just saying that to make me feel better about having to go in?"

"Maybe a little." Marilyn gave him a little grin. "Now go on. I'll see you tonight."

"I love you." Kel leaned down to give her a kiss good-bye.

"Love you, too," Marilyn called after him as he headed for the door.

Instead of going into the garage, he first walked outside and made a complete circle around the house. Once he was satisfied that no one was in his yard, he headed for the garage and got in his car.

He supposed he was still being a bit paranoid, but the image of Halim Karel holding a gun to Marilyn's head hadn't faded in the least. He didn't know how Marilyn was coping so well. In fact, she seemed to be doing better after the kidnapping incident than she had after the bank robbery.

When Kel reached his temporary office, he sifted through his messages and returned a few before it was time to head to the officers' club for a meeting with Admiral Blake. Kel wasn't exactly sure what the admiral wanted to meet with him about, but he guessed that it had to do with the command position of SEAL Team Eight.

A few months ago, he wouldn't have dared dream he would get an opportunity like commanding SEAL Team Eight. Not only would he basically be replacing his own commanding officer, but he would also oversee the operations and training of the Saint Squad as well as the other units within his team. Now that he was faced with the possibility, he wasn't sure he was willing to make the kind of sacrifices that would be required to take such a position or even to continue working in the teams at all.

When he arrived at the officers' club, Kel spotted Admiral Blake across the room standing beside a table occupied by several high-ranking officers. Content to let the admiral finish his conversation, Kel took a seat at the bar and waited.

A moment later the admiral crossed to him. They had barely exchanged greetings and settled into their seats at the bar when a bartender appeared in front of the admiral.

"I'll take a beer," the admiral told him.

The bartender nodded, quickly preparing the admiral's drink and setting it in front of him. Then he turned to Kel. "What about you, sir?"

"I'm fine, thanks."

The bartender nodded and left them alone.

"You know," the admiral shifted to look at Kel, "I'm not sure I trust a man who doesn't drink."

Even with his future in the navy uncertain, Kel couldn't quite muster the energy to placate the admiral. Instead, he stood his ground, refusing to make excuses, and said simply, "Sounds like a personal problem to me."

The admiral narrowed his eyes, a hint of surprise reflected there. "Do you know why I'm here?"

"Rumor has it that you want me to take command of SEAL Team Eight."

"Then you do know." Admiral Blake nodded. He motioned to the bartender again. "And you also know that I can change my mind."

"Yes, sir." Kel nodded. "But that doesn't mean I'm going to change mine." He waved off the bartender once more.

"You've got guts." He let out a short laugh. "I'll give you that."

"Thank you, sir."

Admiral Blake studied him once more. Then he motioned to an empty table. "Let's order something to eat, and we can talk over dinner. I think we have a lot to discuss."

"Yes, sir."

41

Marilyn felt like she was running a race. She could see everything happening as though she were watching it on a movie screen, feeling the characters' emotions as though she were living for them. Her fingers tapped away at the keyboard, the words rapidly appearing on the screen. The story was coming to an end, and it was a race to the finish.

Every day when Kel worked out in the dining room, Marilyn spent time in her office. For days she had been reading over her manuscript, fiddling with parts as it finally came together in her mind. She could see where the characters were heading now, and those last words demanded to be put on paper even though the hour was late and Kel had headed to bed more than an hour before.

She indulged herself for a few minutes more, and then suddenly she was done. Marilyn read through the last few paragraphs, expecting to find that she needed to add more of something. Then she leaned back, surprised that there wasn't any more to do. It was really done. She had finished a novel.

A little awed by the moment, she saved her file and took the extra precaution of making a backup. Then she rubbed a hand over her stomach and realized she was starving.

She debated for a minute whether she was hungry enough to go down to the kitchen alone. She knew if she woke Kel, he would go down with her, but she felt so silly to be afraid of being by herself. She walked out into the hall and made it all the way to the top of the stairs before she realized she still wasn't ready to venture downstairs alone in the dark.

Ignoring her grumbling stomach, she headed for her room instead and hoped that her fatigue would erase her hunger.

* * *

Kel had decided. Never in his life had he spent so much time pondering and praying about what to do with his future, but after seeing all of the miracles that had taken place to bring Marilyn home safely the week before, Kel knew he had to reevaluate his priorities. As much as he loved his career, he loved his wife more.

Admiral Blake had called him earlier that morning and offered him the command of SEAL Team Eight. Kel hadn't accepted it right away as the admiral had expected he would. Instead, he had asked if he could have some time to discuss the decision with his wife. And although the admiral had given him three days to do just that, Kel knew now that he didn't need to. Not anymore.

It was time for him to face the facts, and the fact that continued to overwhelm him was that it was time for him to leave the SEAL teams and pursue a career in another discipline. He hoped Marilyn could help him decide if that new career would be in the navy or in civilian life.

A hollowness settled in his stomach, but Kel hoped that feeling would fade with time. Perhaps once he was actively working toward a new future, he would find a way to leave behind the past that had been such an integral part of his life.

After finishing work early, he had come home hoping to discuss his options with Marilyn, only to find the house empty. After a momentary panic attack, he remembered that she had gone to the doctor for some kind of checkup. He was just debating about whether he should throw some hamburgers on the grill for dinner when he heard the garage door open.

Marilyn rushed into the living room a moment later, her eyes bright, a thick stack of papers in her hand. "Hi." She slowed when she saw him sitting in the chair Amy had given them. "I didn't expect you to be home already."

"I finished up early," Kel told her as she crossed to stand in front of him. "Besides I wanted to talk to you."

"Is everything okay?" Marilyn asked, a combination of concern and curiosity in her voice.

"Yeah. I've just been thinking about work and wanted to talk to you about some ideas I had," Kel told her.

"Okay, but before we talk about that, I really want you to read the end of my story." Marilyn grinned at him. Excitement flashed in her eyes. "I finished it last night."

"Congratulations," Kel said, wishing he were more excited about the words she had written. "But I think I already know how it turns out."

"Just read it."

Kel reached for her hand and drew her close. "Marilyn, I don't need to read it to understand that you need me to put you first," he said softly. "It's the way it should be."

"I need you to put *us* first," Marilyn corrected with a small smile, rubbing a hand over her stomach. "Both of us. But that doesn't mean you have to quit the teams."

Kel looked down at his wife's stomach, at her hand resting there. Then his eyes narrowed as he tried to catch up with what she had said. "Did you say, 'both of us'?"

Tears glistened in her eyes as she nodded.

"You're pregnant?" Kel pulled her closer until she tumbled into his lap. "Really?"

"Six weeks."

Kel rested his hand on her stomach and looked at her, a combination of awe and excitement swelling within him. "We're going to have a family?"

"We already are a family," Marilyn corrected. "And this family needs for you to be happy."

"Marilyn . . ." Kel started, his voice serious once more.

"Here." Marilyn reached for the papers she had dropped onto the coffee table, the last few pages of her novel. "Read this."

Again, Kel's eyes narrowed. "I don't understand."

"Just read it," Marilyn insisted, shifting her weight so that she could lean back against him as he read. She didn't have to see his face when he got to the part that she knew would change his mind, the words that had come to her in the night as she had rolled to the end of the story. She could close her eyes and hear them crashing over her.

Watching him as he slept, she finally understood. If he didn't go, he would stop being the man she loved, the man she wanted to love forever. She would miss him when he left, but she was ready now. She knew that a constant ache would be her companion in the months to come, just as she knew every letter and every call would lift her above it. No distance could truly separate them, and no joy would be greater than the day he made it home.

Kel shifted so he could see her face. "Are you saying . . . ?"

Marilyn nodded. "Kel, you need to be a SEAL, and your squad needs you."

"I'm not sure I'll be going back to the Saint Squad, actually."

"What?"

"Admiral Blake came to meet with me yesterday. I've been offered the command of SEAL Team Eight."

"Exactly what does that mean?"

"The Saint Squad is one of many units that make up SEAL Team Eight. Basically, I would be taking my commanding officer's place."

Marilyn's eyes widened with excitement. "Are you serious? That's huge!" Then their conversations of the past few days came back to her, and she studied his face. "What did you tell him?"

"I told him I needed some time to think about it." Kel paused for effect. "And to talk to my wife."

A smile slowly crept over her face. "In that case, tell him your wife approves completely, provided he'll give you leave in about seven and a half months."

"I think we can arrange that," Kel said. And then he kissed his wife.

ABOUT THE AUTHOR

Originally from Arizona, Traci Hunter Abramson has spent the past two decades living in Virginia. After graduating from Brigham Young University, she worked for Central Intelligence Agency for six years before choosing to stay at home with her children and indulge in her love of writing.

Traci also coaches the North Stafford High School swim team. She currently resides in Stafford, Virginia, with her husband, Jonahtan, and their four children.